l8r, g8r

In the *ttyl* series

ttyl
ttfn
l8r, g8r

Other books by Lauren Myracle

Rhymes with Witches
Twelve
The Fashion Disaster that Changed My Life
Eleven
Kissing Kate

l8r, g8r

lauren myracle

Amulet Books
New York

Library of Congress Cataloging-in-Publication Data:
Myracle, Lauren, 1969–
L8r, g8r / Lauren Myracle.
p. cm.
Summary: Throughout their senior year in high school, Zoe, Maddie, and Angela continue to share "instant messages" with one another about their day-to-day experiences as they consider college, sex, the importance of prom, and the inevitable end of their inseparable trio.
ISBN 13: 978-0-8109-1266-3 (hcj)
ISBN 10: 0-8109-1266-X (hcj)
[1. Instant messaging—Fiction. 2. Friendship—Fiction. 3. Interpersonal relations—Fiction. 4. High schools—Fiction. 5. Schools—Fiction.] I. Title. II. Title: Later, gator.
PZ7.M9955La 2007
[Fic]—dc22
2006031848

Design: Interrobang Design Studio

Printed and bound in U.S.A.
10 9 8 7 6 5 4 3 2 1

HNA
harry n. abrams, inc.
a subsidiary of La Martinière Groupe
115 West 18th Street
New York, NY 10011
www.hnabooks.com

For all the real live Zoes, Maddies, and Angelas out there.
Never stop loving your buds!

Acknowledgments

Oh, bless my stars—so many people to thank! Which is lovely, yeah? Because it just confirms that the world is a big bundle of goodness, with people helping one another all around. So first and foremost: Thank you, world! (I'm cheesy, what can I say? But I totally mean it!)

Smilies galore to the hundreds (omg, thousands?) of girls who have contacted me through MySpace or my Web site. You all keep me real and give me soooo many fab ideas. And, of course, smilies to those sweet guy readers who e-mail me, too. Be proud! There are more of you than you think!

Thanks to Amy Winfrey for being the genius behind Big Bunny, thanks to Amber Kelley and her friend Cherie for helping me figure out my Boo Boo Bear problem, thanks to Brittany Lesser for her insights into the "evil girl" psyche, and thanks to the amazing and talented Melanie Dearman for her incredibly helpful feedback on the first draft of the novel. Thanks to Sarah Burnett for her naughtiness regarding the chicks. And thanks most emphatically to my friends and family, just because.

Thanks to my agent, Barry Goldblatt, for fearlessly embracing the bizarre culture of teenage girls as seen through the eyes of an oldhead (that would be me) who can't quite seem to grow up.

Thanks to everyone at Abrams for making the book so spifftacular, especially: Scott Auerbach, who is so good with details; Celina Carvalho, the gal responsible for the adorable cover art; Jason Wells, publicist and cutie-pie extraordinaire; and the ever brilliant Susan Van Metre, who makes these books what they are. I'm not kidding. Any good things, give credit to Susan. Any crappy parts, blame on me!

Finally, all the thanks and love in the world to Jack, Al, Jamie, and Mirabelle. You guys make my life so sunny, and that's why I'm able to spread some of that sunlight in my books. I love you!!!

lauren myracle

Tuesday, February 7, 4:49 PM E.S.T.

zoegirl: maddie!!! i'm so excited, i can't sit still! i can't *believe* i'm gonna c doug in 2 hrs!

mad maddie: i hear ya—even i'm kinda excited to c the guy. i wonder if he's changed?

zoegirl: it's been SIX ENTIRE MONTHS. *6 months* of no doug!

zoegirl: aye-yai-yai—what if he doesn't like me anymore?

mad maddie: oh, please. doug is doug is doug, and no semester at sea is gonna change that.

mad maddie: anywayz, haven't u guys been writing like 5,000 letters a day?

zoegirl: that's true, and his letters are so sweet. that's 1 cool thing—since internet usage was "strongly discouraged" on the ship, i now have actual love letters to save for when i'm older. sooo romantic.

mad maddie: speaking of romantic, what's doug gonna say when angela and i show up at the airport with u?

zoegirl: er . . . hi, maddie? hi, angela?

mad maddie: he's not gonna be pissed?

zoegirl: why would he be pissed?

mad maddie: that it's not just the 2 of u

zoegirl: course not. 1st of all, his parents r gonna be there. and 2nd of all, i'm way 2 nervous to go by myself.

zoegirl: i have to have my maddie and my angela—he knows that!

mad maddie: how's he gonna feel, waltzing back to school in the middle of our senior yr? is that gonna be weird for him?

Send   Cancel

1

zoegirl:	PAST the middle, u mean. i was *supposed* to have him back at the beginning of the semester.
mad maddie:	i'm still reeling from the unfairness of that, btw. let's pretend i was the lucky 1 who jaunted off to Sea the World. would the administrators let ME take an extra month off to travel with my parents? i don't think so.
zoegirl:	but u don't have straight As like doug—no offense.
mad maddie:	none taken. i'm proud of my Bs.
zoegirl:	doug's mom called it "cultural enrichment." that's the excuse she gave the school. but i say he's seen enuff of the world. now he needs to see ME!
mad maddie:	ah yes, now it's time for him to be enriched in OTHER ways, nudge-nudge, wink-wink.
zoegirl:	maddie!!!
zoegirl:	i'm just glad we're gonna be together again. i mean, he had a great time, and i'm proud of him for doing it, but he's definitely ready to be home.
mad maddie:	god, and i am definitely ready to NOT.
mad maddie:	seriously, if i could graduate tomorrow, i would. i'd be like, hasta la vista, baby! g-bye, atlanta—hello, santa cruz!
zoegirl:	*if* u get in. which u will. i hate that u wanna go so far away, tho.
mad maddie:	blame angela. if we hadn't gone to california with her over the summer . . .
zoegirl:	too ironic. she escapes california to move back to atlanta, and now all u wanna do is escape atlanta and move to california.
mad maddie:	U.C.S.C., here i come. go, banana slugs!

Send   Cancel

zoegirl:	is that honestly their mascot?
mad maddie:	**it honestly is their mascot. it's 1 of the many cool things about them—their whole who-gives-a-damn attitude about typical college stuff like rah-rah football teams. that and the fact that they're 3,000 miles away, heh heh heh.**
zoegirl:	oh, wow
zoegirl:	maddie . . . i just realized something
mad maddie:	**what?**
zoegirl:	things really r changing, aren't they? we're seniors, we're gonna graduate in 3 months, we're all gonna go our separate ways . . .
mad maddie:	**and this comes as a surprise?**
zoegirl:	no . . . i just don't know if i'm ready
mad maddie:	**i sure as hell am**
mad maddie:	**repeat after me: change is good**
zoegirl:	omg—no *way* did u just say that!
zoegirl:	if angela were here, she'd be rolling on the ground.
mad maddie:	**pardon me, but all i said was that change is good. why is that funny?**
zoegirl:	oh, mads. aren't u the 1 who was outraged when they switched brands of soap in the girls' bathroom?
mad maddie:	**the old kind was better! it smelled like lavender!**
zoegirl:	and u have a fit if u can't start the day with your pop-tart and dr pepper. i thought u were gonna stage a riot that 1 day when the drink machine was out!
mad maddie:	**i'm a growing girl. i need my caffeine.**
mad maddie:	**your point?**

zoegirl:	my point is that u *hate* change
mad maddie:	**no i don't**
zoegirl:	yeah, u do
zoegirl:	it's cute
mad maddie:	**i thought we were talking about marching off into the big bad world, not what kind of soap comes out when u squirt the thingie in the bathroom. and all i was saying is that we can't stay in high school forever, even if we wanted to.**
zoegirl:	i know that. but it still feels huge.
mad maddie:	**anywayz, no reason to get worked up about it now. there'll be plenty of time for weeping and gnashing of the teeth before it's over.**
zoegirl:	i already gnash my teeth—that's why i wear a mouth guard at nite. my dentist says it's the curse of being an over-achiever.
mad maddie:	**an over-achiever? U?**
zoegirl:	haha
zoegirl:	hey, can i tell u something stupid that's totally not worth dealing with, but at the same time i'm kinda disturbed by?
mad maddie:	**shoot**
zoegirl:	it has to do with jana. still wanna hear?
mad maddie:	**oh god. not THE J-WORD.**
zoegirl:	u and jana have a past. i'm just trying to be sensitive.
mad maddie:	**i think i can handle it, zo. u might have to excuse me while i retch, but other than that, go ahead.**
zoegirl:	well, right before i left school today, i ran into terri. now,

normally we wouldn't have even exchanged hellos, cuz of the fact she's jana's best friend. but terri had been crying—her eyes were red and her face was all puffy—and i would have been a complete jerk to not say anything.

mad maddie: **if i'd seen terri and she'd been crying, i wouldn't have said anything.**

zoegirl: yes u would've

mad maddie: **and if the situation were reversed, i wouldn't want HER to say anything, either.**

zoegirl: well, i am a good human, so i said, "um . . . terri? u ok?" which made her burst into tears all over again.

mad maddie: **c? that is why u should leave crying ppl alone.**

zoegirl: she was *horrified* to be falling apart like that in front of me, i could tell. she kept saying, "i'm fine, i'm fine," but she obviously wasn't. so i took her to the girls' room and gave her a wet paper towel to press against her eyes, and we ended up sitting down below the sinks and talking.

mad maddie: **so what was wrong? or rather, what terrible and awful thing had jana done to her?**

zoegirl: they'd gotten into a yelling match over terri's hair, if u can believe it. u know how it's now the same shade as jana's? jana had cussed terri out for being a clone, and i guess she took it 2 far and said some really nasty things.

mad maddie: **jana takes everything 2 far. she always has, but this year even more so.**

mad maddie: **she should go thru life armed with an apology and a complimentary bag of peanuts.**

zoegirl:	well, i felt bad for terri, even tho she's not my favorite person. i hate it when i fight with u or angela.
mad maddie:	**what r u talking about? we don't fight.**
zoegirl:	so i said something like, "she shouldn't treat u that way," and terri said, "she treats *everybody* that way." i said she better stop or she won't have any friends left, and terri snorted. she was like, "poor little jana, alone in a corner. just her and her teddy bear."
mad maddie:	**HA**
zoegirl:	that's what *i* said. cuz it's such an oxymoron, the image of jana—mistress of death and destruction—clutching a teddy bear.
mad maddie:	**ooo, nice use of the word "oxymoron." i KNEW i should have taken that SAT prep course.**
zoegirl:	but terri goes, "for real, jana has this mangy old teddy bear that smells like spit. she takes it with her everywhere."
mad maddie:	**???**
mad maddie:	**i've never seen jana with a teddy bear**
zoegirl:	she leaves it in her car. that's what terri says. which is entirely possible. have u seen all the crap in the back of jana's station wagon?
mad maddie:	**it's a mobile junk heap. it's disgusting.**
zoegirl:	according to terri, jana's dad gave her the teddy bear when she was little, and she's unhealthily attached to it.
zoegirl:	its name is Boo Boo Bear.
mad maddie:	**Boo Boo Bear???**
mad maddie:	**omfg, i am loving this so much. Boo Boo Bear!**

6

Send   Cancel

zoegirl:	terri was like, "i can't believe i'm telling u—jana would *die*."
mad maddie:	**heh heh heh, jana whitaker is unhealthily attached to Boo Boo Bear. suddenly the world is a MUCH brighter place!!!**
zoegirl:	er . . . not necessarily. cuz 2 seconds later, jana herself stormed into the bathroom. "*there* u r," she says to terri, all fuming. "ur not even gonna let me apologize?"
zoegirl:	then she noticed me, and her jaw dropped. she was like, "what r U doing here?"
mad maddie:	**plz, it's a public bathroom. does she think it's her private office?**
zoegirl:	my heart got all poundy, cuz—as u know—i'm a wimp, altho jana had already switched to ignoring me. she said to terri, "get up, we're leaving."
mad maddie:	**ok, that is the perfect example of the evilness of jana. she's bossy and she's mean.**
zoegirl:	but amazingly, terri didn't obey. she said, "u can't treat me like dirt and then expect me to be your slave."
zoegirl:	"terri, get up," jana said, still very pointedly not looking at me. "we can talk about your 'issues' later."
mad maddie:	**oh god**
zoegirl:	so terri goes, "*my* issues? ur the 1 with issues! keep acting the way ur acting, and u won't have any friends left!"
mad maddie:	**which is exactly what U said!**
zoegirl:	i know! and for some reason that made me get all stupidly brave, and under my breath i said, "no one but Boo Boo Bear."

Send   Cancel

mad maddie:	**holy shit! u da BOMB!**
zoegirl:	i shouldn't have, tho! it was totally unlike me!
mad maddie:	**that's what's so great!**
mad maddie:	**did jana hear?**
zoegirl:	she whipped her head toward me and was like, "WHAT did u say?" and terri goes, "she SAID no one but Boo Boo Bear."
mad maddie:	**gee, thanx, terri**
zoegirl:	jana was speechless. i've never in my life seen her speechless, but for that single moment she was. big splotches of color bloomed on her cheeks. it was freaky.
mad maddie:	**cuz she IS a freak**
zoegirl:	then she pulled herself together and said to me, "u've got nerve, sticking your nose up. not all of us live in a perfect plastic bubble, u know."
mad maddie:	**exsqueeze me? what is that even supposed to mean?!**
zoegirl:	she was trying to make me feel like a spoiled little baby, in comparison to her, the jaded and worldly jana.
mad maddie:	**who has a teddy bear.**
zoegirl:	her tone said 1 thing—c how cool and detached i am? i could care less that u know about my stupid bear—but her eyes said something else entirely. she looked like she wanted to kill me. i'm not kidding.
mad maddie:	**well, duh. if anyone had to be there for that lovely moment, i'm sure u were the last person she'd pick. u or me or angela, that is.**
zoegirl:	that thought crossed my mind, but i tried to tell myself, "no, ur being silly."
mad maddie:	**except ur not. we have what jana doesn't have—actual**

Send   Cancel

8

	true friends who lift each other up instead of tear each other down—and it's like a knife inside her heart.
mad maddie:	**think of it like this: jana's a dragon (SO not a stretch) and terri exposed her secret place of weakness. so now jana's screwed twice: 1st cuz u know about Boo Boo Bear, and 2nd cuz u know how easily terri would betray her.**
zoegirl:	jana the dragon. i just hope she doesn't flame me.
mad maddie:	**if she does, she'll have ME to deal with.**
mad maddie:	**now isn't it time to pick up your long-lost boyfriend? it's 5:15.**
zoegirl:	it is? EEEEEK! IT IS!!!!!
zoegirl:	go pick up angela from her aunt's house and then swing by here. i'll be the 1 gnawing my fingernails to the quick!
mad maddie:	**i'm heading out the door. l8r, g8r!**

Tuesday, February 7, 5:17 PM E.S.T.

SnowAngel:	mads, thank goodness i caught u
SnowAngel:	i'm not going to the airport after all, k?
mad maddie:	**angela! i was JUST about to log off and come get u, and now i'm staring at u dumbfounded.**
mad maddie:	**of course ur coming. zoe's expecting u!**
SnowAngel:	but c, doug's HER boyfriend, right? why does she need us to go with her to the airport?
mad maddie:	**uh, cuz she's zoe?**
mad maddie:	**and cuz she hasn't seen the guy for a whole semester. more, if u add the time we spent in california over**

Send   Cancel

	summer break. we got back, and she saw him for . . . what? a grand total of 1 week before he took off in his sailor suit to "Sea the World"?
SnowAngel:	r we doing that again? making fun of the name?
mad maddie:	**yes, cuz it demands to be made fun of!**
mad maddie:	**seriously, who goes to "Sea the World" during the 1st semester of their senior yr? senior yr is a time for madcap partying, not for sailing about the globe and stuffing yourself with culture.**
SnowAngel:	*coughs* on a party boat under jet blue skies, surrounded by girls in bikinis . . .
mad maddie:	**like i said. WHAT was he thinking?**
SnowAngel:	i saw a "sex and the city" rerun last nite where carrie meets these guys in the navy, and they were hot in their sailor suits. u wouldn't think it, but they were.
mad maddie:	**i don't think doug would be hot in a sailor suit.**
SnowAngel:	well . . . no
SnowAngel:	but hot or not, i'm not going to be there to c him. it's not that i don't WANT to, it's just that
mad maddie:	**yesssssssss?**
SnowAngel:	i have a flesh-eating virus. i DO!
SnowAngel:	i have a flesh-eating virus and it is attacking my nose and i am DISFIGURED. 😔 don't u dare laff!
mad maddie:	**angela, i saw u at school and u were fine**
SnowAngel:	but it was beginning. i could feel it.
mad maddie:	**uh huh. and how did u suddenly get this flesh-eating virus?**
mad maddie:	**does it by any chance have to do with the fact that we're talking about doug?**

Send   Cancel

SnowAngel:	what? NO!
mad maddie:	**r u sure? cuz i know u, angela. don't think i've forgotten your whole "doug will be my starter husband" spiel.**
SnowAngel:	maddie, that was LAST YEAR, way before doug and zoe even started dating.
SnowAngel:	anyway, did u happen to forget the 1 small fact that i'm going out with logan now???
mad maddie:	**ohhhh, right. logan.**
SnowAngel:	*puts hands on hips* why do u say it that way?
mad maddie:	**what way?**
SnowAngel:	u know what way
mad maddie:	**and U know why. so drop it.**
mad maddie:	**i think it's interesting that u develop a flesh-eating virus on the very day ur supposed to c doug, that's all.**
SnowAngel:	u think i'm making it up? i'm not making it up, maddie. if u insist on being technical, it's a staph infection. it's all nasty under my nose—and even up INSIDE my nose so that it looks very booger-ish and vile—and i'm NOT going out in public like this!
mad maddie:	**wait a sec—i'm having a flashback**
mad maddie:	**didn't this same staph infection thing happen last yr?**
SnowAngel:	yes *sniff, sniff*
SnowAngel:	it happens every year when i get a bad cold, and now i'll have to go on antibiotics and it'll take a week to clear up and until then everyone will think i've got a huge booger oozing out of my right nostril. they'll call me booger girl! that's what it'll say in the senior section of the yearbook. angela silver: booger girl!
mad maddie:	**god, ur vain**

Send   Cancel

11

SnowAngel:	ur calling me VAIN?!! *pops a blood vessel*
SnowAngel:	of COURSE i'm vain. i've been vain my entire life!
mad maddie:	**so suck it up and come with us to the airport!**
SnowAngel:	ur not grasping the full disgusting-ness of this. it's an OPEN SORE under my nostril. it's bubbly and slimy with neosporin, and it's growing even as we speak.
SnowAngel:	it PULSES, maddie
mad maddie:	**what is it with u and things that pulse?**
SnowAngel:	???
mad maddie:	**oh, angela, don't even! 1) your staph infection pulses. 2) u can't bear to touch your wrist cuz the vein there pulses. and 3), dear god, we certainly can't forget your neck.**
mad maddie:	**"woe is me, i can feel my blood pulsing thru my pillow! it jams up wrong against my carotid artery!"**
SnowAngel:	WELL IT DOES
mad maddie:	**then get a new one. u've been complaining about it for frickin ever!**
SnowAngel:	*adopts a wounded expression* i have had a series of unfortunate pillows, thank u very much. aunt sadie is a sweetie, but her pillows r crap. that's the only bad thing about living with her.
mad maddie:	**that and the fact that she burns every single thing she tries to cook.**
SnowAngel:	well, true
mad maddie:	**and she's a shopaholic.**
SnowAngel:	TINY shopaholic. small insignificant problem.
mad maddie:	**ur parents have no idea what they've gotten u into, do they?**

Send   Cancel

SnowAngel: my parents think that aunt sadie is taking very good care of me, which she is!

SnowAngel: anyway, don't u have somewhere to go? shouldn't u be leaving?

mad maddie: yeah, guess i better. u really don't wanna come?

SnowAngel: it's not that i DON'T—it's that i CAN'T.

mad maddie: all right. but remind me to tell u about the latest jana drama, involving an ill-fated stuffed animal named Boo Boo Bear.

SnowAngel: Boo Boo Bear? oh no, plz tell me jana didn't steal some poor kid's teddy bear!

mad maddie: jana didn't steal Boo Boo Bear. she OWNS Boo Boo Bear.

SnowAngel: what??? explain!

mad maddie: sorry, no time

SnowAngel: maddie! u CANNOT throw that out there and leave me hanging!

mad maddie: call me, babe. gotta run!

Tuesday, February 7, 11:01 PM E.S.T.

zoegirl: oh, angela, i am so in love!

SnowAngel: hey, zo. sorry about not making it to the airport.

zoegirl: that's ok. i mean, i'm sorry 2, but no big deal.

zoegirl: doug says "hi," btw

SnowAngel: aw, "hi" to him 2

SnowAngel: so is he bronzed and beautiful? did u fall into a passionate embrace the instant you saw him?

Send   Cancel

13

zoegirl:	well, his parents were there, so more like a really big hug. but omg, it felt *amazing*! it was like my whole body just opened up against his. like, ahhhhhh, this is what i've been missing.
zoegirl:	his arms were so strong, and he smelled so good, and he held me for what seemed like forever.
SnowAngel:	sounds wonderful ♡
zoegirl:	i couldn't keep my hands off him. seriously, it was like an addiction. i can totally c where that expression came from, that absence makes the heart grow fonder.
SnowAngel:	huh, maybe i should i try that with logan. whaddaya think—should i send him off to SEA the world?
zoegirl:	and on the way home, we *did* get to . . . u know. be more physical. his parents had a driver waiting for them in a limo, so for the car ride back it was just me and doug and maddie.
SnowAngel:	doug didn't wanna take the limo?
zoegirl:	no way! he wanted to be with me!
zoegirl:	mainly we just snuggled, since maddie was in the front seat. but it was pure bliss.
SnowAngel:	"pure bliss"? wowzers.
zoegirl:	u know what i mean, cuz u have that with logan.
zoegirl:	hey, let's go on a double-date this weekend! u and me and doug and logan!
SnowAngel:	uh . . . sure. i mean, lemme check with logan, but that would be fun.
zoegirl:	not on friday, cuz on friday i want doug all to myself. but how about saturday? it could be a pre-valentine's thing, since valentine's day falls on tuesday this year.

SnowAngel:	okey-doke—IF my nose is back to normal.
zoegirl:	angela, logan won't care. he worships the ground u walk on . . . which is good, cuz otherwise i might worry that u'd steal doug away. (jk! i'm TOTALLY just kidding!)
SnowAngel:	zoe! it makes me feel bad that u would even say that.
zoegirl:	i'm sorry, i guess i'm just thinking about last year.
SnowAngel:	well, don't. god.
zoegirl:	but i know u would never do that. we're in a totally different situation now. we're both so lucky!
SnowAngel:	not to bring u down or anything . . . but u doing all right with the whole jana weirdness? maddie finally gave me the complete story—sounds icky
zoegirl:	it was. i told doug about it, but he didn't understand why it creeped me out. so i explained jana's whole history with us, and turns out he didn't remember *any* of what happened in 10th grade. doesn't that blow your mind?
SnowAngel:	u think everyone should remember just cuz we do?
zoegirl:	well, yeah!
SnowAngel:	me 2 ☺
zoegirl:	i mean, jana emailed that picture of mads to the whole entire school. u'd think doug would remember a topless photo!
SnowAngel:	maybe he never saw it
zoegirl:	everyone saw it. didn't they?
SnowAngel:	well, doug doesn't travel in the same circles as "everyone." that's part of his charm.
zoegirl:	i told him that from sophomore year on, jana's been nothing but trouble for all 3 of us. how on the 1 hand that made it hugely satisfying to c terri take her on, but

on the other hand it gave me a chill. cuz now jana associates me with her moment of shame . . . and with jana u never know where that's gonna lead.

SnowAngel: pissed and unstable—not a good combination. (plus u know her secret about Boo Boo Bear, hee hee)

zoegirl: but in a way talking to doug about it was good, cuz he didn't c what the big deal was even after i explained. it made me be like, "ok, time to chill. u have better things to do than worry about jana." i have doug back, and that makes everything ok.

zoegirl: g-nite, angela! I'M SO IN LOVE!!!!

Wednesday, February 8, 10:02 AM E.S.T.

mad maddie: **YO! why aren't u at school, missy?! u didn't stay home cuz of your nose, did u?**

SnowAngel: hey now, how shallow do u think i am?!

mad maddie: **angela . . .**

SnowAngel: well . . . yes. yes i did. u wld have 2 if u looked like me!

mad maddie: **ur missing Senior Pet Day! how can u miss Senior Pet Day? ur the prez of the planning committee that came up with this swill!**

SnowAngel: swill! the senior planning committee comes up with delightful activities to celebrate senior-ness. it does not come up with SWILL.

mad maddie: **ted aronson brought a pig. he dressed him in tighty-whities.**

SnowAngel: did u bring chumley the psycho kitty?

mad maddie: yeppers, on loan from my dear bro mark. he piddled on mr. bradley's carpet.

SnowAngel: mark?

mad maddie: good 1. no, chumley.

SnowAngel: i'm so sorry i missed it

mad maddie: u should be. i can't believe your aunt sadie let u stay home cuz u think u LOOK bad. here i am in the flourescently lit media center with chumley the psycho kitty digging gashes into my thighs, while ur languishing about eating bon bons and feeling sorry for yourself.

SnowAngel: the blister is at its peak of foulness, maddie. it is a pustule of terror.

mad maddie: ha. "The Pustule of Terror," coming soon to theaters everywhere.

mad maddie: which actress should we get to play u?

SnowAngel: ooo, excellent question. but if we're gonna make a movie, we have to make it of all 3 of us. and we're not calling it "The Pustule of Terror." we'll call it . . . hmm. "The Winsome Threesome: Senior Year." how 'bout that?

mad maddie: very nice. and now: the cast?

SnowAngel: i know who i want for me: gwyneth paltrow

mad maddie: dude, ur so not a gwyneth. she is icy cool, and u r lovely and warm.

SnowAngel: *preens happily* i am?

mad maddie: how about kirsten dunst?

SnowAngel: i like kirsten, but her hair's the wrong color.

mad maddie: so she'll dye it a lovely light brown

Send   Cancel

mad maddie: or . . . i know! reese witherspoon!

SnowAngel: 2 old. i luv reese, but i don't wanna be played by an old-head.

mad maddie: i've got it! keira knightley, only un-british

SnowAngel: i like keira. she's approachable, not snotty, and she cares about clothes, but not in a show-off-y way.

SnowAngel: she'd have to get off her skeletal kick, tho

mad maddie: what about me?

SnowAngel: oh, ur easy. mary-kate olsen, cuz ur so shy and retiring.

mad maddie: ha ha

SnowAngel: let's c . . . for real?

SnowAngel: we need someone who's beautiful, but not ladylike.

mad maddie: definitely not ladylike

SnowAngel: someone who wears sweats instead of tiny tees. who's not afraid to chug a beer or tell a dirty joke. someone u'd want to party with.

SnowAngel: i know! cameron diaz!

mad maddie: oh yeah, right!

SnowAngel: i'm serious!

SnowAngel: only she's 2 old, just like reese

mad maddie: hate to break it to u, but we're getting old 2

SnowAngel: not THAT old

mad maddie: hold on—ow!

mad maddie: sorry, chumley was doing some nipping.

SnowAngel: her hair would be perfect for u, tho. cameron's, i mean.

SnowAngel: ooo, ooo! i know! amy smart!

mad maddie: who's amy smart?

SnowAngel: she's SO u. she was in "Road Trip," do u remember that movie? and "Just Friends." she's TOTALLY someone who'd be fun to hang out with. and she's gorgeous, but in a very down-to-earth way.

mad maddie: u r so full of it, but whatevs

mad maddie: what about zo?

SnowAngel: hmm, zoe. i'd say katie holmes, but the baby kinda throws a wrench into that. but katie's perfect in terms of the sweet-shy-smart category.

mad maddie: plus the dark eyes and dark hair, especially now that zoe's grown it out. altho personally i liked it better when it was chin length.

SnowAngel: really? i like it long. now she can do french-twist-y things, very elegant.

mad maddie: but if we can't use reese or cameron, we can't use katie.

SnowAngel: how about rory from "The Gilmore Girls"? pre-college.

mad maddie: maybe . . .

SnowAngel: or rachel bilson! how about rachel bilson?!

mad maddie: yeah, rachel's good, altho she'd have to lose the 'tude.

mad maddie: how about this: we'll offer the job to rory and rachel both, and whoever accepts 1st gets the role.

SnowAngel: deal 😊👍

SnowAngel: who should we get for the role of snarky evil dragon lady?

mad maddie: otherwise known as jana?

mad maddie: it's our movie. she's not invited

SnowAngel: good point

Send   Cancel

19

mad maddie: altho i DO have a new chapter in the dragon tales. zoe and i were chatting by our cars this morning, and jana pulled up next to us in her station wagon. i took a sneaky-peek for Boo Boo Bear, but there was waaaaay 2 much crap. mcdonald's bags and coke cans and that ratty army blanket she keeps handy for who knows what.

SnowAngel: her skanky interludes?

mad maddie: probably—with Boo Boo Bear looking on!

SnowAngel: it's weird how a girl who cares so much about her appearance can be such a slob when it comes to her car.

mad maddie: i know

SnowAngel: if i had a car, i'd treat it right.

mad maddie: u could hide a horse in jana's backseat and she'd never know.

SnowAngel: did she say anything when she saw u guys?

mad maddie: she climbed out of her car and gave us an absolute death look, and zoe, being totally un-subtle, elbowed me in the ribs and said, "c? c? i told u!"

SnowAngel: what'd u do?

mad maddie: i burst out laffing—i couldn't help it.

mad maddie: jana was THIS close to marching over and scorching us with her fire-breath, i'm not kidding.

SnowAngel: u just draw ppl to u, don't u? ur so sweet and cuddly. ☺

mad maddie: why yes, i am

mad maddie: and u know who i've drawn to me who i very much wish was UN-drawn to me? and i'm not talking about jana. i'm talking about a certain someone who latched onto U

Send   Cancel

	when u lived in el cerrito last year, and who now, apparently, has latched onto ME.
SnowAngel:	uh oh *chortles into hands*
SnowAngel:	did u get another email from glendy?
mad maddie:	**glendy is YOUR nutcase, not MINE. why is she sending me her stupid frickin chain letters???**
SnowAngel:	why do u keep reading them?
mad maddie:	**u sure r glib for someone who's experienced glendy-love first hand. she STALKED u, angela. and now she's stalking me!**
SnowAngel:	oh, muffin, u don't know what stalking is. has she bombarded u with care bears? noooo. has she invited u to dolphin-themed sleepovers? noooo. if she weren't the daughter of my dad's boss, i would have throttled her long ago. but luckily for her, she's zillions of miles away in california, so i deal with her by ignoring her—which is what u should do, u freak.
mad maddie:	**but why why why is she sending emails to someone she doesn't know?**
SnowAngel:	she must have gotten your addy from some group email i once sent, i dunno.
SnowAngel:	she collects ppl like butterfly collectors collect butterflies.
mad maddie:	**i am not glendy's butterfly!**
SnowAngel:	if u go to her MySpace profile, u'll c she lists over 4,000 friends. now c'mon. does anyone really have 4,000 friends?
mad maddie:	**the email i got from her today was titled "This Is Beautiful . . . And You Will Cry." however, it was NOT**

Send   Cancel

beautiful, and i did NOT cry. it was about some fake 9/11 survivor and a fund we could invest in for her. it made me so mad that ppl would try to exploit all that.

SnowAngel: why don't u just block her messages?

mad maddie: cuz then i couldn't complain about them. duh.

mad maddie: at the end of the email, it said "let's c satan stop this one," followed by instructions to send it to 5 more ppl in 60 seconds, blah blah blah.

SnowAngel: of course glendy probably sent it to 60 more ppl in 5 seconds . . . make that 2,000 more ppl . . .

mad maddie: ack, g2g. chumley is hissing at pete mazer's iguana, and Peaches the Friendly Librarian is trotting over to break up the fray.

SnowAngel: good ol' peaches. give her a squeeze for me.

mad maddie: fo shizzle!

Thursday, February 9, 4:15 PM E.S.T.

zoegirl: hurray for angela! u returned to school—AND U SURVIVED!

SnowAngel: barely. ppl stared, zo. it was 1 of those deals where everyone's eyes wld drift down to my nose then jerk back up, like, "oh, don't mind me. sure didn't notice that horrible blot on your face—nope, sure didn't!"

zoegirl: sweetie, your nose is so much less horrible than u think it is. i mentioned it to doug, and he said he wouldn't have even noticed if i hadn't pointed it out.

SnowAngel: gee, thanks

Send   Cancel

SnowAngel:	speaking of doug, what was up with his whole cheese rant?
zoegirl:	what was up with u giving him such a hard time about it? everyone in the cafeteria was swiveling their heads to c what was going on. they were like, "ok, what's HER deal?"
SnowAngel:	oh please. exaggerate much?
SnowAngel:	i was just giving him a hard time. he sounded so pretentious.
zoegirl:	well i guess they have better cheese in other parts of the world, cuz it's not pasteurized or something.
SnowAngel:	uh huh, whatevs. i LIKE american cheese.
zoegirl:	so do i
SnowAngel:	and not just cheese made in america, but actual orange squares of american cheese. it's the only kind for grilled cheese sandwiches.
zoegirl:	all i'm saying is that *ur* the 1 who made a big deal out of it, not doug. and i guess it seemed a little . . . over the top. even kristin was like, "does it not bother u that angela spent the whole lunch period monopolizing your boyfriend? she talked to him more than u did!"
SnowAngel:	omg, that is so not true! i can't believe kristin said that!
zoegirl:	it wasn't in a malicious way. it was just an observation.
SnowAngel:	friends aren't supposed to make "observations" like that.
zoegirl:	ok, time out. forget i mentioned it, all right?
SnowAngel:	no, it's not all right. what she said was completely rude!

Send   Cancel

zoegirl:	we're changing subjects now
SnowAngel:	says who?
zoegirl:	i passed jana in the hall, and if i'm not mistaken, she actually *smiled* at me. isn't that bizarre? i keep expecting to find pig's blood on my locker or something, as payback for the whole Boo Boo Bear thing, and instead she *smiles* at me?
SnowAngel:	no comment. i'm still annoyed with kristin.
zoegirl:	is it possible that what terri said to her—compliments of me—actually made her change her evil ways?
SnowAngel:	no. a spade is a spade is a spade—which AGAIN is why i'm surprised that kristin would act so uncool, cuz until now i didn't think she WAS a spade.
zoegirl:	okaaaay, time to change the subject
zoegirl:	will u go to planned parenthood with me? i've called and made an appointment for tomorrow afternoon.
SnowAngel:	whoa *jerks back in shock* didn't c that one coming!
zoegirl:	it's just that i'm pretty sure doug and i are gonna have sex, and i'm pretty sure it's gonna be sooner rather than later. i feel bad that i've made him wait this long!
SnowAngel:	he's been AT SEA, zoe. not a whole lot u could do from across the ocean.
zoegirl:	and when we do, i don't wanna be unprepared. i told the lady at planned parenthood that i wanna go on the pill, and she said i have to come in and talk to a counselor.
SnowAngel:	why the pill? why not condoms?
zoegirl:	i don't want my 1st time to be with a condom! yuck! anyway, doug's a virgin just like i am, so disease-wise,

	we're both safe. i've thought about it, and i just think the pill's the right choice for me.
SnowAngel:	u could do the patch, u know. that's what my aunt sadie uses.
zoegirl:	have u seen it?
SnowAngel:	it's just this brown plastic-y thing. it looks like a band-aid.
zoegirl:	i'm gonna go with the pill.
zoegirl:	will u come with me?
SnowAngel:	of course
SnowAngel:	does doug know?
zoegirl:	no, i'm gonna surprise him
zoegirl:	hey! u should go on the pill 2, for when u and logan decide to go for it!
SnowAngel:	i don't think so
zoegirl:	why not? don't u want to?
SnowAngel:	of course i do, just . . . there's no need to rush things. sometimes the wait makes it all the better.
zoegirl:	ur right, ur right, i don't mean to pressure u. i guess i'm just so happy that i'm in love, and i want u and logan to be that happy 2. i mean, u already r, of course. u know what i'm saying.
zoegirl:	if only maddie would find someone!
SnowAngel:	is she coming to planned parenthood with us?
zoegirl:	no, she promised to help her brother move out of their parents' house. can u believe mark and his girlfriend r finally getting a place of their own?
SnowAngel:	it's taken long enuff

Send   Cancel

25

SnowAngel:	how's pelt-woman doing, anyway? hairy as ever?
zoegirl:	hairy as ever, or so i assume. maddie still doesn't call her by her real name, if that tells u anything.
SnowAngel:	do we even know her real name?
zoegirl:	i don't remember. do u?
zoegirl:	omg, how horrible!
SnowAngel:	well, she probably doesn't know our names either. we're just "maddie's little friends."
zoegirl:	maddie's little friends who r off to planned parenthood . . .
SnowAngel:	ppl have no idea, do they? that we're growing up.
zoegirl:	but *we* know . . . and 1 of these days they'll figure it out.
SnowAngel:	just hopefully not until after graduation. *wink, wink*
SnowAngel:	cya!

Thursday, February 9, 9:11 PM E.S.T.

mad maddie:	there is nothing—nothing, i tell u—worse than itchy toes.
SnowAngel:	except for itchy palms. HATE itchy palms.
mad maddie:	toes r worse. the itch is on the knuckle part, and it's driving me nuts.
mad maddie:	but i actually didn't IM to tell u that. i IMed to tell u about vincent. i went to his house today and found him LOOKING AT PORN ON THE INTERNET!
SnowAngel:	ewww!
mad maddie:	i strolled into his room and there it was, up on the screen. i was like, DEAR JESUS, SAVE THIS BOY!

Send   Cancel

SnowAngel: what is it with guys and porn on the internet? do ALL guys like porn from the internet?

mad maddie: hmm. u want the true answer, or the angela-friendly answer?

SnowAngel: u don't think logan looks at porn, do u?

mad maddie: no, no, no. of course not.

SnowAngel: that's the angela-friendly answer, isn't it?

SnowAngel: oh, nvm

SnowAngel: my new friend andre doesn't look at porn on the internet, i know he doesn't.

mad maddie: what, cuz he's gay u think that? poor innocent angela.

mad maddie: and u don't have to say "my new friend." i go to school with andre 2.

SnowAngel: yes, but i feel so cool having a gay boy bud. altho i wish he WASN'T gay, so i could gobble him up.

SnowAngel: and say what u will, i'm SURE he doesn't look at porn.

mad maddie: well, with vincent, it's just who he is. i'm like, "u gotta love him," u know?

SnowAngel: "u gotta love him"??? maddie, PLEASE tell me ur not doing what i think ur doing!

mad maddie: which would be . . . ?

SnowAngel: u know—falling for the bad boy.

mad maddie: VINCENT?

SnowAngel: i personally can't believe ur even friends with him, given that he's so tight with jana. how do u get your head around that?

mad maddie: i don't. don't know what the guy sees in her.

SnowAngel: have u asked him?

Send   Cancel

mad maddie: he says she's fun to party with. is that a guy response or what?

mad maddie: anywayz, why the inquistion? u have andre, who's your "new friend." i have vincent, my spanish class friend. who entertains me.

SnowAngel: and makes u hot.

mad maddie: give me a break. that is not true, angela! and not that it's any of your beeswax, but he's hot for lila.

SnowAngel: uh, hate to say it, but it's not like u've let that stop u before. chive was totally dating whitney when u guys did your little fuck-buddy thing.

mad maddie: i am so not gonna respond to that. ancient history, a.

mad maddie: and "fuck buddy" is hardly the term, since i never even got naked with the guy.

SnowAngel: next thing u know, it'll be U jaunting off to planned parenthood, and i'll be alone in the corner wearing black, a virgin forever.

mad maddie: save the drama for yo mama. vincent and i r just buds.

SnowAngel: u could look at porn together. and eat popcorn.

mad maddie: and as for being a virgin forever, ur way more likely to leave the V-club than i am—that is if things with logan r as good as u say.

SnowAngel: shuddup. when and if logan and i have sex is none of your

mad maddie: yessss?

SnowAngel: hold on—mary kate's IMing, says it's important

mad maddie: dum di dum, dum di dum

mad maddie: i'm practicing my typing ... abcdefg

mad maddie: STILL practicing my typing ... hijklmnop

Send   Cancel

SnowAngel: ok, now THAT was weird

mad maddie: what?

SnowAngel: is something up with zoe? has she been saying things about me 2 anyone?

mad maddie: what r u talking about?

SnowAngel: according to mary kate, paige said zoe thinks i was FLIRTING with doug at lunch.

SnowAngel: *holds out hands in bewilderment* was i flirting with doug at lunch?

mad maddie: angela, u flirt with every 2-legged male on the planet.

SnowAngel: but it doesn't MEAN anything. zoe knows that.

SnowAngel: do u think she seriously has a problem with me talking to doug?

mad maddie: yes, she probably thinks ur trying to STEAL HER MAN

SnowAngel: that's ridiculous!

SnowAngel: omg, i'm gonna IM her and c what's going on.

mad maddie: angela, i was teasing!

mad maddie: angela?

mad maddie: BUT MY TOES R STILL ITCHING!

Thursday, February 9, 9:53 PM E.S.T.

SnowAngel: zo, did u talk to paige jensen at any point today?

zoegirl: i sat in front of her in AP English, but i wouldn't say we talked. why?

SnowAngel: well did u say anything to anybody that could have been passed on to paige? like to kristin, maybe?

zoegirl:	could u be a little more specific?
SnowAngel:	ok, this is stupid, but i'm just gonna say it. i know u think i was hogging doug's attention today, but do u honestly think i was FLIRTING with him?
SnowAngel:	cuz that was a LONG time ago when i somewhat (sorta) threw myself at him, and anyway i would never flirt with him cuz he's going out with U, which i would hope u would know!
zoegirl:	what? i *do* know that. i never said u were flirting with him!
SnowAngel:	and the more i think about it, the more it makes me mad. i don't wanna go around worrying about every last thing i say or do around him, so if u have a problem with the way i'm acting, would u please just tell me instead of talking about me behind my back?
zoegirl:	angela. STOP.
zoegirl:	did paige say i was talking about u behind your back?
SnowAngel:	mary kate overheard paige talking to some junior, and paige said that u said i was embarrassing myself with doug, and that i needed to keep my hormones to myself!
zoegirl:	???
zoegirl:	i never said ANY of that!
SnowAngel:	r u sure?
zoegirl:	angela, i just 6 hours ago asked u as my dear friend to go to planned parenthood with me so that 1 day doug and i can have sex. would i do that if i thought u were still hot for him?
SnowAngel:	well, what about kristin? after all, she already told u what a harlot i am!

Send   Cancel

zoegirl:	kristin made *one comment* about how much u talked to him. i shouldn't have even told u.
SnowAngel:	what else aren't u telling me?
zoegirl:	nothing!
zoegirl:	*r* u still hot for him?
SnowAngel:	NO!
SnowAngel:	but then why would paige say that?
zoegirl:	i have no idea. call her and ask.
SnowAngel:	yeah right. i've never even had a class with her. i'm gonna call her up and be like, "oh, btw, why were u talking trash about me?"
zoegirl:	then call mary kate and ask *her*. or call kristin. somebody is obviously confused.
zoegirl:	seriously, angela, i'm a little hurt u would think that of me!
SnowAngel:	well I'M a little hurt U would think that of ME!
zoegirl:	but i didn't! i *don't*!!!
zoegirl:	listen, i think we better end this convo, ok?!
SnowAngel:	zoe, wait!
zoegirl:	why, so u can yell at me some more?
SnowAngel:	*covers face in shame* i'm SORRY. i'm sorry, i'm sorry, i'm sorry!
SnowAngel:	zo?
zoegirl:	i'm here. i just don't know where this even came from.
SnowAngel:	mary kate thought i should know, that's all.
zoegirl:	except there's nothing TO know. ur getting bent out of shape over nothing.
zoegirl:	remember last semester when u made brownies to cheer

Send   Cancel

	me up, after my mom got mad at me for missing the early decision deadline for princeton? only i didn't *know* that's why u'd made them, and i didn't eat any, and u got really pissed?
SnowAngel:	i used aunt sadie's french chocolate. they were the most delicious brownies ever.
zoegirl:	u told me to tell u the next time u started freaking over nothing. well, here i am telling u.
SnowAngel:	ok, ok, ok
zoegirl:	u need to have faith in me, that's all. i love u, and i would never talk about u behind your back. all right?
SnowAngel:	except u did—with kristin
zoegirl:	ANGELA!
SnowAngel:	*baby deep breath. mama deep breath. big daddy deep breath*
zoegirl:	um . . . is this some new kind of therapy?
SnowAngel:	yes, i learned it from aunt sadie, who got it from 1 of her friends who teaches pre-school.
zoegirl:	and did it work? do u maybe wanna tell me that u love me 2?
SnowAngel:	of COURSE i do. and i'm sorry for freaking. i am.
SnowAngel:	*blinks humbly at friend* r we still on for tomorrow?
zoegirl:	we better be. bye!

Thursday, February 9, 10:20 PM E.S.T.

SnowAngel:	hey mads. zoe denied it all, but i called mary kate and she's SURE that's what she heard.

32

SnowAngel: u don't think zoe's lying, do u?

mad maddie: i've never known zoe to be a big liar

SnowAngel: yeah-huh. she lied to her mom when she said she'd apply to princeton early decision, when she never planned to actually do it.

mad maddie: that was zoe being passive-aggressive, not outright lying. and she DID get her application in eventually.

SnowAngel: well, maybe it's the same thing here. maybe she said something about me and doug in a passive-aggressive sort of way, and it got twisted around.

SnowAngel: but in that case why wouldn't she admit it?

mad maddie: beats me

SnowAngel: and if she DIDN'T say it, who did? i called kristin, and she swears it wasn't her. but who would have made something like that up?

mad maddie: chill, angela

mad maddie: if zoe says she didn't say it, she didn't say it.

SnowAngel: but it bugs me! wouldn't it bug u if someone was saying un-true things about U?

mad maddie: it's probably some dumb misunderstanding, like that someone saw u and doug going at it and jumped to the wrong conclusion.

SnowAngel: we were not "going at it"! why would u say that?!

mad maddie: u know what i mean

mad maddie: listen, angela. it's a stupid rumor, that's all. but i'll keep my ears open tomorrow, and if i hear anything i'll tell u!

Friday, February 10, 4:33 PM E.S.T.

mad maddie: hey, zo. u guys doin' the deed at PP?
zoegirl: we're here right now. eek!
zoegirl: sad posters on walls. sad ppl in chairs. waiting my turn.
mad maddie: IM when u get back, k?
zoegirl: will do. thx for checking in!

Friday, February 10, 6:10 PM E.S.T.

zoegirl: well . . . i did it!
mad maddie: u r with pill?
zoegirl: i am with pill. is that frickin weird or what?
mad maddie: what was it like? i want deets!
zoegirl: it was *crazy*. the woman i talked to was nice, don't get me wrong, but she was very . . . straightforward.
mad maddie: like how?
zoegirl: she had a plastic model of a vulva, for 1 thing. it sat on her desk like a flower arrangement.
mad maddie: ye gads
zoegirl: but more than that, just the way she talked about everything. like, she asked me what kind of "sex play" i'd engaged in, and she went thru this checklist, bam bam bam, as if we were making a grocery list. AND she made angela stay outside in the waiting room, so i was all by myself!
mad maddie: good lord. what kind of sex play HAVE u engaged in?

Send   Cancel

zoegirl:	and she asked me if i smoked—as if!
zoegirl:	she told me that doug and i should use condoms even if i did go on the pill, and that we should *talk* about everything before we actually *do* anything. here's her rule: "the topic should come up and the condom should come out before your zipper goes down."
mad maddie:	**oh, that's classic**
mad maddie:	**u should have a plaque with that needlepointed onto it. u could hang it above your bed.**
zoegirl:	honestly, it made me wanna swear off sex forever. it all sounds so complicated!
mad maddie:	**she's right, tho. if ur gonna have sex with someone, u should be able to talk to them about it.**
zoegirl:	here's another hot tip: she said to use water-based lubricants, not oil-based. and never vaseline.
zoegirl:	am i really gonna be using . . . lubricants?
mad maddie:	**i dunno. r u?**
zoegirl:	AND she asked me if i'd had any abortions, and if so, how many.
zoegirl:	i'm 17! have any 17-yr-olds had multiple abortions?
mad maddie:	**i bet so. depressing, isn't it?**
zoegirl:	angela and i saw this one couple out in the waiting room, they were about our age, and the guy was holding the girl's hand and she was crying. it made me wonder if . . . u know. if that was what she was there for.
mad maddie:	**at least the guy came with her**
zoegirl:	true
mad maddie:	**but ur not gonna get preggo, cuz ur going on the pill.**
zoegirl:	right. RIGHT. i start the 1st sunday after my next period,

Send   Cancel

	which should be coming up in a week or so. and once i've started, we're supposed to wait a month to be safe.
mad maddie:	**u've waited this long, what's another month?**
zoegirl:	that's kinda how i feel, to tell the truth.
zoegirl:	my counselor-lady said there might be side effects, like weight gain, moodiness, and "spotty darkening of the skin." doesn't that sound lovely?
mad maddie:	**lucky u**
zoegirl:	i told angela that part, and she turned pale. she was all, "why is it always the girls who get stuck with this crap? why can't the GUYS get spotty darkening of the skin?!"
mad maddie:	**ah, angela, how i love her**
mad maddie:	**alexis winthrop came up to me today and asked if it was true that she's after doug, btw.**
zoegirl:	oh great
mad maddie:	**i told her no, of course**
zoegirl:	i don't understand. it's like 1 little seed got planted, and now it's growing into this huge thing.
mad maddie:	**ppl like gossip, especially when it's something bad.**
zoegirl:	not me! angela and i made a pact that if anyone says anything, we're just gonna ignore it.
mad maddie:	**it doesn't bother u?**
zoegirl:	r u kidding?
zoegirl:	i asked kristin point blank if she talked about angela and doug with anyone else, and she swore up and down that the only comment she made was that 1 to me.
mad maddie:	**what about paige? did u ask her about it?**
zoegirl:	no. i almost did, but sitting there in english during the actual moment, i felt 2 ridiculous.

zoegirl:	it's all so stupid, i figured just let it go.
mad maddie:	**makes sense. cyas!**

Friday, February 10, 6:35 PM E.S.T.

zoegirl:	hi again
mad maddie:	**hey, long time no talk!**
zoegirl:	maddie, u DO know that i didn't say any of that stuff, right? about angela being 2 flirty with doug?
mad maddie:	**zoe, of course**
zoegirl:	i might have thought it, just for a sec. but i never would have said it out loud.
mad maddie:	**i know**
mad maddie:	**i've noticed she HAS toned down the flirtation, tho. like today, she basically ignored him.**
zoegirl:	yeah, i noticed that 2. part of me feels bad, but part of me's glad.
zoegirl:	altho what am i saying? she's going out with logan, for heaven's sake.
mad maddie:	**oh, right, he's a great deterrent**
zoegirl:	off for real. bye!

Saturday, February 11, 11:01 AM E.S.T.

SnowAngel:	ok, little miss nosy pants. i have a list for u of all the reasons logan is so wonderful.

mad maddie: hey now, i never said logan wasn't wonderful. i'm just not convinced he's wonderful for U.

SnowAngel: *clears throat and shakes out piece of paper*

SnowAngel: Number 1. he loves me and always wants to be with me, even more than with his friends.

mad maddie: can u say "smother"?

SnowAngel: Number 2. he downloads songs onto my iPod and makes romantic playlists.

mad maddie: very sweet, i admit. have u ever made HIM romantic playlists?

SnowAngel: Number 3. he's extremely cute. even u can't deny that!

mad maddie: i never have! altho i wish he'd branch out from the abercrombie look already.

SnowAngel: and Number 4. he doesn't look at internet porn!

mad maddie: hardy har har

mad maddie: is that all u've got?

SnowAngel: noooo, that's not all. that's just all i happened to come up with this very second, off the top of my head.

mad maddie: dude, i love logan—as a PAL. and i know u do 2. i'm just not convinced he gets u hot and bothered.

SnowAngel: we have fun together. he gives great backrubs, and he loves "grey's anatomy."

SnowAngel: he's a terrific catch—even aunt sadie says so. we have a *great* relationship!

mad maddie: then why r u working so hard to defend it?

SnowAngel: and i would like to point out that having a bf who's

	also a "pal" is a good thing. in the long run that's much more important than getting hot and bothered.
mad maddie:	**is it? i personally think u should go for both.**
SnowAngel:	he's gonna inherit his dad's business 1 day, did u know that?
mad maddie:	**u did NOT just say that**
SnowAngel:	and tonite we're doubling with zoe and doug, so there. it's a pre-valentine's day thing.
mad maddie:	**ooo-wee, that's sure to be fun.**
SnowAngel:	well . . . to tell the truth, i'd back out if i could. i don't want to be around doug and have zoe accuse me of throwing myself at him again.
mad maddie:	**angela, zoe DIDN'T accuse u of throwing yourself at him.**
SnowAngel:	or of trying to lure him away or having pent-up feelings for him or whatever. but if she's gonna pretend there isn't all this tension floating around, then so am i.
SnowAngel:	HOWEVER, it's gonna be hard when it's just me and logan and zoe and doug. won't u come with us? please please pleasy please?
mad maddie:	**can't. i'm going over to mark and pelt-woman's new pad for dinner. pelt-woman is making vegetarian lasagna in a desperate attempt to cover up the smell of kimchee.**
SnowAngel:	huh?
mad maddie:	**their new place smells like korean food from the ppl who lived there before them.**
SnowAngel:	☺
mad maddie:	**u know what's weird? i can't get used to the fact that**

Send Cancel

	mark's gone. u'd think i'd be, "wh-hoo, more doritos for me!" but the house feels wrong w/o him.
SnowAngel:	u miss him. that's normal.
mad maddie:	i didn't say i missed him. who said anything about missing him?
SnowAngel:	*deadpans* oh, right, cuz ur tough, strong maddie who takes it all in stride. u luuuuuuuuuuv change. u luuuuuuv change so much u can't wait to dump this town and move to california!
mad maddie:	have u been talking to zoe? r u making fun of me?
SnowAngel:	awww, mads, would i do that?
mad maddie:	oh, nvm
mad maddie:	have fun on your date!

Sunday, February 12, 10:00 AM E.S.T.

zoegirl:	morning, angela. that was great last nite, wasn't it?
SnowAngel:	uh, sure, we should do it more often ☺
zoegirl:	was it weird that during the movie we were all . . . u know? i felt kinda strange about it afterward.
SnowAngel:	don't worry, it was fine
zoegirl:	"fine"? i doubt logan would like hearing u call it that!
zoegirl:	jk
zoegirl:	anyway, we're all consenting adults, right?
SnowAngel:	exactly. of course. no need to talk about it again.
zoegirl:	i'm just so glad the 4 of us were able to spend time together w/o there being any ridiculous undercurrents.

	if anybody ever *did* think u were secretly lusting after doug, they sure wouldn't after last nite!
SnowAngel:	cuz i'm NOT lusting after doug. god!
zoegirl:	i know! i know, angela.
zoegirl:	but *i am* . . . altho it's not lust, it's love. sometimes i think, what would i do w/o him? and then i feel so . . . i dunno, un-me for feeling that way. altho that's silly, cuz it *is* me feeling this way . . .
zoegirl:	didn't u think it was funny when doug did his walking-on-hot-coals impression? can u believe he actually DID walk on hot coals?
SnowAngel:	frankly, no
zoegirl:	he did, in indonesia
zoegirl:	getting to see so many places *did* change him, but all in good ways.
SnowAngel:	he does seem more confident now. the way he holds himself, even.
zoegirl:	sometimes, even tho i know i'm being silly, i get this tiny feeling of wondering whether i'm good enuff for him. isn't that ridiculous? it's just that i know he's gonna do important things in the world. i just *know* it.
SnowAngel:	so r U, zoe
zoegirl:	well, yeah. who said i wasn't?
zoegirl:	hey, i'm outta here. i'm meeting doug to study.
SnowAngel:	at 10 o'clock on sunday morning?!
zoegirl:	just cuz it's spring semester of our senior yr doesn't mean we can slack off. bye!

Send   Cancel

SnowAngel: maddie, i'm sorry to report that our zoe has gone over the edge. i fear she's becoming ONE OF THOSE.

mad maddie: one of what?

SnowAngel: u know, one of those girls whose lives revolve around their boyfriends. she hung out with him all last nite, and now she's off with him AGAIN—on sunday morning when she should be lounging around with greasy hair and eating lucky charms from the box!

mad maddie: let's c, 3 guesses what UR doing right now?

SnowAngel: *sniffs and pops special edition multi-colored whale into mouth*

mad maddie: doug's JUST gotten back in town. she's excited, that's all.

SnowAngel: i guess *looks miffed anyway*

SnowAngel: can i tell u something pervy?

mad maddie: ooo, baby, please

SnowAngel: last nite after dinner, the 4 of us went and played pool at coop's. then we went back to zoe's house and watched HBO, her and doug on one sofa and me and logan on the other. and the lights were off and the door was closed and zoe's parents weren't home . . . and it turned into this weird double macking session. is that sick? that's sick, isn't it?

mad maddie: u were going at it in the same room? all 4 of u?

SnowAngel: i know! and u could hear NOISES! slurp, slurp, fumble, fumble. there was this pretense that we

Send   Cancel

42

were watching the movie, but no one was, and it was just smarmy!

mad maddie: **so why'd u do it?**

SnowAngel: i dunno, cuz everybody just . . . did. AND cuz i didn't have any choice after the whole "angela's after doug" debacle. not that i'm still obsessing over that.

mad maddie: **paranoia will destroy ya . . .**

SnowAngel: it's like, i had to make even more of an effort than normal to be all rah-rah about logan, while at the same time NOT act in any possible way that could be considered flirty toward doug. but i also had to be jokey and normal with doug, cuz otherwise it would be like admitting that those rumors had actually existed. and that i cared.

SnowAngel: it was exhausting.

mad maddie: **so u just said, "what the hell, let's have an orgy."**

SnowAngel: at one point i heard doug whisper something to zoe about "lower, lower," and zoe giggled in an aren't-we-naughty kind of way. it was some random private joke, obviously, but it gave logan ideas. he got all glazed-eyed and moaning, and i had to take his hand and move it higher higher higher. i was like, "logan, NO. we r not doing that in zoe's house with zoe and doug five feet away!!!"

maddie: **u realize ur oversharing**

SnowAngel: and of course it made me think about your "hot and bothered" comment, which pissed me off.

SnowAngel: so then zoe IMed me this morning to do a post-op on the date, and she was all glowing and giddy and a LITTLE embarrassed, but not nearly embarrassed

43

enuff. it just made me think, what is my life coming to?

mad maddie: zoe's in love. it's way sweet.

mad maddie: altho they do need to get their own room.

SnowAngel: *shakes off whole experience*

SnowAngel: i'm going to have a purging ritual, that's what i'm gonna do. aunt sadie bought this high-tech body wash yesterday with glycolic acid in it, and she said i could try it out. 🛁 supposedly it makes u itch like crazy, but afterward ur all silky and soft.

mad maddie: uh, sure, dude. enjoy your acid bath. as for me, i'm gonna park my butt in front of the TV and have a movie marathon. i'm talking all day and deep into the nite . . . cuz tomorrow senior privileges kick in!!! yeah!!!

SnowAngel: aunt sadie is so confused about that, btw. she was like, "u mean, until now u COULDN'T sleep in? even if u had a free period 1st thing in the morning?" she thinks high school is like college or something.

mad maddie: or maybe she just doesn't get the idea of NOT sleeping in. maybe she doesn't realize that other ppl have bosses/teachers who care.

SnowAngel: i am very jealous that u'll be in your warm cozy bed when i'm in 1st period french.

mad maddie: i feel for ya. cyas!

Monday, February 13, 4:15 PM E.S.T.

zoegirl: hey, angela. i'm at java joe's with my laptop . . . and guess who's working the counter?

Send   Cancel

SnowAngel: who?

zoegirl: margo pedersen! i'm the only customer, so she came over and hung out for a while.

zoegirl: angela, she broke up with ian!!!

SnowAngel: ian??? as in maddie's ian?

zoegirl: well, ian who *used* to be maddie's ian.

SnowAngel: yeah, but he never got over her, so i can still call him that.

SnowAngel: when did margo break up with him? and why?

zoegirl: today—and the reason she gave is cuz she doesn't want "a long-term commitment" when she goes to college.

zoegirl: she said she figured that since they were gonna break up anyway, they might as well do it now. she was all, "i don't want to be tied down. i wanna enjoy my senior year."

SnowAngel: she couldn't enjoy it with ian?

zoegirl: that's what i said. and she said, "look, zoe. u and doug, if that's what u want, that's great. but i'm 18 yrs old. i'm not ready to settle down."

zoegirl: she was pretty condescending, actually—like she felt sorry for me cuz i *was* settled down.

SnowAngel: i'm sure she didn't mean it that way

zoegirl: no, she did. but, whatever. that just means that what she and ian had wasn't as real as what doug and i have.

SnowAngel: so ian's a free agent, huh? *taps chin speculatively*

zoegirl: but to break up with him the day before valentine's day, isn't that harsh?

SnowAngel: crap—valentine's day!

zoegirl:	why "crap"?
SnowAngel:	nothing, nvm
zoegirl:	???
SnowAngel:	i don't have anything for logan, that's all. i thought saturday nite was our valentine's day deal, i thought that was our whole celebration. but yesterday logan said something about a "valentine's surprise," which means he's planning something else, which means i have to, 2. crap!
zoegirl:	go out and get him something, it's not hard
SnowAngel:	what r u giving doug?
zoegirl:	a unicycle
SnowAngel:	a UNICYCLE?
zoegirl:	i found it thru the want ads. isn't it the perfect doug gift?
SnowAngel:	great, a unicycle
SnowAngel:	ur gonna make me look bad here, zo
zoegirl:	make logan something homemade, like certificates for one free snuggle. i'm doing that 2. i cut them out of fancy stationery and decorated them with teeny love stickers.
SnowAngel:	i can't do that—he'd think i copied u
zoegirl:	u don't have to get him something big, just give him something from the heart.
zoegirl:	want me to go shopping with u?
SnowAngel:	that's ok. but thanks.
zoegirl:	u sure? i'd be happy to.
SnowAngel:	i'm sure. cya!

lauren myracle

Monday, February 13, 4:46 PM E.S.T.

SnowAngel:	maddie, i'm a bad person!!!!
mad maddie:	**why, what did u do?**
SnowAngel:	tomorrow's valentine's day, and logan has a "surprise" for me. but i have nothing for him!
mad maddie:	**u need a ride to the mall?**
SnowAngel:	zoe already offered, and i turned her down. wanna know why?
mad maddie:	**why?**
SnowAngel:	cuz i didn't WANT to go valentine's day shopping with zoe. i didn't want to hear her go on and on about how in love she is when . . . when . . .
mad maddie:	**when what?**
mad maddie:	**once and for all, just say it.**
SnowAngel:	*turns into a tiny person with a very tiny voice*
SnowAngel:	when maybe i'm not. in love. *crawls under a rock and puts hands over head*
mad maddie:	**bravo, angela. clap, clap, clap.**
SnowAngel:	u've known it all along, i know. and maybe i have 2—or maybe it took seeing how truly head-over-heels zoe is to realize how un-head-over-heels i am.
SnowAngel:	know what the worst part is? all this tension over not feeling in love with logan is making it hard to even have fun with him. when normally i DO have fun with him, lots of fun. just . . . more as a friend.
mad maddie:	**i'm soooo proud of u, a. if i were there, i'd give u a shiny gold star.**

SnowAngel:	the whole stupid rumor thing didn't help either, cuz it was like everybody could c what i couldn't. not that i was lusting after doug, just that i WASN'T lusting after logan.
SnowAngel:	altho i think it finally died out, don't u? the rumors?
mad maddie:	**uh . . .**
SnowAngel:	ok, if u have to say "uh," don't answer.
SnowAngel:	but about logan—what am i gonna do? 😞 just this afternoon he left a cherry mash for me in my locker, cuz he knows they're my fave. he's such a good guy—i don't wanna hurt him!!!
mad maddie:	**u gotta cut him loose, angela. u have no choice.**
SnowAngel:	but not the day before valentine's day! then i'd be just like
SnowAngel:	OMG, I FORGOT TO TELL U! MARGO PEDERSEN BROKE UP WITH IAN!!!
mad maddie:	**whoa, tone it down**
SnowAngel:	isn't that great? *happy dance, happy dance*
SnowAngel:	now u 2 can get back together!
mad maddie:	**angela, u r un-frickin-believable! 1 second ur moaning and groaning over logan, and the next ur jumping up and down about ian?**
SnowAngel:	i feel better now that i've gotten the logan thing off my chest.
SnowAngel:	*pinches arm in surprise* i do! i feel so much better!
mad maddie:	**well lucky u, but what about logan?**
SnowAngel:	i guess ur right—i have to break up with him. just not today, that would be heartless.

Send   Cancel

SnowAngel:	altho it prolly won't be as awful as i think. cuz when 1 person isn't into it anymore, usually the other person isn't either, right?
mad maddie:	**no**
SnowAngel:	what do u mean, no? the correct answer is yes, u blockhead!
mad maddie:	**uh huh. that's why there's so many songs about broken hearts. that's why ppl shoot their exes out of jealousy. cuz everyone's like, "oh, u want to break up? great! no problem! that's what i want 2!"**
SnowAngel:	oh shut up *scowls at friend*
SnowAngel:	i can't believe u suggested that logan might SHOOT me!
mad maddie:	**i did not just suggest**
mad maddie:	**grrrr**
SnowAngel:	logan is not going to shoot me. logan might be sad, but logan'll be ok, and ultimately he'll be better off with someone who appreciates him.
SnowAngel:	and now enuff about logan. aren't u excited to hear about ian?
mad maddie:	**angela . . . don't, k?**
SnowAngel:	but why????
mad maddie:	**i know it's always been this huge fantasy of yours that ian and i get back together, but whatever we once had . . . it was a long time ago.**
SnowAngel:	but
mad maddie:	**shush**
SnowAngel:	if only u'd

Send   Cancel

mad maddie: LET. IT. GO.

SnowAngel: is it cuz of vincent?

mad maddie: omg, ur unbelievable

mad maddie: no, angela, it's not cuz of vincent. it's just that we don't all need a boyfriend to make our lives feel complete, much as that might surprise u.

SnowAngel: ur no fun at all

mad maddie: sure i am. i'm tons of fun.

SnowAngel: guess i better go buy logan a v-day present since ur being such a poop. tootles!

Tuesday, February 14, 5:02 PM E.S.T.

mad maddie: happy valentine's day, zo! wasn't that sweet what the senior guys did?

zoegirl: it *was*! and so out of character!

mad maddie: i wonder who came up with it? i mean, can u imagine a bunch of guys sitting around and 1 of them saying, "hey, i know! let's deliver a bag of candy hearts to every girl in the senior class!"

zoegirl: i can't believe doug managed to keep it a secret. he told me later that he made sure my bag had extra candy, tho. cuz he is a big sweetie.

mad maddie: how'd the big sweetie like his unicycle?

zoegirl: he's out in my backyard right now, trying to get the hang of it. i can c him clinging to a tree branch, trying to get his balance.

mad maddie: ha

mad maddie: what'd he get u?

zoegirl: a pair of hand-crafted earrings from somalia! he bought them when they docked there and saved them all this time. they're gorgeous.

mad maddie: uh huh. well, isn't that nice.

mad maddie: wanna know what i got for v day? go ahead. ask.

zoegirl: uh oh . . .

mad maddie: A FRICKIN EMAIL CHAIN LETTER! FROM GLENDY!!!

zoegirl: oh no! what did this 1 say?

mad maddie: the subject line was "have a heart" (cuz it's v-day, get it?) and the message said, "hi, i am a 29-yr-old father whose baby has some terrible gut-wrenching disease. please forward this to your 2 million closest friends, cuz if u do then we'll get 32 cents a message and we can pay for our poor baby's operation." it ends with, "if u delete this . . . u seriously don't have a heart."

zoegirl: ouch

zoegirl: u deleted it, didn't u?

mad maddie: on the bottom was a picture of a naked baby, butt in air. there was a ribbon wrapped around the baby with a tag that said "from god."

zoegirl: oh no!

mad maddie: ur laffing, aren't u?

zoegirl: i just think it's hysterical that u get chain letters from glendy and u actually read them. u get what u deserve.

mad maddie: gee, thanx for your sympathy

zoegirl: i get her messages 2, but they go straight to "junk" and i delete them. i don't understand why u don't 2.

mad maddie:	**i dunno, cuz i'm perversely curious to c what horror she's dredged up next?**
zoegirl:	then u can't complain about them
mad maddie:	**yes i can. that's the whole point.**
zoegirl:	maybe she'll apply to santa cruz, since she's in-state. maybe u guys can room together.
mad maddie:	**should i kill myself now?**
mad maddie:	**1 of these days i'm gonna write her back. i'm just waiting for the right moment.**
zoegirl:	please tell me when u do. *that* i want to c.
mad maddie:	**hey, have u heard from angela? i called her cell but didn't get her.**
zoegirl:	she's with logan. he found me today after french and told me he's got some great surprise for her. he was verrrrrrrry excited.
mad maddie:	**oh man**
mad maddie:	**u know she wants to break up with him, right?**
zoegirl:	WHAT?
zoegirl:	why???
mad maddie:	**cuz she finally admitted that he's more like a brother than a lover. ooo, that would make a good country song, wouldn't it?**
zoegirl:	that's not true, tho. if u'd seen them on saturday . . . she sure wasn't *kissing* him like a brother.
mad maddie:	**that's cuz she was faking, and deep down u know it. u just wanted her to be in love with logan so that the 2 of them could be twinsies with u and doug.**
zoegirl:	that's ridiculous

mad maddie:	**plus it made it easier for u to blow off those rumors, cuz if she was firmly with logan then of course she wasn't flirting with your bf.**
zoegirl:	oh god, maddie
zoegirl:	u should have seen logan when he was telling me about her v-day surprise. he was like, "she likes blue, doesn't she? i know pink's her favorite color, but pink just wasn't an option. but blue's good 2, don't u think?"
zoegirl:	he was so excited!
mad maddie:	**c, there's the imbalance. he was so excited, and she was like, "oh, crap. valentine's day."**
zoegirl:	ur depressing me. this whole conversation is depressing me.
zoegirl:	1st margo and ian, and now angela and logan?
mad maddie:	**it's senior yr. these things happen.**
zoegirl:	i hate that attitude! just cuz it's senior yr doesn't mean everything has to fall apart—and ppl should just keep their mouths shut if all they're gonna be is negative.
mad maddie:	**by "ppl," do u mean me?**
zoegirl:	no, not u
zoegirl:	but ok, take this for example. do u know what jana said to me today, totally out of nowhere? she stopped me in the hall and goes, "how r things with your boyfriend? keeping him on a short leash?"
mad maddie:	**???**
zoegirl:	she said it with a smirk, as if he *needs* to be kept on a leash. i guess she's been hearing those stupid rumors 2.
zoegirl:	or . . . omg
mad maddie:	**what?**

zoegirl:	was she the 1 who STARTED those rumors???
mad maddie:	**holy frickin crap!**
zoegirl:	all this time i've been thinking, whew, i got off easy with the whole Boo Boo Bear encounter. a couple thousand death stares, but nothing more.
zoegirl:	was this her way of getting me back, by planting rumors about angela and doug?
mad maddie:	**jesus, how could we have been so STUPID?!**
mad maddie:	**AND she has homeroom with paige. we're such idiots!**
zoegirl:	we don't know for SURE that it was her . . .
mad maddie:	**i'm gonna find out. and if it was, she's going to pay!!!**

Tuesday, February 14, 8:42 PM E.S.T.

SnowAngel:	GET YO BOOTIES IN THE CHATROOM! *NOW*!!!!

You have just entered the room "Angela's Boudoir."
mad maddie has entered the room.
zoegirl has entered the room.

mad maddie:	**angela, where have u been? i've been calling fo-evah!**
SnowAngel:	so sorry, but i was unable to answer the phone. wanna know why?
zoegirl:	why?
SnowAngel:	cuz i was 2 busy DRIVING MY JEEP!!!!!! *squeals and laffs spazerifically*
zoegirl:	your jeep? what jeep?

Send   Cancel

mad maddie:	**wait a minute, please don't tell me ...**
zoegirl:	no
SnowAngel:	yes
mad maddie:	**NO**
SnowAngel:	YES! 😁 😁 😁
zoegirl:	LOGAN GAVE U A *JEEP*???
SnowAngel:	i know, isn't it incredible?!
SnowAngel:	he took me to collier park and led me to the playground area, and parked on the street was this sweet baby-blue Suzuki Samurai. he goes, "nice car," and i said, "yeah." he goes, "u should take it for a ride," and i was like, "uh-huh, sure, whatever." and he goes, "no, seriously. look—the keys r in the ignition." and i was like, "what dummy left the keys in the ignition?"
SnowAngel:	finally he took me by the shoulders, looked me in the eyes, and said, "angela, it's yours. happy valentine's day."
mad maddie:	**whoa, that's a helluva v-day present**
SnowAngel:	his uncle IS the decatur car king, u know. i've given him so much hell over those cheesy radio commercials, but now i'm like, "car king, i love u!!!"
SnowAngel:	OMG!!! I HAVE A JEEP!!!!!!!!!!!!!!!!!!!!!!!!!
zoegirl:	but angela ... u can't *keep* it!
SnowAngel:	why not?
zoegirl:	u know why! cuz ur planning on breaking up with him!
SnowAngel:	maddie! *growls at friend*
mad maddie:	**oops—guess i let the cat out of the bag**

Send Cancel

SnowAngel:	*regains composure like a glorious summer day*
SnowAngel:	well OBVIOUSLY i'm not gonna break up with him now! duh!
zoegirl:	cuz he gave u a *car*?
SnowAngel:	yep
SnowAngel:	i mean, what an amazingly generous thing! he's like . . . oprah!
mad maddie:	**i can't believe he gave u a jeep—altho that does show good taste on his part. if your parents were here, no way would they let u keep it.**
SnowAngel:	but they're not, and aunt sadie thinks it's extremely romantic. she's gonna put me on her insurance, and we're just gonna . . . not exactly mention it, that's all. ☺
zoegirl:	angela, i can't get my head around this. how much do u think he spent?
SnowAngel:	$1,200, he told me. his uncle cut him a deal.
zoegirl:	twelve hundred dollars???
SnowAngel:	it's used, natch. but it's been really well maintained.
zoegirl:	angela, i think that's . . .
zoegirl:	i mean, it's incredibly nice . . .
mad maddie:	**MORE than nice**
zogirl:	but it just doesn't seem right. u can't just give someone a CAR!
SnowAngel:	well, he did
zoegirl:	what did u give him?
SnowAngel:	erm . . . a very lovely gift certificate to barnes & noble

mad maddie:	**for how much?**
SnowAngel:	that hardly matters, now does it?
zoegirl:	u need to give it back.
SnowAngel:	i'm not giving it back.
zoegirl:	but u don't even love him!
SnowAngel:	love can grow! love can bloom!
zoegirl:	ANGELA!!!
mad maddie:	**ohhhh, i just figured what's going on here. zoe's rethinking those hand-crafted earrings . . . aren't u, zo?**
zoegirl:	what?! i *adore* my earrings!
zoegirl:	r u suggesting i'd rather have a car?
mad maddie:	**heavens, no. who in their right mind would rather have a car than earrings?**
SnowAngel:	u guys, please don't spoil this for me. u KNOW how much i've wanted a car, for like my whole life. and logan wanted to do this—for me.
SnowAngel:	i think everyone should just be happy, k?
mad maddie:	**come pick us up—i wanna c these wheels of yours!**
mad maddie:	**plus, we've got news to share about our evil nemesis, the dragon lady.**
zoegirl:	we've MAYBE got news. MAYBE.
SnowAngel:	i'll be right over
SnowAngel:	zoe, u in?
zoegirl:	ohhh . . . ok. i've just gotta call doug and tell him i'll be late for our study date.
SnowAngel:	there in a flash, chickies. i'll be the one in the jeep!!!!

Send   Cancel

Wednesday, February 15, 6:33 PM E.S.T.

mad maddie: **hey, a. wassup?**

Auto response from SnowAngel: zoom zoom zoom!

mad maddie: **IM me when u get in. i hunted down jana, and i want to give u the full report!**

Wednesday, February 15, 10:39 PM E.S.T.

SnowAngel: hey, mads, got your message. sorry i missed u.

mad maddie: **that's ok. how's the jeep?**

SnowAngel: *sighs in rapture*

SnowAngel: the jeep is WONDERFUL. i feel like such a princess! 👑

mad maddie: **u R such a princess**

SnowAngel: i'm gonna treat logan right, i really am. i think i wasn't being fair to him . . . before.

mad maddie: **u know what? what will be, will be. i've decided to wash my hands of it.**

mad maddie: **ready to hear what happened with jana?**

SnowAngel: *sits criss-cross-apple-sauce at maddie's feet* spill!

mad maddie: **i was totally straight-up. i cornered her by her locker and said, "did u tell paige jensen that zoe said angela needed to keep her hormones to herself?"**

SnowAngel: *blushes* i really don't like hearing it put that way, even if zoe DIDN'T say it.

SnowAngel: how did jana respond?

mad maddie: **being the callous and soul-less person she is, she laffed**

58

and said, "no, but i wish i did. that's priceless." so i said, "bullshit. u tried to get zoe in trouble with angela, but it didn't work. zoe would have never thought that about angela, and angela would have never thought that about zoe."

SnowAngel: except we both did. just for a teeny tiny second . . . but still.

mad maddie: jana doesn't need to know that. what matters is that your friendship was strong enuff to get thru it.

SnowAngel: OUR friendship, all 3 of ours. u helped talk us thru it, ya know.

mad maddie: nonetheless, jana tried to screw with us, and she must face the consequences.

SnowAngel: IF she really was the 1 who said it . . .

mad maddie: oh, she was. her smugness was undeniable.

SnowAngel: did u tell zo? is she mad?

mad maddie: she is, but not mad ENUFF

mad maddie: i told her i was gonna get jana back, and she was all, "no, no, just leave it." but it's about sticking up for what u believe in—and i believe in us. simple as that.

SnowAngel: so what r u gonna do?

mad maddie: i don't know, but i'll think of something!

Wednesday, February 15, 10:47 PM E.S.T.

SnowAngel: zo?

Auto response from zoegirl: "I want to live where soul meets body, and let the sun wrap its arms around me . . . "

Send   Cancel

SnowAngel: is that Death Cab for Cutie? since when have u liked Death Cab for Cutie?

SnowAngel: ohhhhhh, cuz DOUG likes Death Cab for Cutie. he was talking about them yesterday at lunch!

SnowAngel: well, i was just IMing to giggle about maddie and how bad-ass she's being. i think she sees it as defending our honor, which is sooo sweet. what do u think she's gonna do, do u have any idea?

SnowAngel: i just hope jana doesn't retaliate . . .

SnowAngel: i also wanted to tell u that i've re-thought the whole logan thing for real, and i don't think i've been giving him a fair chance. we were in a rut, that's all. but he's a great guy. he's a wonderful guy, and i would be insane to throw that away.

SnowAngel: and no, it's not just the jeep.

SnowAngel: i thought u'd be happy to hear that, that's all. bye!

Wednesday, February 15, 10:49 PM E.S.T.

SnowAngel: PS—i'm not TOTALLY superficial. i mean, i wanna live where soul meets body 2.

Auto response from zoegirl: "I want to live where soul meets body, and let the sun wrap its arms around me . . . "

SnowAngel: yeah, so u've said

SnowAngel: bye for real!

Send   Cancel

Thursday, February 16, 10:14 AM E.S.T.

mad maddie:	**hungry! hunnnngry!**
SnowAngel:	go to snack machine. buy delicious food item. insert delicious food item into mouth.
mad maddie:	**can't. i'm supposedly recording grades for ms. hathoway. i'm also working on a brilliant way to get back at jana, but don't ask what it is.**
SnowAngel:	what is it?
mad maddie:	**i just told u, i'm not telling! let's just say it's a friendly reminder that all actions come with repercussions.**
SnowAngel:	when will this friendly reminder take place?
mad maddie:	**hopefully tomorrow, so stay alert.**
mad maddie:	**r u in the media center?**
SnowAngel:	yeppers, googling jeep accessories
mad maddie:	**ahhh. what kind of accessories?**
SnowAngel:	any and all, baby. i'm considering a "cherry" theme— do u think that would be stupid? like, they have steering wheel covers and all that, all decorated with cherries.
mad maddie:	**my brother mark has a sheepskin steering wheel cover.**
SnowAngel:	i don't want a sheepskin steering wheel cover. i want a cherry steering wheel cover.
mad maddie:	**then u go right ahead, missy**
mad maddie:	**i talked to vincent after culture studies, and he's having a party tomorrow nite. happy time!**
SnowAngel:	uh-oh. u say happy time, i say DANGER. is this when u

Send   Cancel

61

guys r finally gonna end up in a closet with your hands all over each other?

mad maddie: **god, angela, could we get off that already? seriously.**

SnowAngel: i'm just *teasing*

mad maddie: **well stop. it's like ur refusing to let me be an actual mature adult.**

SnowAngel: an actual mature adult who's salivating over the prospect of a parent-free house party with an endless supply of beer?

mad maddie: **exactly**

SnowAngel: wh-hoo! then i'll be the designated driver—IN MY JEEP!

mad maddie: **i'm all over that. l8rs!!**

Friday, February 17, 9:06 AM E.S.T.

mad maddie: **yes! score! do i rock or what?**

zoegirl: omg, jana must be livid! ur CRAZY, mads!

mad maddie: **that'll show her to mess with my buds**

mad maddie: **did angela hear?**

zoegirl: dunno—didn't c her at her locker

zoegirl: g2g, history quiz. but big high 5!!!!

Friday, February 17, 9:45 AM E.S.T.

SnowAngel: wahhhhh! no fair! mary kate told me i missed it!!!!

mad maddie: **aw, man! it was classic.**

mad maddie: where r u? i thought u had english this period.

SnowAngel: i told mrs. evangelista that i had to run to the media center to print up my bibliography. r u on ms. hathoway's computer?

mad maddie: yes, cuz i am her favorite student aide.

mad maddie: WHY WERE U NOT IN HOMEROOM TO HEAR MY BRILLIANT ANNOUNCEMENT?

SnowAngel: cuz i forgot my shoes. *bonks head on keyboard* i got all the way to school, and then i was like, "oh, crap. i'm barefoot!"

mad maddie: god, angela. only u.

SnowAngel: well if u had TOLD me u were gonna plant a phony announcement, maybe i would have been there on time!

SnowAngel: mary kate said u got the office lady to call jana out as a liar in front of the whole school???

mad maddie: please, it was far more sophisticated than that. do u think the office lady would have read it over the intercom if it just said "jana is a liar"?

mad maddie: it said, and i quote, "congratulations to jana whitaker, winner of our 1st annual liars club award. jana, your free copy of "Lies and the Lying Liars Who Tell Them" can be picked up at the office."

SnowAngel: noooooo! 😄

mad maddie: loretta, she's the office lady, wanted to know what the liars club was, and i told her it was a student organization dedicated to rooting out social injustice. she was like, "it's so nice to c young ppl getting involved in a worthwhile cause."

Send   Cancel

SnowAngel:	is there an actual book called "Lies and the Lying Liars Who Tell Them"?
mad maddie:	**yeppers. i saw it one day on mark and pelt-woman's coffee table, and i remembered the title. i went out last nite and bought 1 at B&N.**
SnowAngel:	that's awesome
SnowAngel:	how did ppl react when they heard the announcement? how did JANA react?
mad maddie:	**megan said jana tried to play it off as "ha ha, very funny," but that it clearly got under her skin. even if ppl didn't know the full story, they know jana, and they could put 2 and 2 together.**
mad maddie:	**she said jana and terri spent all homeroom talking about what a bitch i was, but do i care? no, i do not.**
SnowAngel:	jana and terri r tight again?
mad maddie:	**i guess. but megan said that as soon as jana was out of the room, terri turned to margaret and was like, "i'm sorry, but that was 2 perfect." and then they both cracked up.**
SnowAngel:	i can't believe i missed it. *pouts*
SnowAngel:	what's gonna happen when jana never shows up at the office to pick up her book?
mad maddie:	**i hope loretta will announce it again. and when jana still doesn't show up, i'm hoping she'll have someone deliver it to her in person.**
SnowAngel:	u r bad, maddie—and i lub it.
SnowAngel:	bye!!!!

Send   Cancel

Friday, February 17, 5:18 PM E.S.T.

SnowAngel: hey there, sweetie. what'd ya think of maddie's homeroom announcement?

zoegirl: i thought it was very funny, even tho it was totally unnecessary. but funny.

SnowAngel: u reap what u sow, that's what i say. in fact maybe i'll make that my senior quote.

SnowAngel: have u decided what your senior quote's gonna be?

zoegirl: no, but luckily we have 2 months to decide. i've got too many other things to worry about—ack!

SnowAngel: well to thank maddie for sticking up for us, i had this great idea: to invite ian to vincent's tonite. whaddaya think?

zoegirl: uh, i think maddie would kill u

SnowAngel: so i should go for it?

SnowAngel: she really needs to start going out with ian again. he would be soooooo much better for her than vincent.

zoegirl: u keep giving her a hard time about vincent, but i honestly don't think she's interested in him.

SnowAngel: that's what SHE says. i want ian on her radar anyway.

zoegirl: why do u not like vincent? just cuz he's such good buds with jana?

SnowAngel: there is that, which is a huge strike against him. but it's more that i just don't wanna c her get in trouble again. like with chive.

zoegirl: vincent's not chive, tho

zoegirl: wanna know my theory? i think u give her a hard time

	about vincent cuz she gives u a hard time about logan. that's what i think.
SnowAngel:	WHAT? plz.
zoegirl:	well . . . whatever
zoegirl:	so will jana be at this party?
SnowAngel:	probably. yikes, i didn't think of that.
SnowAngel:	she confronted maddie in the hall today, did u hear? she said, "i know u did it, bitch," and maddie said, "no, but i wish i did. that's priceless."
zoegirl:	oh great—so now jana's doubly mad. i *told* maddie not to do anything!
SnowAngel:	well she did
SnowAngel:	ok, i'm off. i'm gonna call ian right now!

Saturday, February 18, 9:45 AM E.S.T.

zoegirl:	angela, i'm so glad ur awake! i need to talk!
SnowAngel:	*stretches luxuriously and remembers evening of decadence* last nite was a blast, wasn't it? even with jana lurking in the corners and giving us murderous glances the whole time. i almost peed my pants when maddie made that comment about her being a witch, cuz it was so true. like she was muttering incantations and putting curses on us with her evil mind.
zoegirl:	can we not talk about jana?
SnowAngel:	apparently she's got some "plan" up her sleeve to get back at maddie. mary kate overheard her talking

about it, but she shut up as soon as she realized mk
was listening.

zoegirl: seriously, i don't wanna talk about jana, k?

SnowAngel: righty-o *flicks jana into little witchy-poo trash can*

SnowAngel: omg, i've got "pon de replay" totally stuck in my head.
"let the bass from the speakers run through ya
sneakers, move both ya feet and run to the beat!"

zoegirl: u and andre were so cute dancing together.

SnowAngel: i LOVE andre. i should kidnap him and make him live in
my closet, and just take him out to hold every nite
like a teddy bear.

SnowAngel: he said i could be his fag-hag, did i tell u that?

zoegirl: yes, about 1,000 times

zoegirl: what does logan think of that?

SnowAngel: of what? of ANDRE?

zoegirl: it kinda seemed like u weren't hanging out with him
much. logan, i mean.

SnowAngel: we hung out plenty—what r u talking about?

SnowAngel: anyway, how would U know, miss disappearing act?
maddie and i looked all over for u when "sugar, we're
goin down" came on. u were nowhere to be found!

zoegirl: well, that's why i'm IMing. i'm feeling kinda weird about
life, but i don't *want* to be.

SnowAngel: yesssss? tell auntie angela all about it.

zoegirl: well, doug and i somehow ended up alone in vincent's
brother's room. at 1st we were just fooling around, but
then things got . . . pretty involved.

SnowAngel: "pretty involved"? that's such a zoe-way of putting it.

Send   Cancel

l8r, g8r

SnowAngel:	kinda skanky that u used vincent's bro's room, tho.
zoegirl:	i know!
zoegirl:	and then right in the middle, doug stopped and said, "do u want me to put on a condom? i've got one."
SnowAngel:	*shrieks*
SnowAngel:	little dougie had a condom? he actually went out at some point in time and bought A CONDOM??? zoe, that is SO cute!
zoegirl:	it wasn't *cute*, it was awful! it means that he's been thinking about it 2. u know—about having sex!
SnowAngel:	well DUH
SnowAngel:	what did u say?
zoegirl:	i handled it completely wrong. i said, "now?!" and he said, "why not? it's as good a time as any."
zoegirl:	after that i pretty much stopped interacting, and eventually he got the point.
SnowAngel:	have u told him about the pill?
zoegirl:	no, i couldn't make the words come
SnowAngel:	zoe . . .
zoegirl:	why do i act this way?! WHY? i *love* doug. i should be able to talk to him about anything!
zoegirl:	i just didn't wanna have sex with him right that second, in vincent's brother's room, with me afraid the whole time that someone was gonna come in.
SnowAngel:	sweetie. listen. u did the absolute right thing.
SnowAngel:	u and doug will figure it out . . . and until then, there's plenty of other things u 2 can do to keep yourselves occupied. ☺

Send   Cancel

68

zoegirl:	i start tomorrow, btw. the pill.
SnowAngel:	i hope u don't get "spotty dark spots" or whatever.
zoegirl:	gee, thanks
SnowAngel:	just lookin' out for ya
SnowAngel:	so r u good? u feel less weird about things?
zoegirl:	yeah, thanks for listening. bye!

Saturday, February 18, 1:18 PM E.S.T.

mad maddie:	**a word please, angela**
SnowAngel:	*she awakens! she rises! celestial chorus fills the air*
mad maddie:	**now that i've had time to sober up, would u mind telling me how ian ended up at vincent's party???**
SnowAngel:	omg, that was so fantastic, wasn't it? i was like, "ian, wow! what a kawinkidink!"
mad maddie:	**a kawinkidink. Uh huh. i take it u called him?**
SnowAngel:	now, maddie, no need to get hung up on details. he was there, u were there, u guys had fun . . .
SnowAngel:	u DID have fun, didn't u?
mad maddie:	**it was good to c him, i suppose**
SnowAngel:	did u talk about margo?
mad maddie:	**no, we didn't talk about margo. why would we talk about margo?**
mad maddie:	**mainly we talked about college. he thinks santa cruz sounds cool—i liked the way he looked at me when i told him that's where i want to go. like he thought i was brave for marching off so far.**

Send   Cancel

SnowAngel: i wish u WEREN'T so brave. i wish u would just go to UGA with me—athens is only an hour away!

mad maddie: ian's gonna be in athens, u know. he applied to UGA's honors program.

SnowAngel: i applied to the dumbshit program. i need to leave time for my busy social life. ☺

mad maddie: i wish we would hear already. i mean, u and ian have nothing to worry about—u'll both get into georgia. but what if i get a really skinny letter from UCSC and it's a rejection?

SnowAngel: then like i said: just come with me! and ian!!!

mad maddie: go dawgs! woof woof!

SnowAngel: u think i'm joking, but i'm not

SnowAngel: u did apply, didn't u?

mad maddie: as a back-up, sure. but i'm not going to georgia

SnowAngel: but why not???? just think how much fun we would have together. and if we could only get zoe to come, things would be absolutely perfect!

mad maddie: zoe? at georgia? zoe's not going to georgia. zoe didn't even apply to georgia.

SnowAngel: which is stupid, cuz doesn't her mom know the president of the university? she'd be a shoo-in.

mad maddie: she'd be a shoo-in anywayz.

mad maddie: nah, zoe's gonna end up at princeton, cuz that's where her mom went.

SnowAngel: i thought her top choice was kenyon.

mad maddie: it is, but she's gonna end up at princeton, that's my prediction. the pressure from her parents will be 2 strong.

SnowAngel: oh hush. lemme live in my fantasy-land until the very last minute.

SnowAngel: anyway, how'd we get started on college? i thought we were talking about vincent's party.

mad maddie: vincent is wacked. last nite he pulled me aside and offered me a vicodin tablet "to smooth things out." then he changed his mind, saying, "nah, i better not corrupt u."

SnowAngel: doesn't he know ur already corrupted?

mad maddie: not in that way, i'm not

SnowAngel: where'd he get the vicodin?

mad maddie: from his bro, who i'm pretty sure does some farming on the side.

SnowAngel: farming?

mad maddie: as in pharmaceuticals. and i think u should be proud of me for not being tempted.

SnowAngel: i AM proud of u. i'm also proud of u for, u know, not letting vincent be your fuck-buddy.

SnowAngel: i wanted to apologize for that, actually. for assuming u were after him.

mad maddie: i'm NOT after him. i never have been after him. god.

SnowAngel: well, yeah, i realized that after watching y'all last nite. *gulps and sucks it up* i realized that maybe i wasn't being very fair toward him. or u.

mad maddie: thank u! i've been wondering what your deal was!

SnowAngel: he's cool, i admit it! *lashes self with rope of thorns*

SnowAngel: when he and i were in the kitchen, he was totally cracking me up. AND he had only good things to say about u. he thinks ur a good influence, poor guy.

Send   Cancel

71

mad maddie:	a good influence, right. that's why he offered me vicodin.
SnowAngel:	well, we'll just gloss over that bit.
SnowAngel:	u and vincent r pals, just like me and andre.
mad maddie:	amazing, isn't? turns out i AM capable of being pals with a guy and not jumping his bones . . .
SnowAngel:	a HOT guy at that, who doesn't happen to be gay.
SnowAngel:	can i ask a question, tho? why is his brother white, when vincent is tan-colored?
mad maddie:	ha! vincent says they get that all the time.
mad maddie:	frank is irish-puerto rican, and vincent is puerto rican-irish
SnowAngel:	???
mad maddie:	their mom is light-skinned, their dad is dark-skinned. i guess each kid came out looking different.
SnowAngel:	oh. ok.
mad maddie:	so did u talk to zoe, find out where she disappeared to?
SnowAngel:	just as we suspected—off with doug.
mad maddie:	doin' da freak between da sheets?
SnowAngel:	ALMOST doin' da freak b/w da sheets. doug pulled out a condom, and zoe froze up and put an end to things.
mad maddie:	zoe, zoe, zoe
SnowAngel:	it's only gonna make it harder, u know. once they have sex, it's only gonna make it harder for them to split up in the fall.
mad maddie:	who says they're gonna split up?
SnowAngel:	well PHYSICALLY they will, cuz neither of them applied to the same schools. that's what i mean.

Send   Cancel

72

mad maddie:	which in all likelihood means they WILL split up, cuz of the whole long-distance thing. they'll break up . . . and then they'll get together during christmas break . . . and then they'll break up again . . .
SnowAngel:	stop, ur depressing me!
mad maddie:	or who knows? maybe they'll be the couple who proves everyone wrong.
mad maddie:	dude, g2g. i've gotta piss like a racehorse.
SnowAngel:	oh, now that's lovely
mad maddie:	it's a hangover pee. it was worse this morning, and i sooo didn't wanna crawl out of bed to go to the bathroom.
mad maddie:	i found myself thinking, if only i was wearing a Depends . . .
SnowAngel:	delete! delete! *erases image of maddie in diaper*
mad maddie:	that would turn ian on, huh?
mad maddie:	l8r, g8r!

Saturday, February 18, 1:44 PM E.S.T.

mad maddie:	hey, i'm back
SnowAngel:	did u pee?
mad maddie:	i am pee-free
mad maddie:	i realized we hadn't discussed the j-word, and i have a new example of her ridiculosity to share.
SnowAngel:	uh oh, did she put into action her EVIL PLAN? *cues special effects guy for thunder and lightning and a shower of hoppy toads*
mad maddie:	i suppose—altho it was so stupid it just made me laff.

mad maddie: me, megan, vincent, and vincent's bro were standing around talking, right? and vincent and frank were giving megan hell cuz she kept doing that phlegm-clearing thing cuz of her cold.

SnowAngel: she was doing that all nite! it was driving me crazy!

mad maddie: frank was like, "i know—ur a hooker. THAT'S why ur sick."

SnowAngel: huh?

mad maddie: it was mildly funny at the time. megan said no, she wasn't a hooker, and frank goes, "ohhhh, then ur a slut."

SnowAngel: ok, vincent may be cooler than i thought, but i am SO not impressed with frank. *makes disapproving granny face*

mad maddie: anywayz, jana had been lurking about during this whole exchange, and when frank said that, she inserted herself into the convo and goes, "WHO'S the slut? WHO'S the slut?"

SnowAngel: and who WAS the slut?

mad maddie: me, apparently. isn't it shocking? didn't she totally put me in my place?

SnowAngel: i don't get it. what have u done that's slutty recently?

mad maddie: RECENTLY?!!!

SnowAngel: lol☺

mad maddie: omg, i can't believe u!

SnowAngel: sorry sorry sorry, i'm TERRIBLY sorry. *kisses maddie's unslutty butt repeatedly*

SnowAngel: so what did u say?

Send   Cancel

lauren myracle

mad maddie: i said, "jana, jana, jana . . . must we have such a potty mouth? Boo Boo Bear would NOT approve."

SnowAngel: *claps hands in delight* for real?!

mad maddie: no. i just looked at her like *ur such a dumbshit.* it wasn't worth the trouble of a reply.

SnowAngel: damn! i mean, DARN. (sorry, Boo Boo Bear!)

mad maddie: it's 2 bad, really, that after my extremely impressive "lying liars" display, that's all she could come up with.

SnowAngel: um . . .

mad maddie: yesss? u have a comment u would like to make?

SnowAngel: just that it couldn't have been all she could come up with

mad maddie: what r u saying?

SnowAngel: that 1 little remark, it couldn't have been the "plan" mary kate overheard her talking about. cuz if it was, then she's . . . i dunno. feeble.

mad maddie: vincent said she's going thru some tough shit—not that i care. maybe it's affected her brain.

SnowAngel: don't tell me that—then i have to feel sorry for her!

SnowAngel: what kind of tough shit?

mad maddie: i dunno, just that it has to do with her stepmonster. blah blah blah.

mad maddie: and DON'T feel sorry for her. god. if u need to feel sorry for someone, feel sorry for ME. i'm the 1 she called a slut!

SnowAngel: poor old madikins!

mad maddie: and poor old angela-kins. she basically called u a slut 2, or have u forgotten? she just tricked everyone into blaming it on zoe.

Send   Cancel

75

SnowAngel: point taken

SnowAngel: just watch your back, k? betcha a million dollars she's up to something more.

mad maddie: **pah, she's feeble. cyas!**

Sunday, February 19, 10:09 PM E.S.T.

zoegirl: well, i did it. i took my very 1st pill.

mad maddie: **nice work. have u told doug?**

zoegirl: i decided i want to take them for at least a week and THEN tell him. that way i can be, "oh, and btw, i'm on the pill now." u know, very blasé.

zoegirl: it's strange, i feel sometimes like i *need* to be blasé with him—but only when i'm not with him. when i'm actually with him, i *can't* be blasé. does that make sense?

mad maddie: **no**

zoegirl: i know, it doesn't to me either!

zoegirl: it's like i'm being sucked into him. at times i feel this need to resist, but then i get near him and i think, "omg, i would die without him." as in literally die.

zoegirl: i know it sounds crazy.

mad maddie: **u shouldn't let him control u that much, zo.**

zoegirl: he doesn't *control* me. i just love him.

mad maddie: **uh huh, same difference. jk.**

mad maddie: **hey, i found the most awesome website—u've gotta check it out. it's by this chick named amy winfrey who**

Send   Cancel

makes animated cartoons. there's muffin films, making fiends, and big bunny.

zoegirl: uh . . . ok. do u not wanna talk about doug anymore?

mad maddie: big bunny's my fave. it's about 3 kids who go into the forest even tho they're not supposed to, and they meet this humongous bunny who says things like, "do not run, tasty children!"

mad maddie: they ask the bunny if he's seen their dog, and he says, "noooo, i have seen no fluffy crunchy doggies around here. maybe the yummy puppy has gone home."

zoegirl: huh

mad maddie: there's a theme song and everything. go to big-bunny.com.

zoegirl: um, ok, when i get a chance. guess i'm gonna go now. bye!

Monday, February 20, 5:55 PM E.S.T.

mad maddie: angela, ur on my bad list!

SnowAngel: i am? why?

mad maddie: and i quote: "Tonight your true love will realize how much they love you between 1 and 4 in the morning. Tomorrow the shock of your life will occur if you break the chain, and you will have bad luck for 10 years if you don't pass this on to 15 people."

SnowAngel: uh oh *takes big tiptoe steps backward*

mad maddie: u know who it's from, don't u?

SnowAngel: er . . . glendy?

mad maddie: YES, glendy! aaargh!

SnowAngel: can i help it if she likes u? ur very likable, maddie.

SnowAngel: did u break the chain?

mad maddie: what do u think?

SnowAngel: uh oh, hope ur ready for the shock of your life . . .

mad maddie: that stuff is such garbage. who believes that crap?

SnowAngel: i sent out a chain letter when i was 10. a snail-mail chain letter, one of those where ur supposed to put your name on the bottom of the list and send a dollar to the person on the top of the list. i was supposed to receive thousands of dollars within the next month, but i never did.

mad maddie: go fig

SnowAngel: i was very hardcore about it, 2. i sent it to my camp buddies and used all sorts of emotional blackmail, like, "c'mon, trish, i know U won't let me down." i feel bad about it now.

mad maddie: u should. u should write them all an apology.

SnowAngel: um . . . i'll keep it in mind

mad maddie: hey, wanna do something? go somewhere?

SnowAngel: YEAH! i was supposed to go with logan to pick out an interview suit for summer internships, but i'll call and tell him i can't.

mad maddie: should i invite zoe?

SnowAngel: sure, but i bet she's with doug

SnowAngel: cya in a jiff!

Monday, February 20, 6:04 PM E.S.T.

SnowAngel: oh ha ha, maddie. very funny.

Auto response from mad maddie: talkin' on da phone

SnowAngel: i just checked my email, and what should i c waiting for me in my inbox?

SnowAngel: ur supposed to send it to 15 DIFFERENT ppl, u freak!

SnowAngel: ur still gonna get the curse unless u send it to 14 other ppl!!!!!!!!!

Tuesday, February 21, 4:33 PM E.S.T.

mad maddie: angela, ur not trying to play some kind of trick on me, r u? to make me think i'm cursed?

SnowAngel: huh?

SnowAngel: OHHHHH, cuz of that chain letter from glendy. what happened? did u drop a dr pepper on your foot? ha ha!

mad maddie: angela, i'm not joking. i came home to 17 messages on our answering machine, all from guys saying they wanna ... do stuff with me. or TO me.

SnowAngel: what?!

mad maddie: they know my name. and some of them r really really sick.

SnowAngel: OMG

SnowAngel: who r they from?

mad maddie: i don't know, i don't recognize any of them.

Send   Cancel

79

SnowAngel:	could it be vincent? could he be pranking u?
mad maddie:	**these r, like, old guys. all DIFFERENT guys, some with accents and some really gruff and . . . no, it's not vincent.**
mad maddie:	**i don't actually think it was u, either. obviously.**
SnowAngel:	it's jana. it's jana, isn't it?!! THAT'S what the slut remark was all about!
mad maddie:	**she must have written my name and number in a gas station bathroom . . . or maybe put an ad in a singles magazine?**
SnowAngel:	call 1 of the guys back and ask where he got your number
mad maddie:	**NO!**
mad maddie:	**they think i'm a call girl or something. i'm totally creeped out, angela.**
SnowAngel:	ok, listen. if anyone calls, DON'T pick up.
mad maddie:	**i already unplugged the phone. but what if they keep calling? what's gonna happen when my parents get home?**
SnowAngel:	ur there by yourself?!!
SnowAngel:	sweetie, i'm coming over. u shouldn't have to deal with this alone.
mad maddie:	**that would be really really great, actually. thanx, a.**
SnowAngel:	i'm on my way!!!

Tuesday, February 21, 10:00 PM E.S.T.

zoegirl:	how's mads?
SnowAngel:	by the time i got over there, there were 33

Send   Cancel

	messages on the kinnicks' machine. by the time i left, it'd gone up to 68. and the only reason there weren't more was cuz the machine ran out of room!
zoegirl:	were they all the same sort of thing?
SnowAngel:	uh huh. they said things like, "hey, baby, i'll satisfy your every fantasy," and "if u want someone well-equipped, then i'm your man. gimme a ring and let's get dirty."
zoegirl:	ewww!
SnowAngel:	some were even worse. some i couldn't even listen to—i just hit "delete" and then wanted to go take a boiling hot shower.
zoegirl:	did anyone say where they got her number?
SnowAngel:	no—they just said, "i heard u were looking for some action" or "here's my digits. call me, skank."
zoegirl:	poor maddie!
zoegirl:	how could there be so *many*?
SnowAngel:	i dunno. whatever jana did, she did it in a big way—more than just scribbling something on some wall.
zoegirl:	so we're sure it's jana?
SnowAngel:	i am. aren't u?
zoegirl:	i just have a hard time believing that even she would do something so . . . VICIOUS. and dangerous! hasn't she heard about all the girls who've been molested by MySpace lurkers and stuff like that?
SnowAngel:	i can't believe i was almost feeling sorry for her, cuz of her personal problems or whatever.
SnowAngel:	this goes so much further than what maddie did. this is just WRONG.

zoegirl:	did mr. and mrs. kinnick show up? i'm assuming they did, or u wouldn't have left.
SnowAngel:	they got in around 9:00. maddie didn't tell them about the messages cuz she doesn't want her dad thinking about her like that . . . even tho none of it's true.
SnowAngel:	she's really shaken up, zo. and she NEVER gets shaken up!
zoegirl:	i'm gonna do some hunting around on the internet. maybe i can figure out which atlanta newspapers run singles ads.
SnowAngel:	good idea. and tomorrow let's stick close to maddie so she feels safe!

Wednesday, February 22, 4:14 PM E.S.T.

mad maddie:	so much for keeping the parents in the dark. guess how many calls the moms got while i was at school?
zoegirl:	oh no—how many?
mad maddie:	twenty-frickin-six. i guess ppl aren't quite as busy being pervy in the daylight hours as during the nite, but still.
zoegirl:	holy crap
mad maddie:	the 1st guy asked her to pass on a message about his big cock. isn't that charming? and then she answered the 2nd call, assuming the 1st was a wrong number, and that guy said, "is this maddie? u don't sound 18." the moms goes, "this is maddie's mother. who IS this?" and the guy laffed and asked if she was the 1 who taught me to be so nasty.

Send   Cancel

zoegirl:	oh. my. god. she must have had a heart attack.
mad maddie:	**pretty much. she called my cell, and i had no choice but to tell her about last nite. then she called the police, and they said to try and find out where the calls were coming from.**
zoegirl:	if u had caller ID, u'd have a list of their numbers right there.
mad maddie:	**thanx for that, zo. thanx for that oh-so-helpful tip.**
zoegirl:	er . . . sorry
mad maddie:	**so she started asking the callers for their names, but of course no one told her. but eventually this 1 guy said he'd gotten our number from craigslist.**
zoegirl:	who's craig?
mad maddie:	**ha ha, funny**
zoegirl:	no, seriously. who's craig???
mad maddie:	**u've never heard of craigslist?**
mad maddie:	**i guess i should be glad. maybe only half the world has seen the ad instead of the entire population.**
zoegirl:	maddie, i'm gonna ask u 1 more time. who is craig and why does he have a list???
mad maddie:	**he's not a PERSON. well, maybe he is . . . i don't know.**
mad maddie:	**"craigslist" is like a big internet want ad, only for anything in the whole world. roommates, apartments, cars . . . anything. and i didn't know this until now, but there's a "casual encounters" section, and that's where u can find ME, apparently.**
zoegirl:	ohhhh
mad maddie:	**i want u to go find it, ok?**
zoegirl:	the ad?

Send   Cancel

mad maddie:	**the moms tracked it down, but she won't tell me what it said, which makes me think it must be REALLY bad.**
zoegirl:	u don't want to c for yourself?
mad maddie:	**no**
zoegirl:	oh. ok.
mad maddie:	**so go look and then report back.**
mad maddie:	**craigslist. atlanta. casual encounters.**
zoegirl:	got it. be back soon!

Wednesday, February 22, 4:36 PM E.S.T.

zoegirl:	hey angela. i'm supposed to IM maddie, but i wanted to talk to u 1st.
SnowAngel:	about the want-ad thingie? i've seen it. it's sick.
zoegirl:	it literally made me *feel* sick.
zoegirl:	i feel terrible, like it's all my fault!
SnowAngel:	how is it YOUR fault?
SnowAngel:	oh, cuz of Boo Boo Bear. right.
SnowAngel:	zo, this is sooooo much worse than Boo Boo Bear OR the lying liars club. it's in a whole different league.
zoegirl:	i'm gonna tell my mom and c if she knows any lawyer-y rules about sexual harassment and identity theft. there's no way we're letting her get away with this!
SnowAngel:	that is a GREAT idea, zo.
zoegirl:	but about maddie—do i tell her the truth? about *all* of it?
SnowAngel:	well . . . i don't know how u can't. she deserves to know.

Send   Cancel

zoegirl:	u should set up the chatroom, so we can tell her together.
SnowAngel:	oh. um.
zoegirl:	she needs us both for moral support
zoegirl:	so go ahead and do it
SnowAngel:	this very second?
zoegirl:	this very second.
SnowAngel:	fine. just hold on while i . . .

You have just entered the room "Angela's Boudoir."
mad maddie has entered the room.
zoegirl has entered the room.

mad maddie:	**uh oh, i'm not liking the whole "intervention" thing going on here. is it that bad?**
SnowAngel:	tell her, zo
zoegirl:	um . . . hi, mads
mad maddie:	**hi, zo**
mad maddie:	**u gonna tell me?**
zoegirl:	so listen . . . it's bad, but it's not *that* bad.
SnowAngel:	yes it is—don't sugar-coat it! AND it's totally illegal, which is how we're gonna get her back. zoe's gonna get her mom to step in, and jana's gonna be so incredibly busted!
mad maddie:	**will u tell me already???**
zoegirl:	aaargh
zoegirl:	the ad says ur looking for guys to fool around with, and

Send   Cancel

	that u like to . . . do it in front of others. and i wish i didn't have to tell u this, but jana included a picture.
SnowAngel:	that 1 from sophomore year, of u with no shirt on.
zoegirl:	angela!
SnowAngel:	what? i wanted to make sure she knew which 1!
zoegirl:	which other 1 would i mean, her class photo?
SnowAngel:	well we said we were gonna tell her the truth, but ur downplaying it cuz u feel responsible. ur making it sound like some harmless innocent thing!
zoegirl:	saying she likes to do it in front of others is some harmless innocent thing???
mad maddie:	**STOP!**
mad maddie:	**just paste the damn thing in!**
zoegirl:	i thought u didn't wanna c it.
mad maddie:	**i don't, but u guys r making it sound 10,000 times worse than it is, i'm sure.**
mad maddie:	**zoe?**
mad maddie:	**angela?**
mad maddie:	**what, r u both cowering in the corner?**
SnowAngel:	*glowers at zoe for being such a wimp* u heard her, zo. tell her!
zoegirl:	oh GOD. but i'm not including the picture!
zoegirl:	here's the stupid ad, word for word:

"I like to put on a show, so not only do you have to be very hung, talented (long lasting, multiple cummer), but you have to be ok fucking a sexy 18 yr old in front of other guys.

There would never be too many—three, four, or even five. I'm on the chubby side as you can see, but that just means more of me to go around. If you meet the critiria and you're interested, call me, guys! (404) 555-0176"

SnowAngel: maddie? r u there?

mad maddie: she spelled "criteria" wrong

SnowAngel: cuz she's a dumbass, that's why!

mad maddie: the ad doesn't mention my name. how did they know my name?

zoegirl: from the caption on the photo

mad maddie: which says . . . ?

SnowAngel: um . . . "misbehaving maddie"

SnowAngel: but the thing to remember is jana's gonna be in serious trouble for this. she is NOT gonna get away with it!

mad maddie: well, yeah, fantastic—except she is

mad maddie: the moms emailed the craigslist ppl, and there's no way to prove who wrote the ad. nobody's name is attached to it but mine.

zoegirl: but u can just tell them who it was!

mad maddie: and they'd believe me because . . . ?

zoegirl: well, i'm sure my mom'll have some ideas. jana *stole* your identity, that's a criminal offense.

mad maddie: i'm gonna tattle on her like a kindergartener? no way.

zoegirl: but your mom does know, right? that it was jana?

mad maddie: no

Send   Cancel

SnowAngel:	WHY???
mad maddie:	**i told her it wasn't me (duh), but that i didn't know who it was.**
mad maddie:	**i'm not giving jana the satisfaction of seeing me all teary-eyed and hiding behind my mommy's skirt. and don't either of U tell, either. don't tell anyone!**
zoegirl:	maddie . . . don't be like this. u've gotta let us help.
mad maddie:	**u? or your mother?**
zoegirl:	huh?
mad maddie:	**forget it**
mad maddie:	**we're gonna have to change our phone number, that's what the police said. it makes me so frickin mad.**
SnowAngel:	want me to come get u, sweetie?
SnowAngel:	i'm gonna come get u and we'll all 3 go out for ice cream.
mad maddie:	**no, don't. in fact i'm logging off. i don't feel like talking.**

mad maddie has left the room.

zoegirl:	crap crap crap
zoegirl:	i hate jana so much!!!
SnowAngel:	especially cuz u know she's laffing her butt off.
zoegirl:	u realize why maddie doesn't wanna go to the principal, right? and why she doesn't want me going over her head to my mom?
SnowAngel:	cuz she doesn't want them getting involved?
zoegirl:	no, cuz she doesn't want anyone else to c the ad. anyone who already hasn't, that is.

Send   Cancel

SnowAngel: ack—i didn't think of that.

zoegirl: did maddie seem . . . i dunno. mad at me? cuz i know this all started with the Boo Boo Bear thing, but she kept it going with the liars club prank. i mean, she's part of this 2.

SnowAngel: she's mad at the world. wouldn't u be?

SnowAngel: oh, i want to KILL jana!!!!

zoegirl: only the sucky thing is, u can't. i don't want u getting on jana's bad side 2.

SnowAngel: there's gotta be SOMETHING we can do.

zoegirl: i'm serious, angela! don't!

SnowAngel: i'm not just gonna let it go. i refuse.

SnowAngel: i'll figure something out—just wait and c!

Thursday, February 23, 11:01 AM E.S.T.

SnowAngel: did u hear annc. about getting sized for grad. robes? how r we sposed to think about grad robes at time like this?!

zoegirl: impossible. maddie=shattered. trying to hide it, but i can tell.

SnowAngel: does vincent know anything? about jana and the ad?

zoegirl: i asked. he said no.

SnowAngel: i'm gonna get her back big time. saw her in hall and she was gloating—makes me so mad!

zoegirl: really don't think u should!!!

SnowAngel: gonna anyway. bye!

Send   Cancel

Thursday, February 23, 5:14 PM E.S.T.

SnowAngel:	all right, maddie. u can stop worrying about jana!
mad maddie:	**i can?**
SnowAngel:	*beams with satisfaction*
SnowAngel:	i fixed HER wagon, i'll tell ya!
mad maddie:	**u fixed her . . . ? angela, what drug r u on?**
SnowAngel:	i drove over to her house after school. that's right, i went to the DRAGON LADY'S LAIR. *spooky horror noises*
SnowAngel:	i rang the doorbell multiple times to make sure no one was home, and then i went around to the back, turned the doorknob, and wala. breaking and entering, baby.
mad maddie:	**u broke into jana's house?! ur insane!**
SnowAngel:	i had my cover story all ready if anyone had answered the door. but i knew jana herself wasn't there, cuz i mad-dashed out of school right when 6th period ended, and jana's trash heap car was still in the parking lot.
SnowAngel:	anyway, the house was unlocked, so i didn't technically break in. i just entered.
mad maddie:	**yeah, the cops'll give u a medal. what were u thinking???**
SnowAngel:	i was thinking that no one plays such a dirty trick on my maddie and gets away with it. i was thinking that jana needs a taste of her own medicine.
SnowAngel:	so i scoped out the house (smelled like cigarettes) and found the room which had to be jana's, cuz of all

Send   Cancel

the CDs strewn about and the horrible black wall-hanging. and then i left a little something on her pillow. i got the idea from the senior boys.

mad maddie: **u gave jana a bag of candy hearts?**

SnowAngel: nooooooo. and not a dead rat, either, altho i swear i would have if i happened to have a spare dead rat. that's what i WANTED to put on her pillow.

SnowAngel: what i left was a note, which i typed on one of the school's computers so it can't be traced. it said, "hello, jana. what a beautiful room u have. hope u don't mind that i popped by, and hope u don't mind that i . . . never mind. seriously, don't give it a 2nd thought. did i tell u what a beautiful room u have? so many exquisite things, just begging to be touched." and then at the bottom, "p.s. people who are nice don't get visits from strangers."

mad maddie: **angela . . .**

SnowAngel: what?

mad maddie: **well, that's extremely stalker-ish, for 1 thing. is that what u were going for?**

SnowAngel: exactly! *claps hands in glee* now she'll be forever wondering who came in and what they did!

mad maddie: **no she won't. she'll know right away it was u.**

mad maddie: **what DID u do, other than leave the note?**

SnowAngel: nothing, really. i swished her toothbrush in the toilet and shuffled around the makeup on her counter, basic stuff like that. but for all she knows, i could have done anything.

mad maddie: **wow. uh, that's very hardcore, in an angela sort of way.**

Send   Cancel

mad maddie:	**but i still don't understand WHY.**
SnowAngel:	what do u mean? to teach her that she can't mess with the winsome threesome! so that SHE'LL feel violated like U felt violated!
mad maddie:	**who said i felt violated?**
SnowAngel:	maddie . . . why r u being this way?
SnowAngel:	i thought u'd be cackling with delight!!!
mad maddie:	**well i'm not**
mad maddie:	**the moms got our phone number changed, did u know that?**
SnowAngel:	well i'm sorry she had to do that, but at least u won't get any more calls.
mad maddie:	**it makes me so angry. not that it's even that big a deal, a new phone number, but just the fact that jana could waltz in and screw with my life like that . . .**
mad maddie:	**so i decided not to care, only now u've started it all up again.**
SnowAngel:	no i haven't. i've ended it.
mad maddie:	**do u really think that? tell me ur not that naive.**
SnowAngel:	*looks silently and reproachfully at friend*
mad maddie:	**aaaargh**
mad maddie:	**i've got a headache, i'm signing off. and please don't guilt-trip me, that's the LAST thing i need!**

Thursday, February 23, 5:48 PM E.S.T.

mad maddie:	**angela, u still there?**

Send   Cancel

92

SnowAngel:	yes, i'm nursing my wounds and feeling annoyed.
SnowAngel:	i broke into jana's house for u and u can't even say thanks!
mad maddie:	**well that's why i'm back. so . . . thanx.**
SnowAngel:	gee, that was so very heartfelt
mad maddie:	**and to admit that maybe it was a TEENY bit funny . . . and satisfying . . . and brilliant . . .**
SnowAngel:	*perks up* yeah?
mad maddie:	**but why did u say u fixed her wagon?**
SnowAngel:	i dunno, it's an expression my grandmom uses. *adopts crabby old-lady personna*: "i fixed HER wagon, ehh ehh ehh!"
mad maddie:	**it makes no sense**
SnowAngel:	such is life
mad maddie:	**what did zoe think of your little crime spree?**
SnowAngel:	oh, zoe *shakes head*
SnowAngel:	she's not happy. AND she thinks ur mad at her.
mad maddie:	**well frankly, i was. just her whole "i'll bring in my big bad mommy" attitude . . . it pissed me off.**
SnowAngel:	why? she was just trying to help.
mad maddie:	**i know, i know. it's just, i don't want her MOM fighting our battles for us. god.**
mad maddie:	**but then i realized, what else can i expect? it's not like zoe's gonna go storming in herself. that's just who she is.**
SnowAngel:	i did, tho. cuz i am Big Bad Angela. *preens and feels tuffer than zoe*
mad maddie:	**yeah, and now ur gonna be next on jana's hit list.**
SnowAngel:	i don't care. jana is NOT gonna ruin our senior yr.

Send   Cancel

SnowAngel: but thanks for saying "thanks." *gives maddie big wet smoochie* 😙 wuv yas!

Friday, February 24, 11:07 AM E.S.T.

zoegirl: ok, angela, i know ur still on your vigilante justice high, but i just had a run-in with the j-word, and u need to know about it.

Auto response from SnowAngel: doin' the school thing . . .

zoegirl: i'm sitting in the media center doing research, right? i'm not even THINKING about jana, when suddenly she comes barreling over to my computer and says, "u can tell angela i know it was her. tell her i'm gonna kick her a**!"

zoegirl: i was like, who talks like that? r u for real?

zoegirl: i don't wanna demonize her, cuz i know she's a real live human being with wants and needs and all that. yadda yadda yadda.

zoegirl: but face it. she *is*—at this particular point in her life—stunted and immature and oozing with bad energy. she just IS.

zoegirl: and i hope she grows out of it, and maybe 1 day at our 20th reunion we'll, u know, all share a chuckle . . . altho that seems extremely unlikely, if not downright impossible.

zoegirl: AAARGH, i'm getting all worked up, when the only reason i'm IMing is to warn u of her wrath. so watch out, that's all i'm saying!

Friday, February 24, 4:14 PM E.S.T.

SnowAngel: ASS, zoe. ur allowed to say it! ass ass ass! ass-poopy!

zoegirl: did u just say . . . ass-poopy?!

SnowAngel: and GOD, why do u have to be so nice all the time? we will NOT be sharing a chuckle with jana at our 20th reunion. we will not be sharing a chuckle with jana at our 100th reunion! i suppose it's to your credit that ur trying to be all fair-minded or whatever (gag gag gag), but honestly? it's just annoying.

zoegirl: i know ur trying to make this into a joke, but jana was showing serious psychotic break material by threatening u like that.

zoegirl: has she said anything to u in person?

SnowAngel: of course not, cuz i put her in her place and she knows it. *squishes jana with thumb and grinds into icky mess*

SnowAngel: SHE is the ass-poopy. i learned that term on "related," btw. have u ever watched that show?

SnowAngel: or, hrmm. maybe it was ass-booby . . . ?

zoegirl: she's not gonna let this go, u know.

SnowAngel: oh, whatever. blah blah blah.

SnowAngel: let's go out tonite and put it all behind us. wanna?

zoegirl: i can't, i've got plans with doug

SnowAngel: BOR-RRRRING

SnowAngel: i'm gonna call maddie on her new number and c if SHE

Send   Cancel

wants to go out, since ur now being a u-know-what. (here's a hint: it rhymes with gas-woobie)

SnowAngel: cya!

Sunday, February 26, 7:01 PM E.S.T.

SnowAngel: hey, sweet tater. have u figured out what ur going as for alter-ego day tomorrow?

mad maddie: "alter-ego day," good god.

SnowAngel: don't take that tone with me. u love the special senior days as much as anyone!

mad maddie: do i? i mean, seriously. who comes up with this shit?

SnowAngel: *pouts in a steely-eyed sort of way*

mad maddie: oh, wait! it's U! U come up with this shit!

SnowAngel: ha ha, ur soooo hilarious

SnowAngel: so what r u gonna go as?

mad maddie: let's c. i'm normally the coolest chick on the planet, so for my alter-ego i guess i'll go as . . . the president of the senior planning committee!

mad maddie: jk again. whew, i crack myself up.

SnowAngel: i think i'll go as a big ol' slob, since normally i'm so stylish and hip. which means I'LL go as U!

mad maddie: could ya try being the tiniest bit original? could ya?

SnowAngel: i told zoe to go as a stoner, since in real life she's Miss Straight-A Super Student. but she's afraid the administration would disapprove, so she's going as a biker babe.

mad maddie:	**A BIKER BABE???? ZOE????**
mad maddie:	**what is she gonna wear?**
SnowAngel:	i dunno, we didn't get that far.
SnowAngel:	what do u think jana'll go as?
mad maddie:	**hmm, what is the opposite of evil incarnate . . . ?**
SnowAngel:	ZOE!!!! *rolls about in glee*
mad maddie:	**lol. good one, a.**
SnowAngel:	ah, me. *pats self on back with super-extendable hand*
SnowAngel:	i'm gonna go figure out my outfit for tomorrow. see ya in the morning?
mad maddie:	**yeah, only tomorrow's my day to sleep in, so don't look for me before 2nd period. byeas!**

Monday, February 27, 9:02 AM E.S.T.

SnowAngel:	ello, biker babe! ur looking verrry hot!
zoegirl:	ello, rain cloud angela! ur looking verrrry . . . gloomy!
SnowAngel:	seen mads?
zoegirl:	not yet. saw jana in her geek-wear, tho. so tacky.
SnowAngel:	can u say, ego?
zoegirl:	ego!

Monday, February 27, 5:13 PM E.S.T.

mad maddie:	**hey there, sunshine. r u back in your traditional pink?**

SnowAngel:	u kidding? i've decided black is a good look for me. i will soon start using one of those lonnnng cigarette holders and slink about discussing art.
mad maddie:	**only u don't know anything about art**
SnowAngel:	fashion, then. i'll suck in my cheeks and be heroin-chic.
SnowAngel:	didn't u think it was thoroughly egotistical of jana to show up dressed like a nerd?
mad maddie:	**it would be the same as if zoe had come as, like, a drooling idiot, cuz basically she'd be saying, "look how smart i think i am, if this is what i consider to be my opposite." but zoe would never do that.**
SnowAngel:	i liked your preppy attire. the pink-and-green belt was an excellent touch.
mad maddie:	**ms. hathoway said, "well, madigan, u certainly clean up nice." i said, "enjoy it while u can, cuz i am never tucking my shirt into my pants again."**
SnowAngel:	hee hee
SnowAngel:	and andre in his football uniform thingie, i loved that
mad maddie:	**and the captain of the football team in a tutu**
SnowAngel:	he shouldn't have worn tights, tho
mad maddie:	**especially w/o underwear**
SnowAngel:	i'm bored, and aunt sadie's going out with friends. logan said he'd bring me pizza, but i turned him down. if he and i could just hang out and have fun, i'd be all over it. but he always wants to fool around.
mad maddie:	**the nerve**
SnowAngel:	so can i come over?
mad maddie:	**yeah baby!**

Send   Cancel

98

Tuesday, February 28, 4:34 PM E.S.T.

mad maddie: **oh man, u should c my room. i can't stop laffing.**

zoegirl: pourquoi?

mad maddie: **angela came over yesterday, and we took a pad of sticky notes and jumped on my bed and stuck them to the ceiling.**

zoegirl: ha

mad maddie: **then i found 5 more pads, blue green purple pink and orange. we jumped off my chair and desk and stuck them ALL OVER. i totally forgot how trashed it was until i got home from school.**

zoegirl: that's awesome. i wish i could have been there!

mad maddie: **me 2. i need more of that, just good times with my buds.**

zoegirl: we have had some pretty good times over the yrs, haven't we?

mad maddie: **some FABULOUS times.**

mad maddie: **hey, did u ever check out big bunny?**

zoegirl: as a matter of fact, i did. maddie . . . big bunny has teeth.

mad maddie: **yeppers**

zoegirl: and maddie, big bunny ate that poor little puppy.

mad maddie: **nuh uh. didn't u listen to big bunny's story about the giant orange wolf?**

zoegirl: the giant orange wolf who found a puppy whose nose was like an olive and whose legs were like 4 well-stuffed sausages?

mad maddie: **and u will recall that big bunny—i mean the big orange**

	wolf—did NOT eat the puppy, cuz he wasn't hungry at the moment. he put the puppy in a bag for later.
zoegirl:	ick, maddie
mad maddie:	**blame that amy winfrey chick. she made it up!**
mad maddie:	**anywayz, there's 6 more episodes. u have to watch them all to find out what happens.**
zoegirl:	uh huh
zoegirl:	g2g—there's someone at the door.
mad maddie:	**come back and visit me l8r. and be sure to drink plenty of milkshakes and eat lots of sausage!**

Tuesday, February 28, 5:15 PM E.S.T.

zoegirl:	ur *still* on-line?
mad maddie:	**i'm downloading songs from itunes. want me to burn u a cd?**
zoegirl:	yes please
mad maddie:	**who was at the door?**
zoegirl:	2 jehovah's witnesses. that's why i was gone for so long.
mad maddie:	**ooo, lucky they didn't come here. i might have been rude.**
zoegirl:	my natural instinct was to give them the polite brush-off, but then i thought, why? shouldn't i c what they have to say?
mad maddie:	**uh . . . no**
zoegirl:	they're ppl just like we r. it can't hurt.
mad maddie:	**yeah, but it can waste your time—time which would be far better spent downloading itunes, for example.**

zoegirl: plus, it doesn't say much about me if i'm not willing to consider other perspectives.

zoegirl: so i invited them in, and they were nice. they were both women, and 1 of them was not much older than us, like maybe 19 or 20. she just got married last month.

mad maddie: 2 young, 2 young

zoegirl: she goes to Bible study every week, and she and her husband r committed to lifting up their lives to God, well, whom they call Jehovah.

zoegirl: can u imagine believing in something so much that u go door to door trying to spread the word?

mad maddie: no, i really can't, and i think it's obnoxious that they do. organized religion gives me the heebie-jeebies.

zoegirl: they left me a book called "knowledge that leads to everlasting life," which we're gonna discuss the next time they come.

mad maddie: u invited them BACK?

zoegirl: in an up-in-the-air sort of way. they said, "can we come again?" and i kind of agreed.

mad maddie: oh lord, zo

zoegirl: what was i supposed to say?

zoegirl: the girl, tina, was so pretty. she had really long hair, and she wore a skirt and a blouse. she seemed so . . . innocent.

mad maddie: don't let them convert u, that's all i'm gonna say

zoegirl: oh please

mad maddie: don't "oh please" me. i'm serious!

mad maddie: time for din din. tootles!

Wednesday, March 1, 5:01 PM E.S.T.

SnowAngel: my steering wheel cover arrived! my steering wheel cover arrived! *gambols about strewing cherries thru air*

zoegirl: did u end up ordering the seat cover?

SnowAngel: yes, it's spifftacular. plus an ADORABLE dangly cherry to hang from my rearview mirror.

SnowAngel: next i'm gonna get a Barbie to prop in front of the gear shift. mary kate has a Barbie propped in front of her gear shift, and it cracks me up.

zoegirl: u don't wanna be posing off mary kate, tho

SnowAngel: then i'll get a Care Bear! yeah! *gets really excited* cuz isn't there 1 with cherries on its tummy???

zoegirl: last year glendy gave u a care bear and u got all freaked out. u threw it away, remember?

SnowAngel: that's cuz it was from glendy. *makes strangled sound as if being smothered in saran wrap*

SnowAngel: if there's a Care Bear with cherries on it, then i'm definitely getting it. i'm not letting 1 bad experience taint my whole Care Bear career. ☺

zoegirl: what does logan think of your cherry theme?

SnowAngel: he makes fun of it to carl and brannen, but mainly just to tease me. he's like, "i get her a jeep—a tough rugged jeep!—and she's already making plans to doll it up. women!"

zoegirl: i've noticed that he brings that up a lot, the fact that he gave it to u.

Send   Cancel

lauren myracle

SnowAngel:	well . . . but he DID give it to me. i guess he's got the right to brag.
zoegirl:	it doesn't bug u?
SnowAngel:	no. does it bug U?
zoegirl:	why would it bug me?
SnowAngel:	good question, why WOULD it? i thought u wanted me and logan to be hunky-dory, so why r u looking for problems?
zoegirl:	i want things to be hunky-dory if they ARE hunky-dory, but i don't think u should fake it just for the sake of the jeep.
SnowAngel:	what a horrible thing to say! omg, zoe!
zoegirl:	angela, wait, i don't mean it in a *bad* way.
SnowAngel:	what other way IS there?
zoegirl:	well, then i'm sorry
zoegirl:	just delete that whole remark, ok?
SnowAngel:	*crosses arms over chest*
zoegirl:	maybe i'm just having troubles of my own. maybe i'm feeling bad and taking it out on u.
SnowAngel:	why? did something happen with doug?
zoegirl:	he's annoyed with me cuz i don't wanna go to tilman barnwell's party with him on friday. but it's gonna be that whole popular crowd. i feel awkward around them.
SnowAngel:	did u explain that to doug?
zoegirl:	no. i mean, all of a sudden doug IS friends with them, and i don't wanna hold him back. but at the same time, i'm like, "wouldn't u rather spend friday nite with me? *alone*?"

Send   Cancel

103

SnowAngel:	so what r u gonna do?
zoegirl:	go with him, i guess. since he wants me 2.
SnowAngel:	ah-ha! so your rltnshp with doug ISN'T perfect—even u have to make compromises!
zoegirl:	i never said it was perfect! and of course i have to make compromises. i never said i didn't!
SnowAngel:	well, then let's not fight about it. *thwacks all stupidness away* there, it's gone.
SnowAngel:	here's something to change the subject: guess where aunt sadie's going tonite?
zoegirl:	where?
SnowAngel:	to a POLE-DANCING party! *snickers into cupped hands*
SnowAngel:	it's the new rage among the 30s set, apparently. she and a bunch of her girlfriends r getting together, and a real live exotic dancer is going to teach them how to do pole-dances.
zoegirl:	i don't understand. WHY?
SnowAngel:	to learn how to turn on their men?
SnowAngel:	well . . . i suppose it's pretty good exercise . . .
zoegirl:	will they . . . wear costumes?
SnowAngel:	lord, i hope not. some of aunt sadie's friends r, shall we say, rather generously endowed. i'm not really wanting to envision them in g-strings.
zoegirl:	wowzers
zoegirl:	i guess i don't really know what to say.
SnowAngel:	next month she's supposed to go to a lingerie party. and the friend who's hosting that 1 wants aunt sadie to host a sex toy party!

Send Cancel

zoegirl:	good grief, what happened to tupperware? do these 30-yr-olds not need tupperware anymore?
SnowAngel:	no, cuz they're 2 busy gyrating around poles. who can store leftovers at a time like that? ☺
SnowAngel:	want me to ask aunt sadie if u can tag along?
zoegirl:	no thanks
SnowAngel:	if u change your mind, just holler!

Wednesday, March 1, 11:30 PM E.S.T.

SnowAngel:	omg, zoe, i have to give u the report on aunt sadie!
Auto response from zoegirl:	zzzzzzzzzzzzzz
SnowAngel:	yeah, yeah, whatever
SnowAngel:	she stumbled in half an hour ago, all tipsy and giggling and loud, and she woke me up so she could do her dance for me. 😳 😳 😳
SnowAngel:	she had to use the bedroom door since she didn't have a pole, but she's gonna buy 1 from the exotic dancer, who's name was marge. isn't that a terrible name for an exotic dancer? MARGE?
SnowAngel:	anyway, her dance was all full of leg kicks and shimmies and shakings of the boobs, and IT WAS AWFUL!!!
SnowAngel:	it's so weird when u realize that grown-ups r ppl 2, and that they do really stupid and embarrassing things just like we do.
SnowAngel:	she told me her inner thighs r super sore. she also told me (prepare thyself) that the whole thing made

Send   Cancel

105

her really horny. uh huh, she said those very words to me, her chaste and delicate niece.

SnowAngel: my innocence? gone!!!

Thursday, March 2, 9:55 AM E.S.T.

mad maddie: **dude! megan got accepted to clemson!**
SnowAngel: yahootie!!!
mad maddie: **she got her letter yesterday. it was big and fat, so she said she had a good feeling about it.**
SnowAngel: aw, that's awesome
mad maddie: **i know! but at the same time, it's like, YIKES. she's our 1st friend to get an acceptance, u know? not counting bryce's early decision to UVA.**
SnowAngel: first but not last, hopefully!
mad maddie: **can u sneak out of class? i ducked into the media center to IM u, but now i'm gonna go meet megan and mary kate in the quad. come join us!**
SnowAngel: can't. mrs. e = eagle eyes.
mad maddie: **let's take megan out for lunch, then. we need to celebrate!**

Friday, March 3, 6:17 PM E.S.T.

mad maddie: **hey, zo. is tonite tilman's party?**
zoegirl: yes, won't u *please* come? i'd feel so much more comfortable if u were there!

Send Cancel

mad maddie: no way, that crowd's 2 power suit for me.

mad maddie: remember how mean they were to doug back in 9th grade?

zoegirl: they weren't ALL mean to him. anyway, doug says they were ok one-on-one. it was just when they got together that they ganged up on him.

mad maddie: and that makes it soooo much better

zoegirl: paige and holly and those girls r gonna be there, and i'm gonna feel like the biggest dork. i wish i didn't have to go!

mad maddie: u don't! u R allowed to say no, u know!

zoegirl: but i already said i would. doug would be *really* pissed if i backed out now.

mad maddie: has doug changed that much, that he would be "pissed" if u didn't obey his every command?

zoegirl: it's not like that

mad maddie: then what is it like?

zoegirl: just forget about it

zoegirl: i've g2g

mad maddie: well . . . all right. try your best to have fun!

Saturday, March 4, 10:09 PM E.S.T.

mad maddie: hey, girl! i'm over at vincent's—whatcha doin?

SnowAngel: logan fell asleep during "Rumor Has It." he's very cute when he's asleep, but he's not such great company.

Send   Cancel

107

mad maddie:	**maybe u should let HIM pick the movie every once in a while. ever thought of that?**
SnowAngel:	*pushes "reject" button* bleep!
SnowAngel:	i watched the end of it myself, and now i'm getting caught up on emails. but i'd much rather chat with u. HI!
mad maddie:	**vincent and his bro r playing foozball, and later on some other ppl r coming over. u guys should join us.**
SnowAngel:	that's ok. i'm kinda liking having a low-key nite, to tell the truth.
mad maddie:	**i hear ya**
mad maddie:	**vincent gets a kick out of u, tho. your name came up earlier, and he said he thought u'd be good in bed.**
SnowAngel:	WHAT?!
mad maddie:	**he's not crushing on u. he just thinks ur cool.**
SnowAngel:	i am cool
SnowAngel:	why did my name come up?
mad maddie:	**i was telling him about the whole j-word soap opera and why he shouldn't believe anything she says. apparently she bad-mouths me all the time, and vincent gets stuck listening to it all, poor baby. but 2 bad, it's his own fault for being friends with her.**
SnowAngel:	is he STILL friends with her? even after the craigslist thing?
mad maddie:	**he thought that was funny—and yes, i smacked him for it. he thought it was even funnier that u broke into her house and left a stalker note.**
SnowAngel:	u TOLD him?!
mad maddie:	**he says jana's stepmonster is having an affair, that's**

Send   Cancel

what jana thinks, and that's why she's full of rage.
whatevs.

SnowAngel: maddie, i can't believe u told vincent that i was the 1 who broke into her house! what if he tells jana?!

mad maddie: ooo, u'd be so busted! ooo! cuz right now she thinks it was the tooth fairy, u know.

SnowAngel: fine, maybe she has her suspicions. there is no reason for him to CONFIRM it.

SnowAngel: i would like to point out, however, that it's been over a week and she hasn't done anything to get back at me. i don't think she's gonna.

mad maddie: what a nice dream world u live in. u just keep having those happy thoughts, sweetie.

SnowAngel: why did vincent say that about me being good in bed???

mad maddie: no reason, it was just where the convo ended up going. he had digital radio playing on the soul station, and he was like, "B-L-double-M, man."

SnowAngel: what's B-L-double-M?

mad maddie: black love-making music. B-L-double-M.

mad maddie: and u have to say it that way. u can't say B-L-M-M.

SnowAngel: uh . . . ok

SnowAngel: is that a term he made up? sounds racist.

mad maddie: it's not racist. it's amusing.

SnowAngel: just cuz something's amusing doesn't mean it's not racist.

mad maddie: dude, chill. vincent likes soul, and vincent likes sex. AND he's a "person of color," so he can't be being racist.

mad maddie:	anywayz, it's better than U-H-D-H-M
SnowAngel:	what's that?
mad maddie:	uptight honky dry-humping music
SnowAngel:	ha
mad maddie:	what would UHDHM be, u think? faith hill? celine dion?
SnowAngel:	michael bolton
mad maddie:	PERFECT
SnowAngel:	so, not to go on and on about this . . . but did vincent say WHY he thought i'd be good in bed?
mad maddie:	probably cuz u make him laff. plus he thinks u've got CAJONES.
SnowAngel:	hmmph
SnowAngel:	did he say if he thought zoe would be good in bed?
mad maddie:	nope, just u
mad maddie:	i don't think zoe is the 1st person who comes up when guys talk about sex . . .
SnowAngel:	yet if they only knew . . .
mad maddie:	how'd tilman's party go? i thought about calling to ask, but didn't. i think i annoyed her last nite.
SnowAngel:	we talked this morning. turns out it was a party for grown-ups, but the grown-ups could bring their kids, and doug wanted zoe there for moral support. cuz HE was nervous—isn't that funny?
mad maddie:	why was he nervous?
SnowAngel:	cuz even tho doug hangs out with tilman and that crowd at school, he doesn't really know them all that well.
SnowAngel:	plus doug had already told his mom that zoe was coming, so when zoe tried to back out, it made doug

Send   Cancel

get uptight. not that he explained that to zoe at the time . . .

mad maddie: **unneccessary drama, baby**

SnowAngel: but zoe said the party itself was fine. she said it actually ended up bringing them closer, cuz they had to talk that stuff out. she said, and i quote, "he's amazing. i feel soooo lucky."

mad maddie: **that's her problem, that she feels "lucky." HE'S the 1 who should feel lucky!**

SnowAngel: absolutely

mad maddie: **but with zoe these days it's totally one-sided.**

mad maddie: **i miss the old zo, the 1 who thought for herself.**

SnowAngel: i know she's worried about next yr, but who isn't?

mad maddie: **i say live in the present and enjoy each moment as it comes.**

mad maddie: **speaking of—guess who i had coffee with this afternoon?**

SnowAngel: who?

mad maddie: **ian—but don't get all excited! it was just coffee.**

SnowAngel: *squeals in a super high-pitched voice*

mad maddie: **i told u not to get excited**

SnowAngel: *squeals again*

SnowAngel: did u call him, or did he call u?

mad maddie: **he called me. it was sweet.**

SnowAngel: AND?

mad maddie: **and we had coffee. actually, i had chai.**

SnowAngel: *puts hands on hips* madigan kinnick, give me details right now!

mad maddie:	we had a good time talking, that's all. it was nice cuz it made me think maybe things can be normal b/w us again.
SnowAngel:	just "normal"?
mad maddie:	listen, i already broke up with the guy once. no way i'm gonna put him thru that again.
SnowAngel:	AH HA! but ur thinking about it!
mad maddie:	i'm **NOT** thinking about it, that's the point.
SnowAngel:	but ur acknowledging the possibility exists.
SnowAngel:	anyway, if u did start seeing each other again, who says u'd break up?
SnowAngel:	and ANYWAY, shouldn't ian be the 1 who gets to decide whether he's willing to risk it?
mad maddie:	whoa there, bessy
mad maddie:	he asked me out for coffee. he didn't ask me to marry him. altho he did pay for my chai . . .
SnowAngel:	*perks up* he did?
mad maddie:	and my cheesecake
SnowAngel:	he DID?
mad maddie:	and i have to admit, he looked pretty hot. he hadn't shaved cuz he's been sick, and his stubble was so damn sexy.
SnowAngel:	STOP! UR GONNA MAKE ME PIDDLE MYSELF!
mad maddie:	okey-doke, i'm outta here. i'll call u tomorrow—we can go out for donuts.
SnowAngel:	groovilicious!

Send   Cancel

lauren myracle

Sunday, March 5, 3:30 PM E.S.T.

mad maddie: krispy kreme? half an hr?
SnowAngel: cya there!

Sunday, March 5, 9:33 PM E.S.T.

SnowAngel: hey, zo. i wish u could have come out with us today.
we missed u!

zoegirl: next weekend we'll do something together, i promise.

SnowAngel: we better, cuz time is going by way 2 fast and we
have to spend as much of it together as possible.

zoegirl: i know, i know

SnowAngel: i'm SERIOUS, zo!

zoegirl: u don't think i realize that? i do. but the same's true for
doug. i wish u could understand that.

zoegirl: he wanted to go for a walk by the chatahoochee. what
was i gonna do, say no?

SnowAngel: a little time apart's not gonna kill u. in fact, it'd
probably be good for u. isn't that what those
relationship articles say, that ur supposed to
maintain your own friends and interests?

zoegirl: ???

zoegirl: i AM maintaining my own friends and interests. just cuz
we didn't hang out this weekend doesn't make me a bad
friend!

Send Cancel

113

SnowAngel:	i never said u were a bad friend. i just love u, and it makes me sad that i never get to c u.
zoegirl:	well please don't guilt-trip me about it. i feel like i'm under so much pressure these days! and if i don't do everything just right, everyone hates me!
SnowAngel:	???
SnowAngel:	where is THIS coming from?
zoegirl:	never mind. we're *all* under pressure, i know that. that's why doug wanted to go for a walk, cuz he hasn't heard from oberlin yet and it's driving him crazy.
SnowAngel:	take a deep breath. everything's gonna be ok.
zoegirl:	it's just that so much is riding on this year. i feel like if i make 1 false step, everything's gonna come tumbling down. and with the whole college thing looming over us . . .
zoegirl:	i'm gonna miss everyone so much. i'm already dreading saying good-bye.
SnowAngel:	then don't! come to UGA with me! ☺
SnowAngel:	with your record, u could apply tomorrow and get in.
zoegirl:	that's a sweet thought . . . but i don't think so
SnowAngel:	why not? make doug apply 2, and u could BOTH go to UGA.
zoegirl:	i know ur trying to make me feel better, but ur actually not.
zoegirl:	my top choice is still kenyon, assuming i get accepted.
SnowAngel:	*pouts*
SnowAngel:	why kenyon? what makes kenyon so much better than georgia?

Send   Cancel

zoegirl:	cuz it's small, cuz it's got a great liberal arts program, cuz it's got a strong writing faculty. it's just a really good fit.
SnowAngel:	u sound like ur quoting from a brochure
SnowAngel:	anyway, UGA has all of those things
zoegirl:	plus kenyon's 2 hours away from oberlin
SnowAngel:	zoe, u can NOT make your college decision based on doug!
zoegirl:	i'm not!
zoegirl:	i just . . . i don't wanna go to a state school, all right?
SnowAngel:	*draws back*
SnowAngel:	ok, now i'm a little offended. a state school's not good enuff for u?
zoegirl:	*please* don't, angela!
zoegirl:	i just told u how stressed out i feel—ur supposed to be nice to me!!!
SnowAngel:	maddie says ur gonna end up at princeton cuz that's where your mom went.
zoegirl:	maddie's not the ruler of the universe. and i'm not gonna end up at princeton, cuz i'm not gonna get in.
SnowAngel:	u don't know that
zoegirl:	yes i do . . . cuz i sabotaged my application.
SnowAngel:	*faints*
SnowAngel:	for real??
zoegirl:	i wrote my essay about swinging on the playground at memorial park and how liberating it is. which is true, but not exactly princeton material. and how i think there should be a National Pigtails Day, where everyone says

"screw it" to being grown-up and wears their hair in pigtails.

SnowAngel: 🐑 ?

zoegirl: uh huh

SnowAngel: oh

SnowAngel: do u really think that, that there should be a Nat'l Pigtails Day?

zoegirl: don't u? just to escape from the go-go-go of it all?

SnowAngel: i suppose. i'm just kinda surprised that U do.

SnowAngel: 1st u "missed" the early decision deadline, and then u sabotaged your application. why didn't u tell us?

zoegirl: i don't know, i just didn't. but i am now.

SnowAngel: what's your mom gonna do?

zoegirl: what *can* she do?

zoegirl: if i don't get in, i don't get in. case closed.

SnowAngel: i'm floored, that's all i can say.

zoegirl: i've g2g, it's time to take my pill. i have to take them at the same time every nite or they won't work.

SnowAngel: oh yeah?

zoegirl: i picked 10 o'clock, cuz that's when i usually brush my teeth and get ready for bed. but then when i was a week and a half into it, i realized that wasn't such a good idea, cuz when i go out, i have to bring one with me. like at tilman's party. i brought my pill in my pocket, wrapped in a sliver of aluminum foil, and at 10 o'clock i snuck off to the bathroom and swallowed it.

SnowAngel: sounds complicated

zoegirl: welcome to my life. *everything* is complicated!

Send   Cancel

Monday, March 6, 6:14 PM E.S.T.

zoegirl: hey, mads. i needed a distraction from hw, so i watched big bunny episode 2.

mad maddie: YUMMY episode 2, u mean. that's what it says when u click on it. yummmmmmy.

zoegirl: i'm thinking that susie and lulu and the round-headed boy should stop visiting big bunny. the "sofa" he put out for them? it was a giant baguette!

mad maddie: yes, but while they were sitting there, he told that delightful story about the turnip. wasn't that a delightful story?

zoegirl: that story made no sense!

mad maddie: "it is from eating veg-uh-tuh-buls that i got to be sooooo big and strong. yessss, veg-uh-tuh-buls."

zoegirl: uh huh. then why, when lulu said she'd bring him some carrots, did he request a kitty instead?

mad maddie: he wants a delicious tender kitty to pet and love! weren't u paying attn?

zoegirl: i think lulu and the round-headed boy need to listen to susie. that's what i think.

mad maddie: i love susie. susie's my hero

zoegirl: of course she is, she's a mini-maddie.

mad maddie: why, cuz she's surly?

zoegirl: yes

zoegirl: jk

mad maddie: susie's the only 1 with brains. she TOLD lulu and round-headed boy not to go back into the forest, but they did anyway.

Send   Cancel

117

zoegirl:	she went 2, don't forget
mad maddie:	**cuz she's a good friend! she had to take care of them.**
mad maddie:	**u noticed, however, that she was the only 1 of the 3 who did NOT take a seat on the french-bread sofa?**
zoegirl:	i don't want lulu to bring big bunny a kitten. lulu better not bring big bunny a kitty, maddie.
mad maddie:	**watch and c (heh heh heh . . .)**
zoegirl:	ur so weird
zoegirl:	hey, did u hear the latest? supposedly terri spotted jana's stepmom in some guy's car who *wasn't* jana's dad, and terri, being the good friend that she is, let it slip to everyone.
mad maddie:	**what a pal**
zoegirl:	i know, can u imagine?
mad maddie:	**it would totally suck. it would be beyond humiliating. but given that jana has no problem humiliating ME, i can't muster up much sympathy.**
zoegirl:	at least it's distracted her from getting back at angela.
mad maddie:	**true dat!**

Tuesday, March 7, 5:15 PM E.S.T.

SnowAngel:	ah, crap
zoegirl:	what?
SnowAngel:	jana left a DEAD BIRD in the passenger seat of my jeep!!! (and i'm so not kidding, much as i wish i was.)
zoegirl:	noooooo!
SnowAngel:	yessssss!

Send   Cancel

zoegirl:	but we thought she wasn't going to do the evil revenge thing! we thought she'd forgotten!
SnowAngel:	well, she didn't. and u know what's weird? i almost put a dead rat on her pillow, except i didn't have a spare dead rat. where in the world do u think she found a dead bird?
zoegirl:	angela, whoa. u've gotta give me a minute to process this.
zoegirl:	a DEAD BIRD? i don't understand!
SnowAngel:	have u not yet grasped the fact that when it comes to jana, there IS no understanding? maybe it was a voodoo thing. or maybe she's jealous of my beautiful cherry-themed jeep, since her station wagon is such a heap. maybe the bird actually died in her backseat, i wouldn't be surprised!
zoegirl:	how did she put the bird in there? did u leave the jeep unlocked?
SnowAngel:	what is this, blame-the-victim time? it's got zip-up windows. it's not that hard to break into.
zoegirl:	then u should get the window fingerprinted!
SnowAngel:	*hedges just a teeny bit* except that i SUPPOSE it's possible i left the window open myself. *eensy-weensy niggle*
zoegirl:	did u or didn't u?
SnowAngel:	i was in a hurry to get to homeroom! i can't always be leaning over and zipping up windows when i'm late to homeroom, now can i?
SnowAngel:	anyway, i doubt there's any law against leaving dead birds in someone's car.

Send   Cancel

119

zoegirl:	ur *sure* it was jana who did it?
SnowAngel:	ur NOT? who else would it be? who else would have such a psychotic brain as to scoop up a dead bird and deposit it in someone's open window?
zoegirl:	ok, point taken
zoegirl:	so what did u do?
SnowAngel:	i made logan remove the bird with his jacket, and i gave it a proper burial. it wasn't its fault it was the pawn of the evil jana.
zoegirl:	but u don't think she actually *killed* it. that's creepy, the idea of jana killing a living creature.
SnowAngel:	no, it wasn't mauled or anything. it was just dead.
zoegirl:	freshly dead?
SnowAngel:	ewww! how am i supposed to know?
zoegirl:	what r u gonna do? r u gonna say anything to jana?
SnowAngel:	hmm, lemme think. "nice bird, thanks for the memories"?
zoegirl:	i think that once and for all u should just let it go. let her have her moment of triumph, pathetic as it is, and move on.
SnowAngel:	ur saying do NOTHING? just sit here and take it like a . . . dead-bird-taking person?
zoegirl:	yes, cuz ur bigger than this. ur a bigger person than jana.
SnowAngel:	*rolls eyes and fails to feel noble*
SnowAngel:	i'm gonna go lysol the heck out of the place where the bird was. i could get bird flu, u know. and perish.
zoegirl:	ur being very brave. i'm proud of u for not retaliating.
SnowAngel:	hmmph!!!

Send   Cancel

Tuesday, March 7, 11:50 PM E.S.T.

mad maddie: **newsflash! newsflash!**

Auto response from SnowAngel: i'm sleeping, u fools—and u should be 2!

mad maddie: **a bit testy, r we? from all those bird germs?**

mad maddie: **it came to me in a sparkling moment of clarity: jana was GIVING YOU THE BIRD. as in stick up middle finger, fold down others? jana gave u the frickin bird.**

mad maddie: **u've gotta give her points for cleverness, actually. or not.**

mad maddie: **i'm feeling smug for figuring it out, that's all!**

Wednesday, March 8, 11:04 AM E.S.T.

mad maddie: **well hey there, missy! fancy meeting u in a place like this!**

SnowAngel: HUSH! the media center is a very serious place, don't u know?

mad maddie: **whatcha working on?**

SnowAngel: *grins evilly* i'm ordering a crate of baby chicks to be delivered to jana's house. bwahaha!

mad maddie: **wtf???**

SnowAngel: just click on the "submit" button and . . . wala! order #2453 completed and paid for. YES.

mad maddie: **dude, explain**

SnowAngel: well, it's obvious that zoe wasn't gonna do anything, even tho in a perfect universe she would have. but no. she thought we should "let it go," as if that was an option.

mad maddie: **c? now u know how i felt!**

SnowAngel: i never said i didn't!

SnowAngel: u stepped in to defend her when jana started those rumors, and then I stepped in to defend U after the craigslist nightmare. it is soooo her turn!

mad maddie: **IF zoe were an eye-for-an-eye girl. but she's not. she's a pacifist.**

SnowAngel: there is time for peace and there is time for war. and a dead bird in my jeep means war.

mad maddie: **and war means . . . a crate of baby chickens?**

SnowAngel: it was aunt sadie's idea. she and her sorority sisters sent a crate of chicks to some girl in college. u can buy them from www.farmresource.com.

mad maddie: **um, sweetie? jana left a dead bird—i repeat, a DEAD bird—in your jeep. and now, to thank her, ur sending her a crate of fresh victims?**

SnowAngel: omg

mad maddie: **uh huh**

SnowAngel: omg, OMG, OMG!

SnowAngel: what have i done? *bashes in head with keyboard*

mad maddie: **just go back and cancel the order, u doof!**

SnowAngel: right. gotta run!!!!

Send   Cancel

Thursday, March 9, 4:45 PM E.S.T.

zoegirl:	did angela hear back from the farm supply place? were they able to stop her order?
mad maddie:	**nope, by the time she got a human being on the phone, the order was already processed. however, the nice man did offer her a discount on fertilizer.**
zoegirl:	angela is insane. what was she thinking?
mad maddie:	**she was thinking that jana needed to be put in her place, and since it was obvious U weren't gonna do anything . . .**
zoegirl:	*me*? why would i do anything?
zoegirl:	did angela *want* me to do something?
mad maddie:	**???**
mad maddie:	**of course she did. she wanted u to rush in like her knight in shining armor, just like i rushed in for u and she rushed in for me.**
zoegirl:	well . . . but . . .
zoegirl:	it was a dead bird, maddie. not a mortal wound to her soul.
mad maddie:	**dead bird, mortal wound to soul . . .**
mad maddie:	**i'm just sayin**
zoegirl:	great. so u and angela think i'm a sucky friend, and i've basically murdered a crate of baby chicks. that's just great.
mad maddie:	**the chicks r scheduled to arrive tomorrow—they haven't been murdered YET.**
mad maddie:	**l8rs!**

Send   Cancel

Friday, March 10, 8:17 PM E.S.T.

zoegirl: hey, angela! sorry i didn't call u back—i went to R.E.I with doug.

Auto response from SnowAngel: bird murderers should burn in hell!!!

zoegirl: u don't mean *me*, do u?

zoegirl: of course u don't. strike that. ur talking about jana, i know that.

zoegirl: anyway, it's not that i didn't *want* to call u back, i was just busy. and it just happened to be with doug. but that doesn't mean i was picking him over u. u know that, right?

zoegirl: but where r u? r u intercepting the chick delivery???

zoegirl: *please* tell me u made it and they're safe!

zoegirl: call me!!!!

Friday, March 10, 9:09 PM E.S.T.

mad maddie: dude, i heard back from angela, and it's not good. the UPS guy was a tool and refused to give her the package, even after she explained the situation.

zoegirl: so where r the chicks now? and where is she?

mad maddie: well. i had my boy vincent do some detective work, and jana DID receive the crate. angela can be happy about 1 thing: jana's stepmonster was LIVID. i guess the chicks messed up her newly refinished floor or something.

mad maddie: she told jana to get rid of the chicks or else, so jana took them to tony marcus's house, who's gonna use them to teach his doberman how to attack.

zoegirl: WHAT?!!!

mad maddie: so that's where angela is, racing over to tony's to rescue the chicks from the jaws of death. i would have gone with her, but i'm at starbucks waiting for ian. vincent calls it "starfucks," btw.

zoegirl: that's so sick that tony marcus would torture baby chicks. why would anybody do that?

zoegirl: wait a sec, did u say *ian*?!

mad maddie: but i like starbucks. i like their frappuccinos.

zoegirl: i like starbucks 2, and i'm proud of u for not calling it starf***s. i'm even more proud of u for having a date with ian. but now i'm gonna call angela again!!!

Friday, March 10, 10:33 PM E.S.T.

SnowAngel: i got the chicks!!! i got the chicks!!!

mad maddie: yay! they're all safe and sound?

SnowAngel: all but 1, which was dead when i got there. 🙁 tony swears it had a heart attack just from hearing his dog bark, but i dunno. do baby chicks have heart attacks?

mad maddie: did it have any bite marks on it?

SnowAngel: oh god, i'm not sure. i didn't really look . . .

mad maddie: poor chickie

Send   Cancel

SnowAngel:	i know, i feel sooooo bad. like, i should have zoe say a prayer for it or something!
SnowAngel:	but at least i saved the others. they're in aunt sadie's bathtub, slipping and squawking around. and pooping. they poop A LOT. i'm a bit worried about what aunt sadie's gonna say . . .
mad maddie:	**did zoe reach u? she's been hyperventilating all nite.**
SnowAngel:	yeah. we talked. and—omg! she told me u were at starbucks waiting for ian???
mad maddie:	**yep, he's here now, sitting right next to me. we r having a fool-around-on-the-computer date, cuz turns out we're geeks. who knew?**
SnowAngel:	did u just call it a DATE?! and what do u mean, fool around? as in FOOL AROUND fool around?
mad maddie:	**i mean we've both got our laptops and we're doing random computer stuff, u freak. and showing each other. in fact ian's reading over my shoulder this very second.**
SnowAngel:	*shrieks and claps hand to mouth*
SnowAngel:	he's not really, is he?
mad maddie:	**no. but i did tell him about the chicks, and he thinks u did a good thing by saving them.**
SnowAngel:	i had to. i'm the 1 who . . . u know. put them in peril.
mad maddie:	**nonetheless, baby. big thumb's up.**
mad maddie:	**so there's a party at ethan's tomorrow—gonna go?**
SnowAngel:	yep, i'm going with andre. well, technically i'm going with logan, but i told logan i'd meet him there. which didn't make him happy, but . . .
SnowAngel:	bleh. sometimes i just don't want to deal with it.
SnowAngel:	does that answer your question?

Send Cancel

mad maddie: uh, sure, altho a simple "yes" would have been sufficient.

SnowAngel: don't know what i'll do about the chicks, tho . . .

mad maddie: dude, i'm outta here. want me to tell ian "hi" for u?

SnowAngel: i want u to give him a big smoocheroo for me. on the lips, with lots of tongue action.

SnowAngel: bye! 😊

Saturday, March 11, 9:44 AM E.S.T.

zoegirl: hi there, angela. how r the chicks doing this morning?

SnowAngel: they're pooping machines—it's unbelievable! aunt sadie made me take them out of the tub and scrub it with bleach, so now they're living in my room in a box. only they keep hopping out and peck-peck-pecking all over my room.

SnowAngel: hey, would U like a cute baby chick? or 2 or 3? i'm giving them away fo fwee!

zoegirl: no thanks

SnowAngel: rats. can u think of anyone who would?

zoegirl: er . . . maybe a petting zoo? or a farmer?

SnowAngel: ooo, yeah! do u know any petting zoo owners or farmers?

zoegirl: sorry

SnowAngel: *grrrr-ness*

SnowAngel: zoe, listen. i have a question for u and ur gonna think i'm being facetious, but i'm not. do u pray?

zoegirl: um, yeah. why?

SnowAngel:	like, every nite? do u get down on your knees?
zoegirl:	i don't get down on my knees, but yes, i pray every nite. why?
SnowAngel:	what do u pray about?
zoegirl:	just stuff that's going on in my life. i ask for help dealing with it. and i say thanks for all the good things in my life, like u and maddie and doug.
SnowAngel:	honestly? u thank God for me??? *gets teary-eyed*
zoegirl:	i think it's important to be grateful, that's all.
zoegirl:	r u secretly thinking that sounds incredibly stupid?
SnowAngel:	not at all! i think it's awesome.
SnowAngel:	will u say a prayer for that 1 chick? the 1 who died?
zoegirl:	why don't *u* say a prayer for it?
SnowAngel:	cuz u've had more practice.
SnowAngel:	1 little prayer, plz? it would make me feel so much better.
zoegirl:	sure, of course
SnowAngel:	and while ur at it, would u pray that i develop phenomenally lustrous hair and a flawless complexion? and that i win a shopping spree at hot topic?
zoegirl:	angela!
SnowAngel:	jk—but not about the chick ☺
SnowAngel:	u going to ethan's tonite?
zoegirl:	no, doug and i r gonna rent a movie and cuddle.
SnowAngel:	a pox on your head
SnowAngel:	well, if u change your mind, u should come!

Send   Cancel

Saturday, March 11, 9:57 AM E.S.T.

SnowAngel:	1 more thing. i bet u floss, 2, don't u?
zoegirl:	of course. don't u?
SnowAngel:	no comment
zoegirl:	angela! u really should floss EVERY DAY!!!

Sunday, March 12, 11:00 AM E.S.T.

mad maddie: **hey, zo. i thought i'd fill u in on the party u missed, which was extremely soap-opera-ish and filled with angst. perhaps ur thinking, "well, good, glad i wasn't there," but that would be very selfish, cuz if u HAD been there, then . . . well, then it probably all would have happened anywayz.**

Auto response from zoegirl: if this is doug, i'm on my way over! if it's anyone else . . . try me later!

mad maddie: **good lord, zo, r u EVER not with doug?**

mad maddie: **ur starting to look alike, u know. like those ppl who look like their dogs.**

mad maddie: **back to ethan's par-tay. here's the short version: angela made logan cry.**

mad maddie: **if you wanna know more, u'll have to show a little interest in the world beyond doug and call me!!!**

Send   Cancel

Sunday, March 12, 11:09 AM E.S.T.

mad maddie: hey, sweetie. u doin ok?

SnowAngel: hey, mads. i'm FINE, i just feel like a huge jerk.

mad maddie: how's logan?

SnowAngel: *blows out big puff of air*

SnowAngel: he's sad. i dunno.

SnowAngel: but we talked some more after we left ethan's, and i guess we got things resolved. for now, anyway.

mad maddie: it kinda surprised me, the way u were acting last nite. u just ... didn't seem like u.

SnowAngel: i know! i didn't FEEL like me! i get that way whenever i'm around logan these days. it's so bad, maddie. i become this mean callous person who treats him like shit, even tho he's such a great guy. and the worst thing is, he LETS me!

mad maddie: ooo, that's not good

SnowAngel: he likes me too much! i never thought that could be a problem, but it is! *pulls hair from scalp*

mad maddie: angela ...

SnowAngel: what?

SnowAngel: no, don't. i know what ur gonna say. but i CAN'T break up with him. he gave me a JEEP, maddie.

mad maddie: is the jeep really that important?

SnowAngel: aaargh

SnowAngel: no, not as in "i'm so materialistic that i'll keep going out with u so i can have a car." it's more the fact that ...

SnowAngel:	GOD, maddie. HE GAVE ME A JEEP. that's the nicest thing any guy's ever done for me. what kind of heartless bitch would break up with him after that?
mad maddie:	**er . . . the kind of heartless bitch who at least wouldn't be treating him like shit anymore?**
SnowAngel:	i wish HE would break up with ME. that's what i keep hoping will happen. is that horrible?
mad maddie:	**pretty much**
mad maddie:	**but i love u anywayz. u know that.**
SnowAngel:	so does logan, apparently *buries face in hands*
mad maddie:	**i IMed zoe to catch her up on everything she missed, but she was—sooprise—unavailable.**
mad maddie:	**i told her that she and doug were starting to look alike, like those owners who look their dogs, and then u know what i ALMOST said? i almost said, "so hmm, let's c. does that make u doug's dog?"**
SnowAngel:	ouch
mad maddie:	**it's true, tho. the girl's on a leash.**
SnowAngel:	who do u think's worse, me or zoe?
SnowAngel:	nvm, don't answer 😵
mad maddie:	**change of subject: what did jana say when u were playing quarters? i saw your face get all hard.**
SnowAngel:	oh GROAN. it was just jana being jana, as usual. she goes to serena patterson, "it's so sad to c a hottie like logan go to waste, isn't it? cuz he sure isn't getting any from angela. HE'S the 1 who would appreciate a good chick, if you know what i mean."
mad maddie:	**did u say anything back, like "better a good chick than a dead bird"?**

Send   Cancel

131

SnowAngel: ha, i wish

SnowAngel: but no, i took the high road and didn't even mention the dead bird incident. so there.

mad maddie: **that'll show her!**

Sunday, March 12, 4:02 PM E.S.T.

zoegirl: angela, i'm so glad ur on-line! what happened at ethan's party?

zoegirl: maddie started to tell me, but didn't.

SnowAngel: it's really not that interesting. but fine, i'll tell u.

SnowAngel: andre and i showed up around 9, and i could tell logan was all excited to c me. but i wasn't excited to c him. and i guess i kinda . . . didn't make much of an effort. i somehow talked to other ppl for most of the nite, and i guess it made logan feel bad.

zoegirl: cuz u were ignoring him?

SnowAngel: not IGNORING him, just . . .

SnowAngel: i didn't set OUT to ignore him, i just didn't wanna be with him.

zoegirl: why?

SnowAngel: cuz my head is messed up! cuz i'm a mean, stupid, horrible person!

zoegirl: how did he end up crying???

SnowAngel: well, at 1 point i ended up out on the patio with vincent, who was listening to me go on about how frustrated i am with the whole situation. and that in

Send   Cancel

itself was strange. i mean, me? having a heart-to-heart with vincent?!

SnowAngel: part of it was the beer, i'm sure. u know how drinking can either make things better or worse depending on what mood u were in to start with?

zoegirl: not really

SnowAngel: last nite it just made me feel down on everything. it wasn't much fun.

zoegirl: doesn't sound like much fun

SnowAngel: anyway, maddie realized that logan was upset, and she came and told me that i should talk to him. but i said no. so she went to talk to him herself, and a few minutes later he appeared by my side and said, "angela, come on, let's go for a walk."

SnowAngel: we went and sat on a wall outside ethan's house, and he told me he thought he loved me. isn't that just peachy? and that he didn't understand what was going on. that's when he started crying, which made ME cry. it was awful!

zoegirl: poor logan!

SnowAngel: and poor me! don't forget poor me!

zoegirl: so how did u work things out? or rather, *did* u work things out?

SnowAngel: i told him i didn't know WHY i was acting that way, and that i was sorry for being such a terrible girlfriend. and last nite i really did feel sorry. but now i just feel blah about it again.

zoegirl: oh, angela

SnowAngel: usually i'm the 1 chasing after whatever guy i'm

crushing on, u know? and now the situation's reversed, and i can't get my head around it.

SnowAngel: the problem is, i honestly do like him . . . just not in a pulse-racing way. but why can't i just CHOOSE to like him that way? why can't i let my head decide instead of my heart???

zoegirl: i can't believe he said he loves u.

zoegirl: what did u say back?

SnowAngel: i buried my head against his chest and didn't meet his eyes. but i DIDN'T say "i love u, 2." at least i was honest that way.

zoegirl: oh wow

SnowAngel: on the plus side, it's almost spring break, which means we'll be apart for a week. which sounds horrible, i know, but maybe being in california will clear my head.

zoegirl: i wish i were going to california. but no, i get to visit my grandparents in tennessee.

SnowAngel: please remember: i'm going to EL CERRITO, where i will prolly c the dreadful glendy. altho i guess it's better than poor maddie, who has to stay at home and clean out her room.

zoegirl: geez louise, we're pathetic

SnowAngel: u got that right

SnowAngel: i'm gonna log off. i have to go feed the chicks. cya tomorrow!

Monday, March 13, 5:25 PM E.S.T.

mad maddie: **whoa, zoe! ur actually there!**

mad maddie: **how long do i have before doug comes over?**

zoegirl: haha, very funny

mad maddie: **???**

zoegirl: grrrr . . . 30 minutes. we have a physics exam to study for, cuz of course mr. franklin is making us take an exam the week before spring break.

zoegirl: but we can chat til then

mad maddie: **wow, i'm honored**

mad maddie: **did mr. franklin read u guys the announcement about "senior games week"?**

zoegirl: if he did, i missed it. what's senior games week?

mad maddie: **i swiped mr. gerard's copy, lemme read it to u.**

mad maddie: **"Dear Teachers, we are asking that you please mention these following senior lunch games to your classes. If you can, act excited. On Tuesday we will have Ice Sledding in the cafeteria, which will include prizes. On Wednesday we will be having a game called Cheese Heads, in which students will wear fro wigs and try to catch cheese balls in their hair. On Thursday, the big one, we will be holding a root beer chugging contest!!!"**

zoegirl: omg. angela's behind this, isn't she?

mad maddie: **no doubt. isn't it classic?**

zoegirl: they should just give us bonus free periods. if they want to do something for us, that's all they need to do.

mad maddie: **"cheese heads." it kills me. and i love the part about, "if**

Send   Cancel

	u can, act excited." when mr. gerard came to that part, he glanced up with his typical deadpan expression and said, "yippee."
zoegirl:	it's insulting, the idea that throwing cheese balls at each other will make us forget how stressed we r.
mad maddie:	**and don't forget the "big one," a root beer chugging contest!**
mad maddie:	**but I'M not stressed. who says we're stressed? the only one who's stressed is u, zo.**
zoegirl:	ur not stressed? really?
mad maddie:	**spring semester grades don't even matter. u've gotta lighten up, cupcake.**
zoegirl:	ack—maybe ur right
zoegirl:	tina and arlene suggested that 2, altho not in those words.
mad maddie:	**who the hell r tina and arlene?**
zoegirl:	the jehovah's witnesses, don't u remember? they came back today.
mad maddie:	**ur now on a first-name basis?**
zoegirl:	i invited them in and we had a nice chat. i served them pepperidge farm cookies.
mad maddie:	**jesus, zoe. what would your mom say if she knew u were inviting strangers into the house and giving them cookies?**
zoegirl:	but my mom wasn't here, and anyway, all she talks about these days is when i'm gonna hear from princeton.
zoegirl:	*she's* the reason i'm stressed. well, part of the reason.
mad maddie:	**so what did u and tina and arlene talk about?**
zoegirl:	if i tell u, ur gonna be rude, but i don't care.

Send   Cancel

zoegirl:	we talked about everlasting life.
mad maddie:	**uh huh**
mad maddie:	**and what did u learn about everlasting life?**
zoegirl:	i didn't "learn" anything. tina and arlene talked about the peaceful paradise that's waiting for us after we die, and i was like, "yeah, that would be nice."
mad maddie:	**it WOULD be nice. doesn't mean it's true.**
zoegirl:	doesn't mean it's not, either
zoegirl:	tina, she's the one who just got married, she looked so . . . i don't know. open and honest when she talked about it. her whole face lit up.
mad maddie:	**cuz she's trying to suck u in. it's all an act.**
zoegirl:	no it's not. why r u so cynical?
zoegirl:	i haven't figured out what makes jehovah's witnesses so different from normal old Christians. so far it seems like it's just that they call God "Jehovah."
mad maddie:	**and that they go door to door invading ppl's privacy, trying to cram jehovah down their throats.**
zoegirl:	i was thinking how hard that must be, the whole door-to-door thing. i bet ppl are mean to them all the time. (case in point: U!)
mad maddie:	**i wouldn't be mean. i just wouldn't invite them in for cookies.**
zoegirl:	i think they're brave. it may not be what u or i would do with our lives, but that doesn't make it wrong.
mad maddie:	**whatevs**
mad maddie:	**did they give u any more reading material?**
zoegirl:	yeah, a book called "The Greatest Man Who Ever Lived." i gave them a $5 donation for it.

Send   Cancel

137

mad maddie:	**$5 for a book u neither asked for nor wanted?**
zoegirl:	in the illustrations, jesus looks like that cute doctor from "grey's anatomy." patrick dempsey.
mad maddie:	**maybe that's to keep all the j.w. girls hot for christ.**
zoegirl:	uh huh, i'm sure that's what they were thinking
mad maddie:	**whoa—i'm fading here, zoe. i'm gonna go take a nap.**
zoegirl:	it's almost six o'clock! u can't take a nap, u'll be up all nite!
mad maddie:	**vicious cycle, isn't it?**
mad maddie:	**buenos noches!**

Tuesday, March 14, 8:17 PM E.S.T.

SnowAngel:	hey, zo. i just got the saddest email from my sister!
zoegirl:	oh, poor chrissy. what's going on?
SnowAngel:	it's sooooo freshman yr. it's almost laffable, except i know how much this stuff can hurt.
SnowAngel:	her email was all about this girl named mackenzie, who lies.
zoegirl:	mackenzie lies? about what?
SnowAngel:	er, everything? apparently she's 1 of those girls who can win ppl over when she wants to, but then she stirs things up by spreading rumors and everybody gets mad at her.
SnowAngel:	shit—i just realized! she's a 9th-grade jana!
SnowAngel:	anyway, chrissy made the mistake of telling mackenzie some personal private things about this

Send   Cancel

	other girl named jo ellen, and now she's worried mackenzie's gonna blab.
zoegirl:	why would chrissy tell mackenzie anything if she knew mackenzie's reputation?
SnowAngel:	according to chrissy, she was mad at jo ellen at the time.
zoegirl:	so what happened?
SnowAngel:	i'll paste in her email so u can read it yourself.
SnowAngel:	"oh and i'm so smart. i told mackenzie some stuff about my friend jo ellen and i'm scared she's gonna tell to get back at me for not sitting with her at lunch. if she does, i'm in deep doo doo cuz it'll start this whole big war all over again. should i tell jo ellen wut i said about her or lyke leave it alone???"
zoegirl:	sheesh, tough call
SnowAngel:	it's all so silly, and yet i feel bad for her.
SnowAngel:	aren't u glad we're past that? i mean, yeah, we have our problems, but we have learned SOME things, ya know?
zoegirl:	er . . .
SnowAngel:	what? why r u ER-ing?
zoegirl:	not to be rude, but r u *sure* we're past all that?
SnowAngel:	r u referring to jana? the REAL jana? such a different situation, omg!
zoegirl:	how is it so different?
SnowAngel:	for the record, jana started everything, or do u not remember?
SnowAngel:	SHE started it and SHE continued it and SHE is the

Send   Cancel

person to blame. and btw, i've decided not to let her comment about logan go unpunished!

zoegirl: ok, let's try again. *how* is it so different?

SnowAngel: u don't get to have an opinion, cuz u have wimpily refused to get involved. *sticks out tongue*

zoegirl: well . . . i think it's sweet that chrissy writes u for advice, even if she has no idea how unqualified u r to offer any. she misses her big sis.

SnowAngel: she'll c me in 5 days. i fly out to el cerrito on sunday.

zoegirl: what r u gonna do about the chicks?

SnowAngel: holy crap! (literally!)

SnowAngel: what AM i gonna do about the chicks?

zoegirl: i can't take care of them, cuz i leave for tennessee that same day. i'm *dreading* the car ride with my parents. all they're gonna talk about is college, i just know it.

SnowAngel: blech

zoegirl: how r they, anyway? the chicks. when do i get to meet them?

SnowAngel: whenever u get your butt over here, u lame-o. how bout right now?

zoegirl: i would, but i just can't, angela. 2 much hw.

zoegirl: have u named them?

SnowAngel: yes, but i kept getting them mixed up. so now i call all of them "squishy." they're the collective squishy.

zoegirl: *r* they squishy?

SnowAngel: when u squeeze them, yes. but not in a yucky way.

SnowAngel: they're growing on me, the little squishies. altho 1 of them pooped on my pillow.

zoegirl:	u let them on your bed?
SnowAngel:	they like it when i bounce them.
zoegirl:	okaaaay
zoegirl:	moving on . . . how r things with logan?
SnowAngel:	😵
zoegirl:	what does that mean?
SnowAngel:	it means that things r fine and not fine.
SnowAngel:	we're on cruise control. we're both just kinda . . . going along.
zoegirl:	well, could be worse, i guess
SnowAngel:	yeah. thanks for not saying anything obnoxious. *makes face to show idiocy of it all*
zoegirl:	ur a good person, angela. u'll do the right thing.
zoegirl:	bye!

Wednesday, March 15, 5:15 PM E.S.T.

mad maddie:	**dude! i'm at ian's and i've got news. will u set up the chatroom thingie?**
SnowAngel:	coming right up!

You have just entered the room "Angela's Boudoir."
mad maddie has entered the room.
zoegirl has entered the room.

zoegirl:	hey, guys! wassup?

Send　　Cancel

141

SnowAngel:	maddie's got NEWS. she's IMing from ian's house, ooo la la!
mad maddie:	**my news isn't about ian, u doof!**
SnowAngel:	it's not?
mad maddie:	**it's better. ready?**
zoegirl:	hold on . . . lemme tell doug 1 thing . . .
SnowAngel:	dougie's on-line? tell him hi!
zoegirl:	ok, i'm all yours. spill!
mad maddie:	**I GOT ACCEPTED TO SANTA CRUZ!!!!**
SnowAngel:	omg!!!!
zoegirl:	maddie!!!!! yay!!!!!!
mad maddie:	**i know! it's incredible!**
SnowAngel:	*squeals and hugs sweet maddie*
SnowAngel:	tell us every single detail!!!
mad maddie:	**well, i got home from school and saw this big thick envelope on the kitchen counter, with "Santa Cruz Admissions Office" as the return address. i got really fidgety and just started screaming, right there in the house. no one was there but me, so i could be as loud as i wanted.**
zoegirl:	omg!!!
mad maddie:	**i took a deep breath and tried to calm down, but my hands were shaking. i opened the envelope and pulled out a folder that said, "Welcome to Santa Cruz." inside was a letter that said, "Dear Madigan. You're In!"**
mad maddie:	**isn't that cool? i LOVE that, that instead of being all prissy and formal, they're like, "you're in! yahootie!"**
SnowAngel:	oh, maddie, i am soooooo happy for u!

mad maddie: i ran out to my car all jumping and hopping around and drove to ian's, cuz i knew neither of u would be home yet. i showed him my letter and he hugged me really hard and lifted me into the air. it was AWESOME.

zoegirl: i'm so proud of u, maddie!

SnowAngel: me 2!!!

zoegirl: but it's scary, too. out of the 3 of us, this is our 1st college acceptance. which means that others (hopefully) r coming, and which means it's really gonna happen . . . we're really gonna graduate and leave and never be together again!!!

SnowAngel: what r u talking about? we're gonna be together FOREVER. u think college is gonna change that?

zoegirl: well . . . it's not gonna be the same, no matter how much we want it 2.

SnowAngel: don't SAY that!

SnowAngel: we're gonna be friends when we're 90. we'll grab our walkers and meet at maddie's house for a pole-dancing party. we'll gossip about who died and who got divorced and who's got the biggest wattle. OKAY???

mad maddie: who's got the biggest what-ull?

SnowAngel: WATTLE. it's, like, a fold of skin that hangs down low and wobbles under your throat. turkeys have them, as do old ladies. aunt sadie does neck-tightening exercises to prevent 1 from coming on.

zoegirl: my grandmom has a wattle.

zoegirl: u think they're genetic?

SnowAngel: probably. u should get aunt sadie to show u her

Send   Cancel

exercises, altho she looks extremely silly when she does them. *widens eyes and stretches mouth into "O" shape, then rotates lips all around*

mad maddie: **girlies, i've gotta run. the rents will probably wanna take me out to dinner to celebrate.**

SnowAngel: hug hug, kiss kiss! ur amazing, miss college stud girl!

zoegirl: u really r. way to go!!!

Wednesday, March 15, 9:03 PM E.S.T.

mad maddie: **omg, i hate my parents**

SnowAngel: oh no. why?

mad maddie: **this should have been such a happy day, but now it's turned bad and it's all their fault. i HATE them!**

SnowAngel: talk to me. did something happen at dinner?

mad maddie: **at dinner? no, cuz they went to dinner WITHOUT me. i got home and there was a note on the kitchen counter saying they'd gone out for chinese.**

mad maddie: **isn't that cold? the moms must have known what the UCSC letter meant, and even so they went out w/o me.**

SnowAngel: maybe they thought u were celebrating on your own

mad maddie: **they could have called my cell. they could have checked.**

mad maddie: **and then when they DID get home and i told them my good news, the dads didn't say a word. the moms said, "well, congratulations, but u know santa cruz isn't our top choice."**

SnowAngel: ouch

mad maddie: **i started to tell her about going over to ian's and what a**

Send   Cancel

rush it was, and midway thru my story the moms held up her hands and said, "wait, wait, wait. do u realize u've said the word 'like' in front of almost every word u've said?" and then she MIMICKED me, saying "and then ian, like, hugged me, and, like, it was awesome."

SnowAngel: ewww. why was she being so mean?

mad maddie: she goes, "madigan, u say u don't want to be a typical teenager, that there r bigger things in store for u. but talking like that makes u sound better suited to a community college than some fancy school in california. so try not to use the word 'like' at all, just eliminate it from your speech entirely. now start over and tell your story again."

SnowAngel: oh, maddie, ICK. i am not liking your mother AT ALL right now.

mad maddie: i waited until she finished her lecture, and then i looked at her and said, "i can't believe u just said that, when i was so happy and trying to share that with u." i told her that i had absolutely no desire to tell my story again, and then i left the kitchen and came up here.

SnowAngel: *reaches thru computer and gives friend tremendous bear hug* i'm SO sorry!

SnowAngel: DON'T let her ruin your excitement!

mad maddie: she already did

SnowAngel: ☹ ☹ ☹

mad maddie: i'm gonna make a list of things NOT to do when i have kids, including "burst their bubble for no good reason." seriously, what does she stand to gain from making me feel like crap?

Send   Cancel

145

SnowAngel: just remember: u DID get accepted. she can't take that away from u.

mad maddie: thanx, a

mad maddie: nite!

Wednesday, March 15, 9:20 PM E.S.T.

SnowAngel: hey, zo. did u hear how jerky maddie's parents r being?

Auto response from zoegirl: try me at doug's!

SnowAngel: no, i'm not gonna try u at doug's. it's not worth it.

SnowAngel: *shakes it off* tomorrow's another day, full of fresh beginnings and root-beer-y goodness. bye!

Thursday, March 16, 1:03 PM E.S.T.

mad maddie: WHO won the chugging contest?

SnowAngel: U did!

mad maddie: and WHO won the victory lap belching contest?

SnowAngel: U did!

mad maddie: das rite, cuz i da king

SnowAngel: i take it ur feeling better?

mad maddie: well blow me down. reckon maybe i am.

SnowAngel: hurray! and da crowd goes wild!!!!!

Thursday, March 16, 4:19 PM E.S.T.

SnowAngel: i've come up with a plan to pay jana back for her slut-meister remark, hee hee hee.

mad maddie: r u sure u want to keep going with this, a? u saw what she did to me when i didn't let it go.

SnowAngel: which is exactly why i REFUSE to let it go. i am NOT letting her feel all high and mighty, like we're just going to roll over and play dead like that poor bird.

mad maddie: ah, christ. what do u have up your sleeve?

SnowAngel: not telling *hunches shoulders and rubs hands together like mad scientist*

mad maddie: have u decided that u enjoy being devious, angela? r u gonna enter into a life of crime?

SnowAngel: i dunno. think they have a "life of crime" major at UGA?

mad maddie: yeah, it's called poli-sci

SnowAngel: was that some kind of political joke? cuz u know i don't get political jokes.

mad maddie: oh lordie

SnowAngel: but since we're talking about college . . . what about u and santa cruz? is your mom being more normal?

mad maddie: i talked to zo during our free, and her theory is that the moms is scared to let me go. that the whole me-going-away-to-college thing is a big deal for her, and that's why she's being such a snot.

SnowAngel: but ur 18 yrs old, u have to live your life.

mad maddie: i know, that's what i said.

SnowAngel:	so ur gonna go to santa cruz? for sure?
mad maddie:	**well, i haven't sent in my "statement of intent to register," but i will.**
SnowAngel:	i'd have thought u would have mailed that baby back the second u got it.
mad maddie:	**i have until may 1st**
mad maddie:	**when r u supposed to hear from georgia?**
SnowAngel:	WE are supposed to hear from georgia by april 1st (u applied 2, remember!)
SnowAngel:	zoe's supposed to hear from kenyon and princeton around then 2.
mad maddie:	**i kinda wish it would just slow down, don't u?**
SnowAngel:	*faints dead away*
SnowAngel:	what happened to "hasta la vista, baby" and "i can't wait to get out of this dump"?
mad maddie:	**that's all still true. that doesn't mean it has to happen tomorrow.**
SnowAngel:	omg, ur growing sentimental in your old age!
mad maddie:	**what?! no i'm not.**
SnowAngel:	wait til i tell zoe! u R gonna miss us, aren't u?
mad maddie:	**jesus, angela . . . more than u can possibly know.**
SnowAngel:	*hold out arms* c'mere, ya goof!
mad maddie:	**no thanx**
SnowAngel:	c'mere! *clasps maddie to chest and rocks back and forth*
mad maddie:	**erm, i'm leaving now. i'm freeing myself from your clasp and leaving, k?**
SnowAngel:	bye, u old darling! mwah!!!

Send   Cancel

Friday, March 17, 10:10 AM E.S.T.

zoegirl: angela, i just saw maddie in the hall and she told me ur starting the jana war again. i am *not* happy about this!

SnowAngel: i'm downloading fake health service letterhead as we speak. 😊 but don't worry, it's "for entertainment purposes only." *throws back head and laffs*

zoegirl: angela, stop! this has gone on long enuff!!!

SnowAngel: oh piddle

SnowAngel: don't u wanna hear what i'm gonna do with this fake health service letterhead?

zoegirl: NO. i'm serious, angela. what if peaches sees what ur printing? u could get expelled!

SnowAngel: peaches LUVS me. i can do anything i want, cuz i tell her how fabulous her book displays r.

SnowAngel: and now, your attn plz. *clears throat and shakes out paper* "Dear Ms. Whitaker, It has come to our attention that an outbreak of gonorrhea has been traced to your recent sexual activity. Please call our clinic at your earliest convenience to discuss treatment options. You will also need to set up an apppointment with our on-site counselor, who can help you come up with an action plan to cut back on your slutty behavior. This is a matter of the utmost concern."

zoegirl: oh angela

SnowAngel: i know!!! c'est magnifique!

zoegirl: the health service would never use the word "slutty." if anything, they'd say "promiscuous."

Send   Cancel

SnowAngel:	ooo, thanks for the tip
zoegirl:	angela!
SnowAngel:	what? jana made a comment suggesting that i don't put out enuff. fine. i'm just suggesting that being a slut isn't necessarily the way to go, either.
zoegirl:	please don't send it to her. please?
SnowAngel:	who said anything about sending it to her? i'm gonna print up multiple copies and accidentally-on-purpose drop them in various school bathrooms.
SnowAngel:	bye!

Friday, March 17, 5:16 PM E.S.T.

mad maddie:	**IT'S SPRING BREAK!!! WOOT! WOOT!**
zoegirl:	i feel like a huge load has been lifted off my shoulders! except for the fact that i still have to go to tennessee with my parents, who r gonna drive me insane. and except for the fact that yes, i saw angela's health service handiwork, which means that everyone in the school saw, which means that jana once again is going to be on the warpath.
zoegirl:	but except for that, i feel so much better!
mad maddie:	**let it go, baby. just let it all go.**
zoegirl:	right, ur so right. and as a reward for getting thru another tough week, i treated myself to big bunny episode #3.
mad maddie:	**"as a reward for getting thru another tough week"? is that really how u operate?**

Send   Cancel

zoegirl:	u say that as if it's weird. do u think it's weird?
mad maddie:	**i just think u should give yourself rewards any time u feel like it.**
zoegirl:	but then they wouldn't be rewards. they would just be . . . random good things.
mad maddie:	**and the problem is . . . ?**
zoegirl:	u have your pop-tarts and dr pepper; i have my rewards. kay?
mad maddie:	**whatevs**
mad maddie:	**so u saw that lulu DID bring big bunny a kitty, hmmm?**
zoegirl:	yes. and when susie told lulu to take the kitty back, big bunny told that horrible story about "another" susie who sold herself to the devil and had a pet hell-hound.
mad maddie:	**ah, yes. and then the faux susie repented at the last second and went to heaven. a classic morality tale.**
zoegirl:	i do like ol' susie
mad maddie:	**cuz u have good taste. she is a prophet of the modern times.**
zoegirl:	let's do something tonite, wanna? just u and me and angela, since we won't c each other for a week. i won't even have internet access, cuz my grandparents live in the boonies!
mad maddie:	**i think that's a great idea. u sure doug won't mind?**
zoegirl:	don't be silly. let's meet at angela's so we can play with the chicks. i'll give her a call and tell her we're heading over!

Send   Cancel

Saturday, March 18, 12:46 AM E.S.T.

SnowAngel: hello, hello, sleepy maddie! i KNEW u'd still be awake!

mad maddie: i had to check my myspace comments before going to bed. myspace is the devil, u know.

SnowAngel: that was fun tonite, huh? i love u guys with every single bit of my heart, and sometimes i feel like we haven't been making enuff time for each other. i'm so glad zoe suggested it!

mad maddie: did u like how it turned out that doug was out with HIS buds, and that's why she was available all of the sudden?

SnowAngel: i'm not gonna quibble. but yeah, i did notice when she let that slip.

SnowAngel: oh well, we got to have her all to ourselves. that's all that matters.

mad maddie: u, me, zo, and the collective squishy.

SnowAngel: speaking of . . . r u sure they can't come live with u over break? pretty please with chicken feed on top?

mad maddie: no can do, the moms has all these spring-cleaning plans that don't involve 11 baby chicks.

SnowAngel: well, have u called your brother yet to c if he and pelt-woman can take them?

mad maddie: chill, i'll call them in the morning. ur not leaving till sunday!

SnowAngel: be sure to tell them how extremely cute and lovable they r! and how hugging a chicken is good for your soul!

mad maddie: will do. catch ya on the flip side, homie!

Send   Cancel

Saturday, March 18, 3:33 PM E.S.T.

SnowAngel: uh oh

mad maddie: uh oh, what-oh?

SnowAngel: well . . .

SnowAngel: i crashed the jeep

mad maddie: WHAT?

SnowAngel: but not bad! just a little! *holds thumb and forefinger verrrry close to show how teeny*

mad maddie: angela! r u ok?

SnowAngel: i'm fine, but before i go any further, u need to know that honestly, it wasn't my fault. it was aunt sadie's. she's the 1 who ordered "The Firm." "The Firm" is this set of exercise videos she's been wanting, and it arrived today.

mad maddie: what happened to pole-dancing? didn't she just buy that ridiculous pole thing?

SnowAngel: a girl needs variety in her exercise routine—that's what she said. plus the pole was giving her bruises.

mad maddie: ack, didn't really wanna hear that

mad maddie: so what does this have to do with crashing your jeep?

SnowAngel: u c, the mailman left the package at the end of the driveway by the mailbox, which he shouldn't have done. he's not supposed to leave it at the end of the driveway, he's supposed to bring it to the door.

SnowAngel: omg, it's the POSTMAN'S fault!

mad maddie: dude. WHAT HAPPENED?!

SnowAngel: so i was driving back from jamba juice, and there was

Send   Cancel

153

aunt sadie's package, just sitting by the side of the road. being the good niece that i am, i thought i'd bring it to the house.

SnowAngel: so i opened the door of the jeep and leaned down to get it.

SnowAngel: and . . .

SnowAngel: well . . .

mad maddie: yes?

SnowAngel: i kinda fell out

mad maddie: u "kinda" fell out?

SnowAngel: ok, i DID fall out. the jeep is very high off the ground! u know that!

SnowAngel: and it was still in gear, and of course aunt sadie's driveway *would* go downhill, so there i was sprawled on my butt while the jeep rolled along on its merry way!

mad maddie: oh, angela

SnowAngel: i was like, wait! come back!

mad maddie: and . . . ?

SnowAngel: it ran into the garage door 🙁

SnowAngel: it's not TOO banged up, mainly just the fender. and there's a big ol dent in the garage door. but logan is so pissed!

mad maddie: why? it's not HIS car.

SnowAngel: he's just . . . i dunno. he thinks i wasn't being careful enuff. i thought he would laff when i told him—i honestly did—but he got all silent on the other end of the phone and then said, "c? this proves that u don't care as much about me as i care about u."

Send   Cancel

mad maddie: cuz u wrecked the jeep?

SnowAngel: i know!

mad maddie: i mean, it's true what he said, but that's kinda a random connection to make.

SnowAngel: i was like, "logan, this has nothing to DO with u!" it's so exhausting, soothing his ego all the time.

SnowAngel: anyway, he's gonna take the jeep to this guy his uncle knows who does body work, which i do appreciate.

mad maddie: unbelievable

SnowAngel: i know, he's taking offense over NOTHING

mad maddie: no, unbelievable that he's coming over, BAM, to fix the jeep for u.

mad maddie: doesn't that make u feel bad, angela? doesn't it make u feel icky inside?

SnowAngel: well . . . well . . .

SnowAngel: hmmmph *gazes off with look of unresolved anguish*

mad maddie: ???

mad maddie: what do U have to be anguished about?

SnowAngel: logan's part of this relationship 2, u know. if he thinks i don't care enuff, then he should break up with me! god!

mad maddie: have u told him that?

SnowAngel: i scraped my knee on the driveway, i'll have u know. i could have lost a limb!

mad maddie: good lord

SnowAngel: yes, and ur being a big poopy pants for not being more sympathetic.

SnowAngel: but lookie here, logan just pulled up—so i guess i'll go to HIM for solace and comfort. at least he'll give me the attention i deserve!

mad maddie: **and what will u give him?**

SnowAngel: i'll give him . . . a great big hug!

SnowAngel: *thumbs nose at friend and flounces off*

SnowAngel: make that *LIMPS*!

Saturday, March 18, 3:50 PM E.S.T.

SnowAngel: *hobbling back to computer*

SnowAngel: i forgot to ask due to all the trauma. did mark and pelt-woman say they'd take the squishies?

mad maddie: **maybe**

SnowAngel: did they???

mad maddie: **yes, fine, they did. but how u gonna deliver them, huh?**

SnowAngel: i will very nicely ask logan to drop them off after he takes care of the jeep. so there!

Saturday, March 18, 11:32 PM E.S.T.

zoegirl: angela, yay! i get to say good-bye before u leave!

SnowAngel: i was just emailing pelt-woman instructions on taking care of the squishies. i sent written notes with logan, but i wanted to add a few small details, like that the smallest squishy really likes music, anything by eisley.

SnowAngel: what's up?

Send   Cancel

zoegirl:	i'm kinda wired. i just gave doug his very 1st blow-job.
SnowAngel:	*falls backward out of computer chair*
SnowAngel:	WHAT?!!
zoegirl:	it was a going-away present, since i won't c him for a week. i feel so proud of myself!
SnowAngel:	well, for sure. u can list it right up there with your other accomplishments: straight As, honor council, giving head . . .
zoegirl:	it wasn't all that fun for *me*, but i think he really liked it, and that made me happy.
zoegirl:	but my jaw got really tired.
zoegirl:	have u ever given logan a blow-job?
SnowAngel:	no, and i don't plan 2. i have . . . odor issues.
zoegirl:	hmm. yes, i can c that.
zoegirl:	but i was just like, "this is doug, and i love him." and i hope u don't think it's bad that i'm talking about all this, i just needed someone to process it with! i mean, it's a really big deal!
SnowAngel:	sweetie, of course
SnowAngel:	anyway, he prolly talks to his friends about what u guys do and don't do, don't u think?
zoegirl:	oh god, he better not!
SnowAngel:	so: spit or swallow?
zoegirl:	i swallowed, but i don't think i'm going to next time. i'll just tell him very politely so he's not offended.
SnowAngel:	erm, i bet he'll be ok with it. what's he's gonna say, "nuh uh, no way! in that case, no blow-jobs for U, missy!"

Send   Cancel

157

zoegirl:	i don't *want* a blow-job
SnowAngel:	u know what i mean
zoegirl:	doug tried to go down on me (geez, that sounds dorky), but i was like, "no no no no no. that's ok."
SnowAngel:	why?
zoegirl:	like u said, the whole odor thing. but in reverse. ack, i'm blushing just talking about it!
SnowAngel:	what about plain old sex? if ur embarrassed to have him go down on u, won't u be embarrassed to have sex?
zoegirl:	that's different
zoegirl:	but . . . maybe
zoegirl:	i'll cross that bridge when i come to it, which i guess will be soon, cuz pill-wise i'm 1 day away from being safe. can u believe it? but i leave for tennessee tomorrow, so there goes that good timing.
SnowAngel:	which means u'll have more time to get ready.
zoegirl:	exactly
zoegirl:	i'm gonna go brush my teeth (again!), and then i'm going to bed. and then i guess i won't talk to u for a week! sad!
SnowAngel:	i know, but we'll be reunited soon!!!

Sunday, March 19, 8:19 PM P.S.T.

SnowAngel:	hey, madikins. i'm IMing from the lurvely el cerrito to tell u to have a good spring break!!!

Auto response from mad maddie: cleaning out my room so that the moms can turn it into a study. wrong! wrong!

SnowAngel: ooo, that's bad

SnowAngel: your mom obviously hasn't been keeping up with dr. phil. parents aren't supposed to convert their kids' rooms until they've been gone for at least 1 year, otherwise it sends the wrong message.

SnowAngel: omg, it's WEIRD to be here! chrissy looks so much older. her clothes r hipper than mine, which is extremely scary and wrong.

SnowAngel: well, they're not REALLY hipper. c'mon. but 2 hip for comfort.

SnowAngel: anywaysie, i'm glad i'm here, despite the fact that my right ear is all pluggy from the airplane. and u know what occurred to me as i was in the cab? next year when i visit my family in el cerrito, i can pop over and visit U in santa cruz! IF u send in your thingie, that is. have u yet? cuz ur kinda taunting me by not, u know! it makes me get my hopes up for georgia!

SnowAngel: okey-dokey, smokey. we're going out for thai. 🙂

SnowAngel: kissies!!!

Tuesday, March 21, 3:33 PM E.S.T.

mad maddie: i just made myself a whomping good peanut-butter-and-banana sandwich. anyone who slices their banana instead of mushing it up with the peanut butter is tragically misguided.

Send   Cancel

159

Auto response from SnowAngel: off to chinatown, land of souvenirs!

mad maddie: **what? do u really think it's appropriate to be jaunting off to chinatown when i'm trying to IM u?!**

mad maddie: **u better bring me some of that cantaloupe-flavored gum u got last time. and i want a t-shirt with "i heart san francisco" on it, or your ass is grass.**

mad maddie: **speaking of asses, i saw logan at the drugstore this morning, and he was wearing those khakis that make his butt look fat. why oh why haven't u plucked those from his closet and burned them?**

mad maddie: **i went over to say hey, and he was totally no-eye-contact-boy, like he didn't wanna talk. wassup with that?**

mad maddie: **la la la, la la la . . .**

mad maddie: **ok, i feel pathetic enuff for now. l8rs!**

Thursday, March 23, 6:12 PM P.S.T.

SnowAngel: yay! ur there!

mad maddie: **and so r u! the planets r aligned!**

SnowAngel: i can't talk for long, cuz we're going over to mr. boss' for dinner, where i will have to c the dreaded glendy. *sticks arms out and walks stiffly like a zombie*

SnowAngel: want me to pass on any messages for u? 😮

mad maddie: **yeah, to quit sending me her stupid chain letters. i got one yesterday about those damn bonsai kittens FOR THE 2nd TIME. she already sent me one about the damn bonsai kittens, and now here she is doing it again!**

Send   Cancel

SnowAngel: what bonsai kittens?

mad maddie: **u don't know about bonsai kittens??? there's someone in the universe who hasn't heard of bonsai kittens?**

mad maddie: **here, let me enlighten u. 1st i'll paste in what she said at the top of the email:**

i'm crying as i'm typing. this can't be happening!!!!!!!!!!!!!!!! we HAVE to stop this!!

mad maddie: **and here's the body of the message:**

A site that we were able to shut last year has returned. We have to try to shut it down again! (www.bonsaikitten.com) A Japanese man in New York breeds and sells kittens that are called BONSAI KITTENS. That would sound cute, if it weren't kittens that were put into little bottles after being given a muscle relaxant and then locked up for the rest of their lives!! The cats are fed through straws and have small tubes for their feces. The skeleton of the cat will take on the form of the bottle as the kitten grows. The cats never get the opportunity to move. They are used as original and exclusive souvenirs. These are the latest trends in New York, China, Indonesia, and New Zealand. This petition needs 500 names, so please put your name on it!!! Copy the text into a new email and put your name on the bottom, then send it to everyone you know! THIS NEEDS TO BE STOPPED NOW!!

Send   Cancel   **161**

SnowAngel:	omg, that is the most awful thing i have ever heard in my life!
mad maddie:	**yeah, only IT'S NOT TRUE. there is no such thing as bonsai kittens, nor is there rat urine on your coke can, nor is there a mass murderer out there who lures women from their homes with a crying baby. NONE OF IT IS TRUE!!!!**
SnowAngel:	a mass murderer lures women out of their houses with a crying baby?! ooo, that's freaky. what does he do, leave the baby on the porch or something? what does he do with the baby afterward???
mad maddie:	**ur yanking my chain, right?**
mad maddie:	**THERE IS NO CRYING BABY! THERE ARE NO BONSAI KITTENS!!!!!**
mad maddie:	**just go to urbanlegends.com. u can look up anything and c if it's real or bogus.**
SnowAngel:	oh, wow, u just used the word "bogus." *touches maddie reverently*
mad maddie:	**shuddup**
mad maddie:	**so i talked to zo yesterday. she's stoked cuz she's officially safe birth-control-wise. (like how i used "stoked"? i'll try to work in "bitchin" before long.)**
SnowAngel:	has she told doug?
mad maddie:	**yeb'm. she couldn't muster the courage in atlanta, but she was able to from tennessee when they didn't have to be face to face. isn't that so zoe?**
SnowAngel:	awww. was he excited?
mad maddie:	**they didn't have phone sex, if that's the kind of excited u mean.**
SnowAngel:	no, that's not what i meant 😝

SnowAngel:	she prolly told him long-distance cuz she wanted to give him something to look forward to. something to keep her on his mind.
mad maddie:	**why? doug wouldn't stray, not in a 1,000 yrs.**
SnowAngel:	i know, but it's part of zoe's weird deal with him to be paranoid anyway. i'm sure she's missing him like crazy.
mad maddie:	**r u missing logan like crazy?**
SnowAngel:	hmm, how to respond . . .
SnowAngel:	well, i saw a really cute boy at the embarcadero, and i totally lusted after him. like, bad hormone crazy-lust. does that answer your question?
mad maddie:	**it should tell U something, that's for sure**
SnowAngel:	i know, which is why—*deep breath*—i'm gonna break up with logan as soon as i get back in town. i am, and no wimping out. and no worrying about the jeep, which of course i'll offer to give back.
SnowAngel:	r u proud?
mad maddie:	**yes, i am**
SnowAngel:	this trip has been good for me, just to give me clarity on it all. it's NOT fair to logan to keep going out with him. he's such a good guy. he deserves better.
mad maddie:	**right on. i mean, BITCHIN.**
SnowAngel:	and i'm gonna drop the whole jana thing, i truly am. even if she does something to get back at me for the health center letter (which u've got to admit was frickin brilliant).

Send   Cancel

SnowAngel: but we're seniors. we should be above this crap.

mad maddie: wow, i almost believe u. but let's hold off on that 1 till ur back in the same state with her, k? i don't want u holding yourself to unreasonable standards.

SnowAngel: i just wanna rid my life of pointless shit, that's all. i want my life to matter.

mad maddie: i hear ya. l8rs!

Friday, March 24, 10:00 AM P.S.T.

SnowAngel: hey, sweetness! just leaving u a message so u'll feel loved!

Auto response from zoegirl: happy spring break, everybody! cya in a week!

SnowAngel: well, more like 3 days. and once we get back, it's only a little over a month until we graduate! YAY!!!

SnowAngel: omg, that means we have GOT to figure out our senior quotes. when r we supposed to turn them in? the end of april?

SnowAngel: ok, so back to el cerrito. i saw glendy last nite. the girl is internet-obsessed. she made me look at her myspace profile with her, where she now has—yes, it's true—5,987 friends. ridiculosity!

SnowAngel: k, off to get a latte. hope ur having fun with the grands!

Send   Cancel

zoegirl: i'm back! i'm back! i am no longer trapped in the car with my parents!!!!

mad maddie: welcome, dude!

zoegirl: they would not shut up about princeton the *entire* trip, i'm not kidding. they were bragging about it to my tennessee relatives—and i haven't even gotten in! "well, when zoe's at princeton . . . ," as if my aunts and uncles r these big hicks who r gonna be impressed by an ivy league school. aaaargh!

mad maddie: what r they gonna say when u DON'T get in?

zoegirl: i don't know, and i don't care. i should get my rejection in a week, and then it'll all be over.

zoegirl: maybe they'll even feel sorry for me, poor sad zoe who didn't get into princeton.

mad maddie: pity is good. pity could work to your advantage, cuz then u can win them over to kenyon more easily.

zoegirl: that's the plan

zoegirl: hey, how'd pelt-woman do with the squishies?

mad maddie: pelt-woman is in 7th heaven. pelt-woman is fulfilling her destiny as earth-goddess-chicken-lover, making the squishies homemade chicken feed and letting them run loose around their apartment. she loves them so much she wants to keep them fo-evah.

zoegirl: seriously?

mad maddie: i think they're good for her image—it makes her seem authentically eccentric. 1 of her friends has a ferret . . . but what's a ferret compared to 11 squawking chicks?

Send   Cancel

zoegirl:	very true
mad maddie:	**i brought ian over to c the chicks, and he let them walk on his tummy, it was very cute.**
zoegirl:	so u hung out with ian over break, very interesting. does this mean . . . ?
mad maddie:	**that he has nerves of steel? yes it does. he put 1 of the chicks on my stomach, and it was like some terrible tickle torture. pokey scratchy chicken feet, trip-trip-tripping along.**
zoegirl:	nooooo. does it mean that things r moving forward with u and ian?
mad maddie:	**hmmm**
mad maddie:	**i don't know how to answer that question. i am confused in my own head about that question.**
zoegirl:	why?
mad maddie:	**cuz think about it! we're graduating in may!**
mad maddie:	**when i broke up with ian last year, it was awful. i was just so stupid about it. and i never told u or angela, but part of me really regretted it.**
zoegirl:	we knew that. u didn't have to tell us.
mad maddie:	**well . . . i've always thought that if i ever DID get back together with ian, it would have to be for real. for the long haul, u know?**
mad maddie:	**but even tho i tell myself and tell myself that neither of us is ready for that, i DO like him. a lot. and he told me he . . . oh god. please don't make a big deal of this, ok?**
zoegirl:	he told u what???
mad maddie:	**we were outside my house, just leaning against his car and talking, and suddenly he got all solemn. he said, "i**

Send   Cancel

can't believe this. after last year . . . i never thought we'd be doing this."

zoegirl: oh my gosh

mad maddie: and he took my hand, and we just . . . looked at each other for a really long time. in a soul-touching way.

zoegirl: oh, maddie

zoegirl: i'm getting the chills!

mad maddie: but i can't talk about it anymore. it's 2 scary.

mad maddie: what about u and doug? have u planned a date for the big wonka wonka love-fest?

zoegirl: this friday. eeeek, talk about scary!

zoegirl: i'm telling my parents i'm going to the senior daze camp-out, but really doug's gonna get us a hotel room.

mad maddie: very cool

zoegirl: i'm nervous, tho

zoegirl: it's all so big. everything about this year is big.

mad maddie: and there's nothing we can do about it—we just have to hang on and enjoy the ride.

Sunday, March 26, 2:20 PM E.S.T.

SnowAngel: hiya, madikins. yes, pelt-woman can keep the chicks— as long as i get visitation rights.

mad maddie: hey hey! u back on atlanta soil?

SnowAngel: just flew in an hour ago, and boy my arms r tired. (hardy-har-har . . .)

mad maddie: that's great about the chicks—pelt-woman will be so happy.

mad maddie:	and now, time to report the results of a very scientific experiment. ready?
SnowAngel:	uh, sure
mad maddie:	the tacky gold glitter polish u made me put on my toes is finally gone.
SnowAngel:	what gold glitter polish?
mad maddie:	from last summer. remember?
SnowAngel:	from last . . .
SnowAngel:	u mean that time u borrowed my sandals and your toes looked like little crabs, so i gave u a pedicure? THAT gold polish???
mad maddie:	i was 2 lazy to ever use nail polish remover, so i just clipped off little moons of glitter as virgin growth inched up my toes. and today i clipped off the very last bit! my toenails r pure once more!
SnowAngel:	r u telling me u left that nailpolish on for . . . let's c . . . 8 months???
mad maddie:	that's the scientific experiment part! now we know that it takes 8 months for toenails to completely cycle thru!
SnowAngel:	no, now we know that ur an unhygienic slob!
mad maddie:	didn't we already know that?
SnowAngel:	wow. i'm kinda disgusted and kinda impressed.
mad maddie:	why thank u
SnowAngel:	and now i'm outta here. i'm biking over to logan's to do the deed.
SnowAngel:	wish me luck!

Send   Cancel

Sunday, March 26, 9:31 PM E.S.T.

SnowAngel:	hey again. and before u ask: NO, i didn't break up with him. but it's not my fault! it's like, where is he? he's not at home and he's not answering his cell. what's up with that???
mad maddie:	**i told u he was acting weird that day i saw him at the drugstore. maybe he's avoiding u.**
SnowAngel:	why would he be avoiding me? i've been gone for a week—u'd think he'd be DYING to c me.
SnowAngel:	oh well, u can't say i didn't try!

Monday, March 27, 10:04 AM E.S.T.

SnowAngel:	logan = acting V odd. almost rude!!!
mad maddie:	**did u break up w/ him?**
SnowAngel:	not here at skool. gonna meet to talk this afternoon.
mad maddie:	**maybe he knows it's coming?**
SnowAngel:	maybe, i dunno. strange, that's all!

Monday, March 27, 8:15 PM E.S.T.

SnowAngel:	well, i did it. i broke up with logan.
zoegirl:	oh, sweetie. how'd he take it?
SnowAngel:	not so great. hold on just a sec—i don't wanna have to tell u and maddie separately.

Send   Cancel

169

l8r, g8r

You have just entered the room "Angela's Boudoir."
zoegirl has entered the room.
mad maddie has entered the room.

mad maddie: **so how's the ol' guy doing? is he suicidal?**

SnowAngel: gee, mads, how sympathetic

SnowAngel: no, he's not suicidal, unless by suicidal u mean uncharacteristically antagonistic.

zoegirl: what do u mean?

SnowAngel: remember how i told y'all he was acting strange in the hall? well, that's how he acted when we talked after class, 2. like . . . i dunno. pissy. like he'd forgotten my b-day and knew he was gonna get reamed for it, so he was trying to head me off by being mad 1st. does that make sense?

mad maddie: **but your b-day's in july**

SnowAngel: uh, yeah. that was me giving an example, duh.

zoegirl: i know what u mean, i think. like, 1 time doug forgot to call when he said he would, and i was upset, but he didn't think i *should* be, so he acted defensive rather than just apologizing. is that what it was like?

SnowAngel: but what did logan forget to do? meet me at the airport? call me when i was in el cerrito? what does he have to be defensive about?

mad maddie: **give us the play-by-play, maybe that'll shed some light**

SnowAngel: SIGH

SnowAngel: i waited till we were alone, and then i told him i needed to tell him something. in this hostile voice he goes, "yeah? what?" and i said i thought we should

Send   Cancel

170

	break up, cuz things hadn't been good b/w us for a while and we both knew it.
mad maddie:	**and?**
SnowAngel:	and there was a super long silence—a BAD silence— and then he just said, "fine." i reached out to touch his arm, and he jerked away.
SnowAngel:	i feel absolutely awful. did i do the right thing?
zoegirl:	yes, angela, u did the right thing. u've just gotta give him time.
mad maddie:	**and if u find yourself having a moment of weakness (cuz u will, i guarantee it), just remind yourself: plump bottom. got it?**
SnowAngel:	plump bottom, right. *smiles wanly*
SnowAngel:	it just didn't go the way i expected. but maybe that's part of the hardness of it? maybe break-ups aren't supposed to go the way u expect?
zoegirl:	did u bring up the jeep?
SnowAngel:	he said, "keep it," and i said, "no, no, that wouldn't be right. once it gets out of the shop, U keep it." and he said, "fine."
mad maddie:	**oh man, that's harsh**
zoegirl:	shop? why's it in the shop?
SnowAngel:	i can't believe the jeep is gone! poof, just like that!
mad maddie:	**but your conscience is clear—that's the thing to remember.**
zoegirl:	i'm still not getting the "shop" bit. would somebody plz explain?
mad maddie:	**teeny repair work, ok? now stop talking about the jeep. ur not exactly being Miss Sensitive.**

Send   Cancel

zoegirl:	right, right. sorry.
SnowAngel:	don't worry, zo. there's nothing u could say to make things worse than they already r.
zoegirl:	oh. um, ok.
zoegirl:	but in that case . . . can i ask u something else? altho it might be on the insensitive side 2, so i'll wait if u want.
SnowAngel:	go ahead, i don't care
zoegirl:	what about senior prom? who r u gonna go with now that u and logan have broken up?
mad maddie:	**zoe! wtf?!**
zoegirl:	i'm not trying to be a jerk. just . . . it's 2 weeks away!
SnowAngel:	oh god. what have i done?
mad maddie:	**zoe, ur not only Miss Insensitive, ur Miss Complete and Utter Idiot.**
mad maddie:	**angela, I'LL take u to prom. u can go with me and ian.**
SnowAngel:	u asked ian to prom? U ASKED IAN TO PROM?
mad maddie:	**er . . . guess i did. but u can come with us, and i swear u won't be a 3rd wheel.**
zoegirl:	oh, now that's reassuring
mad maddie:	**shuddup, u started this!**
zoegirl:	i deliberately didn't mention it BEFORE she broke up with him, ok?
zoegirl:	angela, i don't wanna make things more complicated. i just didn't know if u had considered this 1 particular aspect, and i thought maybe u'd wanna figure something out before it's 2 late. u've been looking forward to prom your whole life!
SnowAngel:	omg

Send   Cancel

SnowAngel:	i think everyone's gonna have to go away now. i think my brain has had enuff.
mad maddie:	**nice work, zo**
SnowAngel:	it's not zoe's fault. it's nobody's fault—except my own!

Tuesday, March 28, 5:14 PM E.S.T.

zoegirl:	maddie, i have something big to say, and it's not about angela—altho i did feel very sorry for her today wandering around all mopey.
mad maddie:	**yeah, me 2. but she's tuff. she'll be ok.**
mad maddie:	**wassup?**
zoegirl:	well . . . my mom just got a call from ms. kelley.
mad maddie:	**ms. kelley, the college counselor? pourquoi?**
zoegirl:	i got into princeton. i got into *princeton*, mads.
mad maddie:	**whoa! for real?**
zoegirl:	i'm, like, stunned. i'm technically not supposed to know yet, but ms. kelley heard from princeton's admissions office and she was so excited she let the secret slip.
mad maddie:	**what happened to the sabotage?**
zoegirl:	that's the ironic part. they *loved* my essay on nat'l pigtails day—they thought it was "indicative of an independent thinker" and that it was a refreshing change of pace from the essays they usually get!!!
mad maddie:	**holy shit**
zoegirl:	i know!
mad maddie:	**so how do u feel?**

Send   Cancel

mad maddie:	i mean, crap, zo, u got into PRINCETON. that's gotta make u a little happy?
zoegirl:	that's what's so confusing! it *does* make me happy. or proud, or whatever. especially cuz my mom is so happy and proud.
zoegirl:	but even tho princeton is a great school and has a great reputation, blah blah blah—it's not where i want to go! it's not me, maddie. it's stodgy and elitist and pretentious. they have "drinking clubs," if that gives u any idea.
mad maddie:	drinking clubs? i'm liking that idea. what's wrong with drinking clubs?
zoegirl:	ur imagining some rowdy, casual, bar scene kind of deal. it's not like that. it's more of an old boys network, where u sit around a polished oak table and make witty literary references while drinking beer from a stein. sooo not my cup of tea, especially cuz i don't even like beer.
mad maddie:	have u told that to your mom?
zoegirl:	no
zoegirl:	yes
zoegirl:	i dunno. she thinks once i go there i'll love it, just like she did. and when i bring up kenyon and how that's where i really wanna go, she blows it off like i'm a little kid who doesn't know what she's saying.
mad maddie:	so just say, "no, i'm not going."
zoegirl:	uggggggghhhhhh
zoegirl:	u don't understand. u've known since day 1 that u wanna go to santa cruz, and even tho your parents aren't thrilled, they're not psycho about it. for u everything's simple.

Send   Cancel

mad maddie: yeah? what if it's not?

zoegirl: what's not simple about going to your dream school? what's not so simple about, and i quote, "getting the hell out of this dump"?

mad maddie: nothing, ur right. what was i thinking?

zoegirl: i've g2g, my mom and dad wanna take me out for a celebratory dinner. isn't that sad?

mad maddie: yes. i get into a school i want to go to, and my parents do nada. u get into a school u don't want to go to, and your parents lavish u with fine cuisine. "sad" is exactly right!

Wednesday, March 29, 4:30 PM E.S.T.

SnowAngel: i passed jana in the hall today, and she thoroughly laffed in my face. she whispered something to terri that i KNOW was about logan, and then she smirked like she knows something i don't.

mad maddie: she just wants u to THINK she does. anywayz, why do u care? u've risen above the whole jana malarkey, remember?

SnowAngel: i know, i know. but when i saw logan in the hall—not at the same time as jana, but later—he didn't even look at me—and not in a "i am hurting so i will ignore u" kinda way. it was just . . . stone-cold nothing.

mad maddie: well, u broke up with him. not to be harsh, but that's just the way of it.

SnowAngel: it's not that i want him to be devastated . . . but maybe i do? at least a little?

Send   Cancel

SnowAngel:	it's so out of character for him to be totally "whatever" about it.
mad maddie:	**let it go, that's my advice. think about something else.**
SnowAngel:	like what?
mad maddie:	**like . . . the fact that ian got accepted into georgia's honors program! i knew he would, but i'm still happy for him.**
SnowAngel:	which means we'll prolly hear soon ourselves. eeeek, that makes it feel so real! u and zoe have already gotten your 1st acceptance, but not me!
mad maddie:	**i was thinking that instead of the senior daze camp-out, we should drive to athens to visit your soon-to-be-home. wanna?**
SnowAngel:	yeah!
mad maddie:	**do u mind if ian comes 2?**
SnowAngel:	the more the merrier. and i promise i'll be in a better mood!!!

Thursday, March 30, 8:12 PM E.S.T.

SnowAngel:	hey, zo. i just got off the phone with mary kate, and she says mr. pittner authorized a bonfire for the camp-out tomorrow nite. he said they can do it in the faculty parking lot as long as they have an adult chaperone present at all times.
zoegirl:	that's awesome. 2 bad we're all gonna miss it!
SnowAngel:	i know, it almost makes me wish i was going. they're gonna make s'mores and tell ghost stories and sing

songs, and practically the entire senior class is planning to be there. it'll be so corny!

SnowAngel: but athens'll be fun 2 . . . and i do need a break from the whole school scene. did i tell u my secret plan to show maddie such a good time that she decides to go to UGA after all?

zoegirl: omg, i would be sooo jealous if u 2 ended up at the same school.

SnowAngel: well we can't all go to princeton, ya big stud. *winks*

zoegirl: all day long, ppl have been congratulating me. it's so weird. ms. aiken pulled me over during french and told me how pleased she was for me, and then she goes, "but don't let it define who u r, zoe. we all like positive strokes, but what's important is who we r inside."

SnowAngel: that's random

zoegirl: but true, tho. sometimes, even if i work really hard for something, i don't feel good about it unless i get praised for it. that's stupid, isn't it?

SnowAngel: praised, like getting good grades?

zoegirl: and having ppl be impressed that i got into princeton. having my parents be so proud. like that.

SnowAngel: that's a pretty high-class problem, as aunt sadie would say.

SnowAngel: let's talk about something juicier, like your big nite with doug. while the rest of the seniors r warming their bods by the campfire, u'll be warming yours in a cozy hotel room. r u ready???

zoegirl: i'm excited, but antsy. and no, i'm not ready. how *could* i be??

zoegirl:	what i hope is that i get swept away by the moment. i wanna be . . . seduced, if that makes sense. that would be the greatest thing, just to be carried away by the passion so that i don't have to THINK about anything.
SnowAngel:	just relax and enjoy it—and don't put 2 much pressure on yourself. OR doug. this is a once-in-a-lifetime thing. u don't wanna screw it up.
zoegirl:	angela!!! "relax and enjoy it—but don't screw up cuz it's a once-in-a-lifetime thing"?!!
SnowAngel:	oops—guess that's not so helpful?
SnowAngel:	anyway, it's not like i have a clue what i'm talking about! i'm the perpetual virgin, and apparently will be for the rest of my life.
zoegirl:	about that. u know how u said logan seems totally fine with y'all's break-up? i think he's less fine than u think. it's like he's trying to be all frat-boy-tough and punch-'em-in-the-shoulder, but at lunch, even when he was joking around with his buds, there was something that made it seem like an act.
SnowAngel:	that actually makes me feel better—isn't that sick?
SnowAngel:	when u really think about it, he's being WONDERFUL. i mean, he could be being super snotty, u know?
zoegirl:	he's a good guy. just not the guy for u.
SnowAngel:	u think i should call him? just to tell him i appreciate how cool he's being?
zoegirl:	no! angela, i
zoegirl:	u should *not* call him. NO.
SnowAngel:	i think i will . . . and i'll tell him i'm not planning on going to senior daze. that way he won't feel strange

Send Cancel

about going, if it's true what u said and he's just
trying to be strong whenever he's around me.

zoegirl: angela, ur just gonna make it harder for him. don't do it!

SnowAngel: he's still an important person in my life. i don't wanna NOT call him when i feel like calling him, cuz then i'm, like, validating the weirdness. anyway, he deserves a nice fun nite. bye!

Thursday, March 30, 8:49 PM E.S.T.

SnowAngel: zoe, i called logan . . . AND JANA PICKED UP!!!

Auto response from zoegirl: hw, my dears. but i still love u!

SnowAngel: what? nooooo!

SnowAngel: didn't u hear what i said? JANA is at logan's house. JANA picked up the phone. WHAT THE HELL IS GOING ON?!!

SnowAngel: omg, she prolly saw my name on caller ID. she's prolly cackling hysterically. but why is she there in the 1st place???

SnowAngel: all she said when she picked up was, "yeah?" i didn't recognize her voice, so i said, "uh, is logan there?" and she started LAFFING, cuz that is evidently the theme with her these days, to laff her butt off whenever she sees me. or hears me, whatever.

SnowAngel: and then she goes, "sorry, we're a little busy right now." and hangs up!

SnowAngel: oh screw it, ur no help at all. i'm calling maddie!!!!!!!

Send   Cancel

Friday, March 31, 9:58 AM E.S.T.

mad maddie:	**hiyas, media-center girl. u surviving the day?**
SnowAngel:	no, cuz i keep worrying that i'm gonna run into jana. ever since last nite i've been feeling very insecure, even more than when she spread that rumor about me hitting on doug!
mad maddie:	**u know this is what she wants, right? u've got to fight it, a.**
SnowAngel:	do u think she's fooling around with logan? for real?
mad maddie:	**as i said before, that's what she WANTS u to think.**
SnowAngel:	i'm having serious flashbacks to that time in 10th grade when i caught rob tyler macking with tonnie wyndham. remember?
SnowAngel:	what is WRONG with me? why am i the girl who everyone screws around on?!!
mad maddie:	**point 1: logan is not rob tyler. point 2: dude, sweetie, U broke up with HIM. he's hardly screwing around on u if ur not going out. and point 3: we don't know that he's screwing around at all!**
mad maddie:	**why would he even WANNA mess around with jana??? is he that desperate?**
SnowAngel:	she's pretty, even if she's a bitch. she's never had any trouble finding guys to mess around with before.
mad maddie:	**skanky guys. skurvy guys.**
SnowAngel:	i can't believe i called him to tell him how wonderful he was being, and that's how i caught him with jana!

Send   Cancel

mad maddie: u didn't CATCH him with jana, u just ...

mad maddie: ack. could we talk about something else, like the fact that our very own zoe is gonna have her cherry popped tonite?

SnowAngel: don't say "cherry," that's reminds me of the jeep, which reminds me of logan. *stomps around feeling like a weenie*

mad maddie: ok, forget zoe and her cherry. let's discuss our lurvely trip to athens. when do u want me to pick u up?

SnowAngel: u and ian go on without me. i'm gonna make a surprise appearance at the senior camp-out and spy on logan and jana. *makes slitty eyes to show she means business*

mad maddie: oh, man, angela. not a good idea.

SnowAngel: tuff, i don't care

mad maddie: all right, it's your grave.

mad maddie: call me when u need me to pick up the pieces!

Friday, March 31, 7:25 PM E.S.T.

mad maddie: has the cherry popping commenced?

zoegirl: maddie! no, but we're at hotel.

mad maddie: which 1? ian and i will come visit.

zoegirl: as if!

mad maddie: in that case, off to athens. have big fun!

Saturday, April 1, 11:01 AM E.S.T.

mad maddie: i have been extraordinarily patient and i have NOT called for over 12 hours, even tho i wanted to many times.

mad maddie: SO?!!!

zoegirl: u make me laff. and yes, i'll tell all—but not til i'm home. have angela set up chat!

mad maddie: i'm giving u 10 minutes or i'm calling the nat'l guard!

Saturday, April 1, 11:18 AM E.S.T.

You have just entered the room "Angela's Boudoir."
mad maddie has entered the room.
zoegirl has entered the room.

zoegirl: hey, girls

mad maddie: hey, zo. it's a good thing ur finally home, cuz angela has just informed me that SHE has news 2 . . . only she's not gonna tell us till after u.

zoegirl: u have news, angela? about what?

mad maddie: about logan and the j-word, i'm assuming. she blew off our athens trip and went to spy on them at the senior camp-out.

zoegirl: what?!

zoegirl: omg, tell us!

SnowAngel: NO *glares at maddie*

SnowAngel: after u, zo. cuz mine is bad.

Send   Cancel

zoegirl:	then u should go 1st!
SnowAngel:	i'm not going 1st. will u plz just tell us?
mad maddie:	**yeah, u non-virgin, we're DYING for details!!!**
zoegirl:	well, it was a *wonderful* night. wonderful, wonderful, wonderful.
zoegirl:	but actually . . . i'm still a virgin.
mad maddie:	**pardon?**
zoegirl:	we didn't . . . make it to completion. well, *he* did, but it was before he . . . u know.
mad maddie:	**squeezed it in u?**
zoegirl:	maddie!
zoegirl:	afterward, he was all, "ah, crap. zo, i'm sorry!"
mad maddie:	**well, yeah! nice way to blow your wad, doug!**
zoegirl:	i didn't care. afterward we just held each other. it was nice.
mad maddie:	**did he at least finish u off? return the favor, as it were?**
zoegirl:	he offered, but i just wanted to cuddle. we watched HBO and snuggled and made each other laff, and it was perfect.
zoegirl:	i felt good that i made *him* feel so good. that's all that mattered.
mad maddie:	**but it's supposed to be MUTUAL, little miss fifties housewife.**
zoegirl:	i'm not allowed to wanna please doug?
mad maddie:	**oh good lord. angela? a little help here?**
zoegirl:	yeah, u've been awfully quiet. u still there?
SnowAngel:	yes, i'm still here. and i say, so what if doug couldn't go the distance? at least he really loves her, and at

Send   Cancel

183

least he wasn't humping the 1st available female just to get his cheap thrills! at least he's not a total asshole fuckwad!

mad maddie: **whoaaaaa. what r u saying here, a?**

SnowAngel: i'm sorry. i'm such a loser. but i DID wait, u have to give me credit!

zoegirl: sweetie, what's going on?

SnowAngel: i'm just a little wrecked right now, that's all. i'm trying to hold it together, but . . . but . . .

mad maddie: **angela, i think u better explain what happened at the senior camp-out.**

SnowAngel: i don't know if i can! it's 2 horrible!

mad maddie: **we're right here. we're not gonna let anything bad happen.**

zoegirl: unless the bad thing already *did* happen. were logan and jana . . . together?

SnowAngel: they were sitting in the parking lot by the bonfire, and logan had his arm around her!!! i was so shocked, i just stood there looking like an idiot. and then logan's friend dan came up and was like, "dude, i've gotta give u props. most girls would be flipping."

zoegirl: what did u say?

SnowAngel: i was in a fog. i said something like, "why? he's allowed to go out with other girls if he wants."

mad maddie: **other whore-sluts, u mean**

SnowAngel: dan made this expression like i was being 2 nice for my own good, so i said, "dan, logan and i broke up. didn't u hear?"

Send   Cancel

SnowAngel: and he goes, "sure, but wasn't that AFTER spring break?"

zoegirl: uh oh

SnowAngel: i said, "yeah, so?" and he said, "dude—they hooked up when u were out of town. i thought u knew."

mad maddie: NO!

SnowAngel: i felt like i was having a panic attack, i swear to god. so dan pulled me over to the curb and sat me down, and i made him tell me everything.

zoegirl: which was . . . ?

SnowAngel: well, dan says that jana and logan "happened" to run into each other at a party the 1st weekend of break, and jana flirted with logan all nite. like basically threw herself at him, that's what dan said. apparently they talked about ME, about that night at ethan's when i was such a jerk.

mad maddie: and lemme guess: jana was a VERY sympathetic listener.

SnowAngel: uh huh, so sympathetic that she led him to an empty bedroom so they could be alone. AND THEY SLEPT TOGETHER!!! THEY SLEPT TOGETHER!!!!!!! as maddie would say, he squeezed it in her. now do u understand why i'm such a mess?!!

mad maddie: that lying scheming skanky bitch!

zoegirl: oh, angela, i am sooooo sorry!

SnowAngel: and YES, i wasn't in love with him, and YES, i wanted to break up with him, but that is so not the point. he fucking screwed me over for JANA!

zoegirl: how could he do something like that? how could she?!!

SnowAngel:	it hurts so bad. i feel so STUPID. i told u jana's been laffing at me!
mad maddie:	**the 2 of them won't last, angela. u know they won't.**
SnowAngel:	no, i don't know that, cuz i don't know anything anymore.
SnowAngel:	all i know is that jana fucking won. that's what it comes down to, doesn't it?
zoegirl:	what do u mean?
SnowAngel:	don't u get it? i called jana a slut in that stupid health center letter, so she was like, "fine, i'll show u a slut."
SnowAngel:	jana. fucking. won.
mad maddie:	**we're coming to get u, angela. right, zo?**
zoegirl:	we're on our way!!!

Sunday, April 2, 11:01 AM E.S.T.

mad maddie:	**man, she's really shattered, isn't she?**
zoegirl:	it kills me that she's gonna end her senior year feeling like our arch enemy stomped all over us. it's just wrong!
mad maddie:	**so what r we gonna do about it?**
zoegirl:	i don't know. i just don't know.
zoegirl:	what i *do* know is that it puts things in perspective, tho. on friday nite—when doug and i went to the hotel? there's a little more to the story that i never told u guys, cuz of the angela stuff.

Send   Cancel

mad maddie: that's funny—cuz there's more to the athens story 2. but the timing wasn't right to tell it, once angela shared her news.

mad maddie: u wanna go 1st, or should i?

zoegirl: i will, cuz i need to get it out. it's making me feel icky in my stomach

mad maddie: ???

mad maddie: i thought u said the nite was wonderful, wonderful, wonderful.

zoegirl: it was! but then . . . oh god.

mad maddie: what?

zoegirl: it was *so* wonderful that as i was lying there on doug's chest, i found myself thinking, "how am i going to live without him? seriously, how am i gonna survive next year when we're not together?" and then i had the thought that i'd rather die than be without him, which i know is ridiculous. but it wasn't like i CHOSE to think it. it just crept in!

mad maddie: zoe, that IS ridiculous. completely and absolutely ridiculous.

zoegirl: i know! but i was thinking that, and listening to doug's heart and feeling how warm he was, and the next thing i found myself wondering was, does he care as much as i do? what would he do if i actually did die?

zoegirl: so i pretended i *was* dead. i stopped breathing and let my eyes go vacant and went limp in his arms, right there in the hotel bed.

mad maddie: no

zoegirl: yes

Send   Cancel

mad maddie:	ur more messed up than i realized, girl! i mean, i love ya, don't get me wrong . . . but sheesh!
zoegirl:	doug said, "zoe? zoe?!" he shook me by the shoulders, and i *kept* playing dead. in my head i was like, "why r u doing this?" but i did it anyway. doug's breathing got fast and he was like, "zoe, oh my god!"
zoegirl:	finally i came back alive and giggled. he was REALLY mad.
mad maddie:	u must have scared the piss out him!
zoegirl:	i know—and i know that giggling was the wrong move. i knew it even then. but what else could i do? pretend i'd had an epileptic fit?
zoegirl:	that crossed my mind, actually, but it was 2 late to go back.
mad maddie:	holy crap
mad maddie:	u do realize that u need to chill out on the whole doug front, right? ur not gonna die without him. u shouldn't WANT to die without him. good lord.
zoegirl:	duh, that's my whole point
zoegirl:	angela, she legitimately has something to be upset about. but me? i've got a boyfriend i love and who loves me. what do i have to complain about?
mad maddie:	nothing
zoegirl:	but sometimes i can't help it, i feel this huge gaping hole at the thought of not being with him. i don't want to, i just do.
mad maddie:	what did doug say, after he got over being scared?
zoegirl:	he made me promise not to ever do that again, and i said i was so so sorry. we hugged, and eventually things got good again. after that, we just didn't bring it up.

Send   Cancel

mad maddie:	**u've gone over the deep-end with this co-dependency shit.**
zoegirl:	i know
mad maddie:	**it's not the zoe i'm used to.**
zoegirl:	i know
mad maddie:	**so snap out of it, will ya?**
zoegirl:	i'll try, i swear
zoegirl:	um, what about u and ian during your nite in athens? what's *your* news?
mad maddie:	**i don't know if i wanna tell u anymore, cuz if i do, it'll make it official that ian and i are a couple. and then I'LL lose my head and fall into couple-land and the next thing u know, I'LL be playing dead!**
zoegirl:	don't be cruel
zoegirl:	u and ian r a couple????? does this mean . . . ?
mad maddie:	**this means that if u hush, i'll tell u. we drove to athens, right? and on the way we had a really fun convo, as we always do. i was bummed angela wasn't there, but not TOO bummed, if ya catch my drift. we took ian's car, and it was weird sitting there in the front seat and remembering all the times we'd fooled around on that very mock-leather upholstery.**
zoegirl:	good weird?
mad maddie:	**good weird. it was . . . relaxed. that was the best part. like, neither of us was trying to impress the other or prove anything. none of that 1st date shit. we just talked about music and movies and ian's recent trip to the dentist.**
mad maddie:	**he called his teeth his "pearly whites." i love that.**

zoegirl:	ian does have a great smile
mad maddie:	**doesn't he?**
mad maddie:	**so then we got to the uptown lounge, and there was a huge crowd. i got out to put our name on the list while he parked, but ian, genius boy with his 4.0 average, has zero ability when it comes to a sense of direction.**
zoegirl:	oh no. did he get lost?
mad maddie:	**yes! he frickin got lost 2 blocks from the club! he texted me on my cell, cuz there was a super-loud frat party going on, and i was like, "ok, take a left on lumpkin." then he'd text back and say, "i'm in front of a florist. is this right?" and i'd be, "nooo! your OTHER left, fool!"**
mad maddie:	**i'm standing in front of the restaurant, craning my head looking for him, and i get a text that says, "uh . . . should i be seeing fireworks?" so i type, "what?! NO, u shouldn't be seeing fireworks! there r no fireworks anywhere NEAR here!" he texts, "u sure? turn around."**
zoegirl:	oh my gosh! omigosh omigosh omigosh!!!
mad maddie:	**so i turned around, and there he was. and he kissed me.**
zoegirl:	ohhhhhh!
zoegirl:	and were there fireworks?
mad maddie:	**bright crazy sparkling fireworks, boom boom boom. and for the whole rest of the nite we didn't let go of each other. we just kept grinning and kissing and laffing all goofily.**
zoegirl:	aw, mads!!!
mad maddie:	**but now comes the part of the story that reveals my own pathetic-ness.**
zoegirl:	oh yeah? please tell—it'll make me feel so much better.

Send   Cancel

mad maddie:	**i can't stop wondering if maybe, just MAYBE, i should go to georgia instead of santa cruz. assuming i get in, that is.**
zoegirl:	omigosh. cuz of ian?
mad maddie:	**AND angela. it's not just ian.**
mad maddie:	**i'm not gonna actually DO it, obviously.**
zoegirl:	r u not excited about santa cruz anymore? santa cruz has been your dream forever!
mad maddie:	**not forever, just since last summer. and yes, i'm still excited. i mean, when i think about living in california . . . and being near the ocean . . . and going to a super-liberal school . . .**
zoegirl:	that all sounds perfect for u
mad maddie:	**but then i also think about everything i'd be giving up.**
mad maddie:	**it's like, why do i wanna start over at some place new when i've got so many great things going on here?**
zoegirl:	that's true, that's absolutely true
zoegirl:	sometimes i think it's good that doug and i *didn't* apply to any of the same schools, cuz if we did, and we both got in, i'm not sure i'd be able to say no.
mad maddie:	**grrrr. why do i have to think about having to say "good-bye" to ian when we just re-said "hello"?**
zoegirl:	would u regret it, later in life? if u didn't go to santa cruz?
mad maddie:	**yes. no. i dunno!**
zoegirl:	oh, maddie, it's so hard!!!
zoegirl:	tomorrow's when i can check on-line to see if i got into kenyon. after that, i'll have to have the big discussion with my parents.

mad maddie:	**i wish we all didn't have to be split apart. i know this is supposed to be a time filled with excitement—but sometimes it feels like a time of sadness instead.**
zoegirl:	which makes me wanna cry
mad maddie:	**and add to that the angela suckiness . . .**
zoegirl:	we're just a barrel of laughs, aren't we?
zoegirl:	but i am awfully glad about u and ian. that's awesome.
mad maddie:	**thanx, zo. i'm glad, 2.**

Monday, April 3, 1:05 PM E.S.T.

mad maddie:	**dude! i just checked my application status on hathoway's computer—i got into UGA!**
zoegirl:	yikes! i mean, congrats congrats congrats! but . . . yikes! what does this mean?!!
mad maddie:	**i called the moms. she's soooo much more excited than she was about santa cruz.**
zoegirl:	did angela get in 2?
mad maddie:	**she doesn't wanna check till she gets home, but i'm sure she did.**
mad maddie:	**what about kenyon?**
zoegirl:	site is "experiencing delays," so i have to wait for snail mail. aaargh!

Monday, April 3, 5:32 PM E.S.T.

zoegirl:	hey girl. did u check your UGA status? did u get in???

Send   Cancel

192

SnowAngel: yes, i got in. blah. who cares?

zoegirl: angela! i care, and i know u do 2. u can't let jana and logan take that away!

SnowAngel: whoop-di-do! *makes expresionless face while dixie-land band marches thru bedroom*

SnowAngel: wanna know what i did after i found out? i took a bath, cuz that's how exciting my life is. and cuz i feel so SORDID knowing that jana and i are grotesquely connected by logan's spit.

zoegirl: angela . . .

SnowAngel: his tongue touched my tongue, and that same tongue has now touched HER tongue. i dated a jana-licker! i can't stop thinking about it!

zoegirl: but logan is nothing to u, remember?

SnowAngel: what do u mean, logan is nothing to me?! i might have broken up with him, but he's still someone i care about. or DID.

zoegirl: i didn't mean "nothing" like that. i'm sorry.

SnowAngel: but now jana has tainted everything. in the future when i think back on logan, SHE'S what i'll remember. and when i think back on senior year, SHE'S what i'll remember! 😆

zoegirl: i'm so sorry, sweetie!

SnowAngel: in the bath, when i was trying to cleanse myself of her evil spirit, i looked thru the water at my body, and it's like i was this pasty disconnected FLESH thing. especially my fingers, which were floating there looking flat and weird.

SnowAngel:	i thought to myself, "i am a piece of fruit, suspended in Jell-O." that is what my life has come to.
zoegirl:	uh . . . ok. well, let's think about the positives: fruit is good. Jell-O is good.
SnowAngel:	oh WHATEVER. i'm gonna go eat all of aunt sadie's chocolate truffles and get fat. bye!

Tuesday, April 4, 7:27 PM E.S.T.

mad maddie:	**hey, zo. what r we gonna do about angela???**
zoegirl:	and prom, u mean?
mad maddie:	**prom, sure, and EVERYTHING. watching her mope around is making ME depressed!**
zoegirl:	i felt so bad for her at lunch. she was sitting with me and mary kate and kristin, and we were all talking about our dresses.
zoegirl:	mine came back from the alterations lady, btw. i love it so much. now the hem hits about 4 inches above my knees, and i am tres sexy.
mad maddie:	**ooo la la**
zoegirl:	when am i gonna get to c yours?!! ur not gonna make me wait until saturday nite, r u?
mad maddie:	**yep, sorry. it's cool, tho. it's black and long and the entire back is cut away in a diamond shape. i'm gonna have to go bra-less.**
zoegirl:	ian's gonna love that
zoegirl:	have y'all decided which pre-party ur going to?
mad maddie:	**macee mcgovern's—she's having it catered by piebar.**

Send   Cancel

mad maddie:	**u?**
zoegirl:	if ur going to macee's, we probably will too. unless doug has other plans. i don't really care, just as long as we don't end up at some hotel afterward to have sex. i am *not* gonna be that girl!
mad maddie:	**er . . . aren't u already that girl?**
zoegirl:	that was different. our 1st real time isn't gonna be in a post-prom hotel room with 3 other couples and everyone (except me) drunk on cheap champagne.
zoegirl:	and to make sure, i have a plan.
mad maddie:	**which is?**
zoegirl:	i told doug that i wanna spend the nite *before* prom with just him. he's got the key to his church's basement, so i'm gonna suggest we go there. it's not perfect, but it's better than prom nite insanity!
mad maddie:	**very nice. and i think it IS perfect that ur gonna lose your maidenhood in the house of the lord. u'll be like a nun!**
zoegirl:	uh, no, i'll be the opposite of a nun
mad maddie:	**an anti-nun! yeah!**
mad maddie:	**but back to angela: WHAT R WE GONNA DO???**
zoegirl:	well . . . i do have 1 idea
zoegirl:	i think she should go to the prom with andre.
mad maddie:	**omg, that's brilliant! i'm gonna call her right now and suggest it. unless u want 2?**
zoegirl:	that's ok, i've gotta finish my hw.
mad maddie:	**but . . . why?**
zoegirl:	some of us still care about our final grades!

Send   Cancel

Tuesday, April 4, 8:19 PM E.S.T.

SnowAngel: well . . . guess i've got a date. *smiles bravely in face of adversity*

mad maddie: way to go, u!

SnowAngel: andre said there's no one he'd rather go with except a lusty sea captain, but since atlanta has a shortage of sea captains, he's my man. 😇

SnowAngel: he also said—and i thought this was interesting—that when it comes to affairs of the heart, it's even harder being gay than it is being, well, me. which kinda put me in my place, u know?

mad maddie: i think that's terrific. (not that it's hard being gay, but that u'll be joining us at prom.)

mad maddie: whatcha gonna wear?

SnowAngel: WELL. aunt sadie has a silver sequined cocktail dress that i've been salivating over, and i'm gonna ask very nicely if i can borrow it, along with her stuart weitzman slingbacks. and her diamond studs.

mad maddie: that's the way to get back on that horse.

mad maddie: ya glad u asked him?

SnowAngel: yeah

mad maddie: and do u attribute it all to ME, your angela-lovin' friend?

SnowAngel: yeah *huggy hug hug*

mad maddie: then my job here is done. cheers!

Send   Cancel

Wednesday, April 5, 5:55 PM E.S.T.

zoegirl:	i got accepted to kenyon!!!
mad maddie:	**wh-hoo! ur such a stud muffin!**
zoegirl:	i can't believe it. i mean, i *can* believe it, but it's just so HUGE. i got accepted to my 1st-choice college!
zoegirl:	i have to tell u how i found out, k? cuz it's, like, full of cosmic unconsciousness.
mad maddie:	**cosmic unconsciousness, nice. tell away.**
zoegirl:	well, i'd just finished big bunny #4, which was just as disturbing as all the others.
mad maddie:	**disturbing? i dare say u mean DELIGHTFUL.**
mad maddie:	**didn't u love the story about the bluebird who rose from the dead and preyed on the flesh of the living?**
zoegirl:	no. that bluebird ate a girl's eyeball!
mad maddie:	**a girl who looked an awful lot like susie, did u notice? cuz big bunny knows that susie's onto him. lulu and the round-headed boy, they're all, "la la la, we'll do whatever u tell us to do." but susie thinks for herself.**
zoegirl:	good ol' susie
mad maddie:	**but, ok. u'd just finished big bunny, when all of a sudden . . .**
zoegirl:	the doorbell rang, and it was the jehovah's witnesses. tina and arlene.
mad maddie:	**oh joy. did u invite THEM in to watch big bunny?**
zoegirl:	uh . . . no
mad maddie:	**pity**
zoegirl:	we were at the door talking about how god has a plan for

Send   Cancel

all of us—that's the cosmic unconsciousness part, that we would be talking about that very thing in terms of the future and what we're supposed to do with our lives and all that—when the postman pulled up. i was like, "tina, arlene, i've gotta go. i've been expecting something really important."

zoegirl: and there it was in the mailbox! my kenyon acceptance!!!

mad maddie: that rocks!!! have u told the rents?

zoegirl: not home yet. ack.

mad maddie: they can't MAKE u to go to princeton. just remember that. when it comes down to it, they'll want u to go where U wanna go, right?

zoegirl: u don't know my parents.

zoegirl: well, actually u do . . . so u know what i'm up against.

mad maddie: i can c the headlines: GIRL FORCED AT GUNPOINT TO ATTEND ELITE IVY LEAGUE UNIVERSITY. PARENTS CHARGED WITH GROSS ABUSE.

zoegirl: no, not at gunpoint. they'd have a psychiatrist prescribe zoloft and analyze me into submission.

mad maddie: now c, that's good humor

zoegirl: but i'm not gonna give in, so there.

zoegirl: what about u—have u figured your own stuff out, in terms of georgia vs. santa cruz?

mad maddie: i think about it all the time

zoegirl: and?

mad maddie: and as much as i might want to, i can't pick georgia over santa cruz. i just can't.

zoegirl: yeah. i kinda figured that's what it would come down to.

Send Cancel

mad maddie:	**i can't NOT do something cuz i'm afraid of change, u know?**
zoegirl:	i think that's good, maddie. i think ur making the right decision.
zoegirl:	have u told ian?
mad maddie:	**not yet**
zoegirl:	have u told angela?
mad maddie:	**r u kidding?**
mad maddie:	**1st i'm gonna give myself time to get my own head around it and really make sure this is what i want. then, once i've officially mailed my acceptance in, i'll deal with telling ian and angela.**
zoegirl:	well, i'm proud of u. and i'm proud of me, 2, for my good news. and now i wanna call and tell doug, k?
mad maddie:	**whoa. u told me before u told him?!**
zoegirl:	erm . . . he had track practice, so i couldn't reach him. but that doesn't change the fact that ur the 1st to know!!!

Wednesday, April 5, 9:12 PM E.S.T.

SnowAngel:	maddie told me about your acceptance—that's awesome! what did your parents say?
zoegirl:	oh, they were sooo supportive. my mom said, "if kenyon's your top choice, we won't stop u from going. but u'll have to pay for it yourself."
SnowAngel:	*winces*
SnowAngel:	well . . . can u? like with financial aid?

Send   Cancel

zoegirl:	the deadline for financial aid has already passed, which i'm sure my mom knew.
zoegirl:	i feel like such a dumb little rich girl! i didn't even *think* to apply for financial aid!
SnowAngel:	your parents never gave u any reason to think u should, that's why.
zoegirl:	i'm tempted not go to college at all. i'm tempted to get a job and live on my own and save up the tuition money myself, even tho it would take a zillion years. ppl our age DO do that, u know!
SnowAngel:	your parents would freak if u didn't go to college.
zoegirl:	so?
SnowAngel:	U would freak if u didn't go to college. u were born for college, zo.
zoegirl:	it just sucks, that's all
SnowAngel:	u got that right. the world sucks in general, that's what i'm sadly coming to realize.
SnowAngel:	life sucks and then u die. THAT'S gonna be my senior quote!

Thursday, April 6, 8:08 PM E.S.T.

SnowAngel:	hey, mads. wassup?
mad maddie:	**nmjc. u?**
SnowAngel:	feeling sorry for myself, that's what. i keep thinking about how tomorrow zoe and doug r going to make love for the 1st time.
mad maddie:	**and this makes u feel sorry for yourself becuz . . . ?**

SnowAngel:	U know. cuz yay for them, it'll be this wonderful moment cuz they'll be sharing it with someone they love. UNLIKE SOME WEAK AND SHALLOW PPL I HAPPEN TO KNOW.
mad maddie:	**uh oh**
SnowAngel:	i called logan tonite—can we say "masochist"?
mad maddie:	**masochist!**
SnowAngel:	i asked him outright how he could have slept with jana while we were still going out. i was like, "that REALLY hurt, u know? like stabbed-me-in-the-heart-with-an-icepick kind of hurt."
mad maddie:	**what did he say?**
SnowAngel:	NOTHING. nada, zilch. didn't deny it, didn't fight back, didn't do anything but sit like a lump on the other end of the line. i could hear him breathing, that's it.
mad maddie:	**so lame. he should at least be a man about it and apologize.**
SnowAngel:	yeah, but he didn't. and that's why he sucks. bye!

Friday, April 7, 9:00 PM E.S.T.

mad maddie:	**oooo! doug and zo must be going at it in the church basement by now!**
mad maddie:	**think he's gonna blow his wad again?**
SnowAngel:	that's not nice. this is a big and tender moment for zoe.
mad maddie:	**i know, but it's still funny to think of doug blowing his wad ...**

Send   Cancel

201

SnowAngel:	i hope he doesn't. after all the stress she's been dealing with, she deserves something that's just plain good.
SnowAngel:	i had an idea for her about that, btw. her college stress. i told her that even tho she didn't apply to UGA, she should write them a letter and tell them how cool she is . . . and of course throw in who her mom is and how she's buds with the president of the university.
mad maddie:	**her mom's not gonna help her get into georgia**
SnowAngel:	she wouldn't have to TELL her mom. she'd just mention it as background info. plus, what university wouldn't want zoe???
mad maddie:	**how would she pay for the tuition? georgia's cheaper than kenyon, but there's still a lot of money to be forked over.**
SnowAngel:	duh! the Hope Scholarship!
mad maddie:	**oh yeah!**
SnowAngel:	zoe didn't even KNOW about the Hope Scholarship. i was like, "girl, there is free money just waiting for smart chickies like u!"
mad maddie:	**u have to have a "B" average and your tuition is paid for, right?**
SnowAngel:	as long as ur a georgia resident, which she is. and btw, i happen to know someone else who's a georgia resident . . . *looks meaningfully at friend*
mad maddie:	**a free ride, that's pretty amazing**
SnowAngel:	u can thank the state lottery for that 1
mad maddie:	**what did zoe think of your great idea?**

SnowAngel:	she said something very zoe-ish about how it was sweet of me to try and help, but that it would never work. what she DIDN'T say, but what i know she was thinking, was that georgia's not good enuff.
SnowAngel:	sometimes she's waaaaay more like her parents than she realizes.
mad maddie:	**true dat**
mad maddie:	**however, and not to be a downer, but u don't want her to end up somewhere she doesn't want to go, do u?**
SnowAngel:	if it's b/w 2 schools she doesn't wanna go to, then heck yeah, i'd rather her come to georgia!
mad maddie:	**i want us all to go to our dream schools. and be the super cool studs we r.**
SnowAngel:	whatEVer. what I want is for us all to be together.
SnowAngel:	so i'm gonna keep working on her. AND u. k
mad maddie:	**well, don't hold your breath**
SnowAngel:	i AM gonna hold my breath. l8r, g8r!

Friday, April 7, 10:09 PM E.S.T.

zoegirl:	well . . . i did it!
SnowAngel:	OMG!!! for real? all the way???
zoegirl:	get mads into the chatroom and i'll tell all!

You have just entered the room "Angela's Boudoir."
mad maddie has entered the room.
zoegirl has entered the room.

Send   Cancel

zoegirl:	hey, girls. yes, it's true: i'm a woman now.
mad maddie:	**way to go, u sexy beast!**
SnowAngel:	*squeals!!!*
mad maddie:	**just to be clear, we're talking full insertion here?**
zoegirl:	we made love. it was amazing. and now all i can think is, "holy cow, i'm no longer a virgin! i will never be a virgin again!"
SnowAngel:	what was it like???
zoegirl:	hmm, where to start?
zoegirl:	it was more complicated than i thought it would be, for 1 thing. i'm sooo glad it was doug i was with, cuz i can't imagine doing that with some stranger. it's so incredibly intimate!
SnowAngel:	in what way was it complicated? and don't leave anything out, cuz as u know i am going to be a virgin-for-life. my only solace is to live thru u. ☺
zoegirl:	i'll tell u, but 1st u both have to promise that u'll keep it to yourselves and not tell a single soul. and that u'll be respectful of doug in your minds and not make any crass jokes, MADDIE.
SnowAngel:	i promise
mad maddie:	**yeah, yeah, whatevs. of course!**
zoegirl:	cuz it really is a big deal. it's something i'll remember forever, and it's something doug will remember forever. we will always be each other's firsts.
SnowAngel:	we get it! now spill!
zoegirl:	the complicated part was . . . getting it in. it wasn't effortless like in the movies. i *knew* it wasn't gonna be like in the movies, i'm not clueless, but part of me still

	expected that it would happen naturally, u know? (the getting it in part)
mad maddie:	**it DIDN'T happen naturally? what r u saying, that u used a**
mad maddie:	**nvm, i'll be good**
SnowAngel:	what were u gonna say, a forklift?
mad maddie:	**no, a crowbar. but a forklift's even better, more complimentary to doug.**
zoegirl:	u guys! no jokes!!!
SnowAngel:	ok, so how DID u get it in? *sits attentively with pen and paper*
zoegirl:	he kinda guided it in. with his hands. i tried to help, but i felt pretty fumbly.
SnowAngel:	did it hurt, when it finally happened?
zoegirl:	a little. and i think i bled some, but doug had brought a quilt which we'd spread on the floor. he also brought candles and roses, and afterward he held me tight and told me he's never loved anyone as much as me.
SnowAngel:	awwwww!
mad maddie:	**did u have the Big O?**
zoegirl:	what's the big o?
mad maddie:	**don't play coy with me, missy! U know!**
zoegirl:	no, i really don't! what r u
zoegirl:	ohhhhhhh
mad maddie:	**yeah, OOOOOOOO**
zoegirl:	erm . . . not exactly
zoegirl:	but that's ok. lots of girls don't their 1st time. that's what i've read.

SnowAngel:	did HE have the Big O?
zoegirl:	well, yeah!
mad maddie:	**guys always do! der!**
zoegirl:	we'll get better with practice, that's what i think
zoegirl:	plus doug wore a condom, which i've read can inhibit the woman's pleasure. he's gonna look into different brands for next time.
SnowAngel:	doug wore a condom? but ur on the pill!
zoegirl:	he wanted to be doubly safe.
mad maddie:	**oh my god**
zoegirl:	what?
mad maddie:	**that is so doug, that's all. *and* so u. u've found your soul-mate, haven't u?**
zoegirl:	i know ur saying that to tease me—but yes, i have.
zoegirl:	i love him so much. i already *did* love him so much, and now i love him even more. it's like that song by cascada, "everytime we touch." that's *exactly* how it is!
SnowAngel:	*rocks out to pulsing bass line* "cuz everytime we touch i get this feeling! and everytime we kiss, i swear i can fly!"
zoegirl:	"forgive me my weakness, but i don't know why. without u it's hard to survive!"
mad maddie:	**"w/o u it's hard to survive"?**
mad maddie:	**zoe . . . PLEASE tell me u didn't play dead again**
SnowAngel:	huh?
zoegirl:	no!
SnowAngel:	when did u play dead? u guys aren't . . . ur not into kinky stuff, r u?

Send   Cancel

mad maddie:	**oh man, i am enjoying this so much**
zoegirl:	no, angela, we're not into kinky stuff. (maddie, BE QUIET)
zoegirl:	when ur in love, all u need is each other.
SnowAngel:	AND your friendz!
zoegirl:	of course, and your friends
mad maddie:	**but not in bed with u. that WOULD be kinky!**
zoegirl:	u know what the strange thing is?
zoegirl:	this gigantic tremendous life-changing event happened, and now here i am back in my bedroom like a good girl, doing my (cough cough) hw.
SnowAngel:	and your parents have no idea
mad maddie:	**neither does the minister of doug's church, or all the little old church ladies. if they did, they'd have brought u pineapple upside-down cake.**
SnowAngel:	"here u go, sweetie. what a fine young woman u've grown up to be. and u 2, dougie! my, my!"
zoegirl:	very funny
mad maddie:	**well, zo, that's awesome. like u said, ur a woman now.**
mad maddie:	**quick change of subject—unless there's more u wanna tell?**
zoegirl:	i'm good, go on
mad maddie:	**i just wanna know: r we getting ready for prom together tomorrow?**
SnowAngel:	spa day! spa day! just for us girls! ☺
mad maddie:	**excellent**
SnowAngel:	come over around 3:00, and we can raid aunt sadie's makeup cabinet. she's got this new bobbi brown

Send   Cancel

cheek-sparkle stuff that's supra-cool, plus 5,000 shades of lipstick. ⬡

mad maddie: **good by me**

zoegirl: good by me, 2. and now i've *got* to go to bed.

SnowAngel: nitey-nite, non-virgin! mwah!

Saturday, April 8, 1:12 PM E.S.T.

mad maddie: prepare thyself: my UCSC accep. has been mailed!

zoegirl: omg! way to go!!!!

mad maddie: gonna tell ian tonite. might as well get it out in the open.

zoegirl: he'll be thrilled for u, mads. gonna tell angela 2?

mad maddie: um, i'm thinking no, not at prom. but i'll def'ly tell her tomorr

mad maddie: hold on, incoming call

mad maddie: crap!

zoegirl: ?

mad maddie: we can't go to macee's pre-prom—just heard from vincent that jana & logan r gonna b there!

zoegirl: together?

mad maddie: uh, yeah! will doug care if we go to jocelyn's instead?

zoegirl: ugh, j lives sooooo far out. will our limo take us that far?

mad maddie: if we pay them 2. aargh, guess i better call angela. she's not gonna b happy, but better to find out now than l8r!

Saturday, April 8, 2:02 PM E.S.T.

SnowAngel: zoe, why aren't u here?! we're supposed to be getting ready for PROM!!!

zoegirl: i thought we were meeting at 3

SnowAngel: change of plans—i need u now. if i'm gonna have to face jana and logan, i need to be smokin' hot. 😈

zoegirl: ur already smokin hot

SnowAngel: AND i need a drink. i really really need a drink to calm my nerves. should i raid aunt sadie's liquor cabinet?

zoegirl: NO! not a good plan!

SnowAngel: no time for arguing. just get your booty over here!!!

Saturday, April 8, 9:15 PM E.S.T.

SnowAngel: hahaha! aren't i clever? i'm IMing u from the limo driver's blackberry!

mad maddie: yes, angela, i know. i'm sitting right next to u?

SnowAngel: hiiiiii! 👋

mad maddie: oh good god. hi!

SnowAngel: stop whispering to zoe. i can hear u, u know! and no i have NOT had too much peppermint schnapps. i'm offended u'd even

SnowAngel: woops, sorry! is ian's foot ok?

mad maddie: foot's fine. will u stop with the damn computer? ur pissing off the limo driver.

Send   Cancel

209

SnowAngel:	he's looking verrrrrry yummy, btw. ian, not limo guy. and what's this BIG THING u need to tell him? i heard u say u've got some BIG THING to tell him. it better not be that ur pregnant with his child!
📱 mad maddie:	**good grief, a. as if.**
SnowAngel:	i wonder what logan's wearing, tux or suit. prolly something stupid to match stupid jana. i'm NERVOUS to c them, maddie. why am i nervous?
📱 mad maddie:	**u have no reason to be. can we quit IMing & talk like normal ppl, plz?**
SnowAngel:	only if u pass me the schnapps. i know u hid the flask!
SnowAngel:	HEY! ur whispering again! u said something about jana, i heard u.
SnowAngel:	she's WHAT?
SnowAngel:	tell zoe to stop trying to turn off the blackberry. stop it zoe! i can still type with only 1 hand! haha!
SnowAngel:	is that vincent on yr cell? hand it to me. i wanna talk to him.
SnowAngel:	ok fine, i'm signing off since clearly ur not reading this. ur a very bad girl and u should be spanked.
SnowAngel:	now give me the frickin phone!!!

Saturday, April 8, 10:56 PM E.S.T.

📱 mad maddie:	**zo, where r u? did u & doug have a fight?**
📱 zoegirl:	this is the worst prom ever!
📱 mad maddie:	**come back—I'LL dance with u!**

Send   Cancel

zoegirl: thanx but no thanx. i'll just stay here in the parking lot
              where i can't be 2 "needy."

mad maddie: don't be that way. just come back and we'll

mad maddie: ah shit, g2g. angela trouble!

Sunday, April 9, 12:12 PM E.S.T.

SnowAngel: oh. my. god.

mad maddie: u can say that again

SnowAngel: i am MORTIFIED. was i as drunk last nite as i think i
              was?

mad maddie: drunker. i'm surprised ur even conscious. how ya feeling?

SnowAngel: like crap (x x)

SnowAngel: my mouth is soooo dry, and i've got a killer headache.
              and i smell like barf. did i barf, mads?

**mad maddie: yes, all over logan u'll be happy to know. this was after
              your whole "no touching allowed" speech. do u
              remember?**

SnowAngel: i threw up on logan? *cringe*

SnowAngel: i remember him coming up to me all hang-dog, and i
              very clearly remember jana storming up after him.
              she looked SPOOKY, didn't she? all glittery-hard, but
              with her words coming out slurry and wrong.

**mad maddie: cuz she'd had even more to drink than u, that's why.
              altho she's also had way more practice.**

SnowAngel: did something happen b/w me and her? i have this
              vague itchy thought that it did.

Send   Cancel

mad maddie:	u don't remember?
SnowAngel:	der, that's why i'm asking
mad maddie:	well, logan wants u back—do u remember that? he kept trying to apologize, and u kept pushing him away and telling him he wasn't allowed to touch u anymore. and jana snorted and said, "that's for sure," meaning the "no touching" rule was what drove logan away in the 1st place.
mad maddie:	and then she laffed, and that's when u threw up. on logan.
SnowAngel:	christ
mad maddie:	2 bad u didn't throw up on her
SnowAngel:	*conks head on desk and wants to die*
SnowAngel:	why did SHE have to be there to c me do that? why???
mad maddie:	she wasn't especially supportive, i'll give u that. i believe her exact words, after she jerked back to avoid the splatter, were, "what a fucking loser."
SnowAngel:	oh, how original
mad maddie:	yep, that's jana
SnowAngel:	it's still humiliating. it's BEYOND humiliating.
SnowAngel:	did u say anything back, when she said that?
mad maddie:	i was 2 busy cleaning u up
SnowAngel:	so u didn't stand up for me?
mad maddie:	i just sorta
mad maddie:	no. what good would it have done?
SnowAngel:	fine, whatever
mad maddie:	angela . . .

mad maddie: r u mad???

SnowAngel: no, i'm not mad

SnowAngel: i'm just depressed. and bitter. and pretty much disillusioned with life in general.

mad maddie: cuz i didn't stoop 2 jana's level?

SnowAngel: yes, cuz it makes me lose faith.

mad maddie: in what? in ME?

SnowAngel: in all of us

mad maddie: angela, it was PROM. i needed to get u out of there before a chaperone noticed!

SnowAngel: i'm not trying to argue, i'm just stating the hard cold facts. i spent my senior prom puking my guts out while jana stood there and sneered. once again she had the final laff.

mad maddie: sheesh, angela

SnowAngel: *shrugs*

SnowAngel: it's how i feel

mad maddie: then i'll do something to get back at her. again. whatever u want me to do, i'll do it.

SnowAngel: don't bother. if anyone was gonna do something, it would need to be zoe. but she won't . . . so there it is.

mad maddie: why would it need to be zoe?

SnowAngel: don't give me that. cuz i already have and u already have, but she hasn't. and that's why the power of 3 is no more.

mad maddie: so tell her

SnowAngel: what's the point? she'd go all doe-eyed and whimper-y, but she still wouldn't DO anything.

Send   Cancel

mad maddie:	**ur being pretty melodramatic, even for u. u sure ur not just looking for a reason to be hopeless?**
SnowAngel:	why wasn't she there when jana was calling me a fucking loser, huh? cuz she was with doug, that's why. doug's more important to her than we r!
mad maddie:	**that's crap, angela. anywayz, she and doug had a fight.**
SnowAngel:	they did?
mad maddie:	**she was hiding in the parking lot for the whole last half of the nite. THAT'S why she wasn't there to c u puke your guts out.**
SnowAngel:	what was the fight about?
mad maddie:	**i dunno, he said something that made her feel bad. something about how she's 2 codependent.**
SnowAngel:	well . . . it's true. she IS codependent. she cares *way* 2 much about what he
SnowAngel:	omg—another horrible memory is intruding. no, no, no!
mad maddie:	**sweetie?**
SnowAngel:	it has to do with u NOT being codependent, and something u said to ian in the limo.
mad maddie:	**oh. that.**
SnowAngel:	is it true??? did u really send in your acceptance to santa cruz???
mad maddie:	**maybe this isn't the best time to be talking about this**
SnowAngel:	noooooo! *puts hands over ears*
mad maddie:	**i didn't wanna tell u before prom, cuz i knew u'd take it badly.**
SnowAngel:	but u told ian?

Send   Cancel

mad maddie: well, yeah, but just cuz i couldn't NOT tell him, once i'd actually done it and sealed the envelope and put it in the mailbox. it would be 2 big a thing b/w us.

SnowAngel: why DID u do it and seal the envelope and put it in the mailbox? why?!!

mad maddie: angela . . . u know it was the right thing for me to do. and so does ian, who was great about it, btw.

SnowAngel: of course he was. he's perfect. but i'm not perfect—i just want my world back!

mad maddie: it would be nice if u could be happy for me, u know.

SnowAngel: i'm sorry, but i can't

mad maddie: ur kinda being impossible here. u come down on zoe for being co-dependent, and u come down on me for NOT being co-dependent. does that seem very fair to u?

SnowAngel: logan cheated on me with jana, i made a fool of myself at prom, and in three months my 2 best friends r leaving me forever. does THAT seem very fair to U?

mad maddie: ok, like i said, maybe we should talk about this l8r.

SnowAngel: whatever

SnowAngel: oh look, zoe just got on-line. maybe i should stop being "impossible" with u and be "impossible" with her instead.

mad maddie: um, maybe u should

SnowAngel: might as well be pathetic with her. misery loves company!!!

Sunday, April 9, 12:59 PM E.S.T.

SnowAngel: hey, zo. maddie just dropped the bombshell that's she's going to santa cruz. did U already know, 2?

zoegirl: uh . . . well, actually . . .

SnowAngel: she's being so selfish! she's being so . . . stupidly mature!

zoegirl: i don't think u can call her "selfish" for following her heart . . .

SnowAngel: fine, forget it. should have known u'd take her side.

SnowAngel: so i hear u and doug had a fight?

zoegirl: yeah, and i hear U threw up all over logan. how in the world did that happen?

SnowAngel: no, that's not what we're discussing. story, please.

zoegirl: i don't know if i can. it makes me feel so pathetic— probably cuz i *am* pathetic.

zoegirl: crap, he just came on-line. what should i do?

SnowAngel: tell him ur 2 busy talking to me

zoegirl: i can't say that!

SnowAngel: why not?

zoegirl: he wants to know how i'm feeling, but i'm not in the mood to get into it. aaargh.

SnowAngel: tell him ur fine, but super tired, and that ur gonna go take a nap. then log back on in stealth mode so u can talk to me w/o him knowing.

zoegirl: i can do that?

SnowAngel: yeah—it's under "settings"

zoegirl: ok, hold on

Send   Cancel

Sunday, April 9, 1:07 PM E.S.T.

zoegirl:	i'm back. ur sure he can't tell i'm on-line?
SnowAngel:	as long as u selected his name, then yeah
SnowAngel:	now tell me about the fight!
zoegirl:	i'm just . . . i'm having bad feelings toward him and i really don't want 2, cuz i love him.
SnowAngel:	what r the bad feelings about?
zoegirl:	about him being a weiner, that's what.
zoegirl:	NOOOOO, not really. but kinda.
SnowAngel:	tell me what happened
zoegirl:	at 1st everything was great. jocelyn's pre-party was a blast, and i didn't mind that he was hanging out with tilman and those guys, cuz i knew i had all nite to spend with him. plus that meant i got to hang out with u and andre and maddie and ian, and that was awesome.
SnowAngel:	it was the only good part of the whole nite.
SnowAngel:	god, i feel sorry for andre. he got stuck with such a loser date.
zoegirl:	u don't think he had fun?
SnowAngel:	not once i was covered in barf, i don't. but whatevs, go on.
zoegirl:	so we got to the actual prom and i thought, "at last, now we get to be romantic." i asked if he wanted to dance, and he was like, "sure, sure, in a sec." and then he *kept* talking to tilman. i mean, he had his arm around me and he kept rubbing my shoulder, but still.
zoegirl:	a slow song came on, and i said, "doug? let's dance."

Send   Cancel

SnowAngel: i saw u guys out there, u looked cute.

zoegirl: except for the fact that even tho he was pretending to be into it, i could tell that he wasn't. i asked and asked and asked what was wrong, and finally he said he didn't really feel like dancing after all. i said, "fine! let's not, then!" i told him i really didn't care what we did, and that if he had a preference 1 way or another, then we should do that.

SnowAngel: i thought u DID wanna dance.

zoegirl: i didn't care *that* much

SnowAngel: so then what?

zoegirl: so then we walked over to where tilman and pete had been, but they were gone. i asked if he wanted to go find them, and he shrugged. he was still acting all gloomy, and when i asked why, he was like, "now i feel bad that we're *not* dancing."

SnowAngel: oh good grief

zoegirl: he said, "i feel like ur 2 dependent on me, and even tho i like that sometimes, sometimes i don't. if u wanted to dance, we should have danced."

SnowAngel: this was 1 of those no-win situations, wasn't it?

zoegirl: it kills me to think that he thinks i'm so weak i wouldn't stand up for myself. that i'd change what i felt to suit his needs, even if that meant giving up something i wanted to do.

SnowAngel: erm . . .

zoegirl: but at the same time, maybe i'm afraid i *am* that way a little. i know i let him be 2 important to me sometimes . . . but that's normal, right?

Send   Cancel

lauren myracle

SnowAngel:	well . . .
zoegirl:	whenever we hang out with tilman and pete, i turn into the biggest blob. i just sit there with a smile pasted on and feel so boring. have u ever had that experience?
SnowAngel:	do u mean boring or bored?
zoegirl:	both! i'm bored by them *and* i'm boring. and now to find out that doug feels the same exact way—that i *am* a big codependent blob—it just sucks!
SnowAngel:	so ur gonna punish him by not talking to him?
zoegirl:	do u have a better plan?
SnowAngel:	no. only . . .
zoegirl:	only what?
SnowAngel:	nothing, just that sometimes—like in life in general— ur so passive. and i just wondered, i suppose, if that was working for u.
zoegirl:	i'm "passive"?
SnowAngel:	i don't mean to offend u. i just . . . i dunno. i don't even know what i'm talking about.
zoegirl:	i'm not passive, angela. name 1 time (other than prom) that i've ever been passive!
SnowAngel:	u don't wanna go there, zo. trust me.
zoegirl:	???
SnowAngel:	i'm gonna sign off before i get myself into trouble!!!

Sunday, April 9, 1:45 PM E.S.T.

zoegirl:	angela says i'm passive. can u believe that?

zoegirl:	i told her to give me an example, just 1, and she couldn't. that right there says it all, don't u think?
mad maddie:	**the whole jana deal—that's what she was talking about. but she didn't wanna get into it cuz she thinks there's no point.**
zoegirl:	i don't understand
mad maddie:	**plus she's mad at me for going to santa cruz, which is ridiculous. the 2 things r totally not related.**
zoegirl:	what 2 things?
mad maddie:	**well . . . i'm not supposed to tell u, but i will.**
mad maddie:	**angela thinks jana stole our power cuz we haven't been a united front. cuz even tho she and i fought back against her, u never did.**
zoegirl:	oh
mad maddie:	**and add to that the fact that i'm leaving for california . . . and u'll be leaving for either princeton or kenyon . . .**
mad maddie:	**she thinks her whole world is crashing down.**
zoegirl:	cuz we're going to different colleges? she's always known we'd be going to different colleges!
mad maddie:	**if everything else was going well, maybe she could handle it. but as it is, it's just 1 more thing that's out of her control.**
zoegirl:	and the other thing that's out of her control . . .
mad maddie:	**. . . is jana. exactly. so she's turned it into this passion play, with us on 1 side and jana on the other. and in her mind, jana came out on top.**
zoegirl:	let me c if i've got this straight. angela thinks jana robbed us of our power cuz i wouldn't stand up for the 3 of us. and doug thinks i'm needy and weak, cuz i

wouldn't stand up for myself.

zoegirl: wow. i'm feeling even more depressed than i already was.

mad maddie: i wanted u to know what was going on, that's all.

zoegirl: and now i do

mad maddie: just don't tell angela i told u!!!

Sunday, April 9, 9:18 PM E.S.T.

zoegirl: i've spent all afternoon thinking, and u know what? angela's right.

mad maddie: ah, zo. i felt really bad after u logged off. u didn't need that shit on top of your whole fight with doug.

mad maddie: how r things with him, btw? have u talked?

zoegirl: i set my cell to voicemail, and i turned the ringer off our landline. that way, even if he does call, i won't know.

mad maddie: ur still pissed?

zoegirl: more like embarrassed, that he would think that of me. that he would c me as so . . . spineless.

mad maddie: all he made was that 1 comment. he still loves u, zo.

zoegirl: don't try to downplay it when u know there's truth to it. u personally have told me 5,000 times that i'm under doug's thumb.

mad maddie: i never said under his thumb

zoegirl: the worst part is, i don't know how it happened. i was gutsy last yr, wasn't i? when u made me parade thru the mall with marshmallows on my nipples?

zoegirl:	what happened to that girl?!
mad maddie:	**2 words: doug came back**
mad maddie:	**wait, that's 3. lemme try again: doug returned.**
zoegirl:	no, cuz doug was still in town when i did the marshmallow dare. remember?
mad maddie:	**yeah, but then he did his Sea the World thing, and when he came back it was a whole new ball game.**
zoegirl:	???
mad maddie:	**u became pod girl. maybe u didn't mean to, but u did.**
zoegirl:	no i didn't
mad maddie:	**before he left, the power b/w u guys was equal. maybe even in your favor, since he was head-over-heels for u and u were kinda resisting. but then he came back, and he was so much more wordly and confident, and for some reason u let that matter. u fell into the role of letting him call the shots.**
zoegirl:	but that's pathetic
mad maddie:	**u were all, "oh doug, what is life w/o u? ur soooo important to me!"**
zoegirl:	ok, i get the picture
mad maddie:	**angela and i wished u'd snap out of it, but u didn't.**
zoegirl:	ok! i get the picture!
mad maddie:	**it actually helped me when it came to going to santa cruz, tho. cuz in my head i was like, "i love zoe, but i refuse to BE zoe," in terms of the whole neediness thing.**
zoegirl:	gee, i'm glad i could be of service
mad maddie:	**as for the jana thing, it's more of the same. more of u saying, "i'll just study and be stressed and hang out with doug, and nothing else matters."**

Send   Cancel

mad maddie:	**that's what angela meant by u being passive.**
zoegirl:	well that's why i'm IMing. if i'm gonna stop being passive—if i'm gonna get jana back once and for all—then i need your help.
mad maddie:	**ha! ur cute.**
zoegirl:	i'm serious, mads
mad maddie:	**for real?**
zoegirl:	what do u mean, "for real"? of course for real!
mad maddie:	**it's just that**
zoegirl:	just that what?
zoegirl:	i can't believe i'm finally willing to do something, and ur telling me not to!
mad maddie:	**i'm not telling u NOT to . . . i just don't know if it's worth it, frankly.**
zoegirl:	why???
mad maddie:	**jana didn't "steal" our power. it's not your job to steal it back.**
zoegirl:	except that it is!
zoegirl:	look at the facts: JANA SLEPT WITH LOGAN. jana had SEX with angela's ex-bf, who at the time *wasn't* her ex, for the sole sake of messing with her. u know it's true!
mad maddie:	**well . . . yes**
zoegirl:	and she planted rumors about me and angela . . . and put sex ads about u on craigslist . . . and put a dead bird in angela's jeep! a dead bird—how sick is that?
mad maddie:	**pretty frickin sick, i'll give u that**
zoegirl:	and throughout it all i sat there and did nothing, cuz that's me, do-nothing-girl. BUT NO MORE.

mad maddie:	**ok, fine**
mad maddie:	**so what r u gonna do?**
zoegirl:	well, that part i don't know yet. but i'll think of something!
mad maddie:	**yes ma'am, non-passive zoe**
zoegirl:	and don't be sarcastic
mad maddie:	**me???**
mad maddie:	**hey, i'm outta here. i'm meeting ian at starbucks.**
zoegirl:	oh good—ian needs some quality maddie-time. i feel so bad for him, spending prom alone while u babysat angela!
mad maddie:	**yeah, wasn't that lovely?**
zoegirl:	and c? that's just 1 more example of my being a lame friend. i should have been there. i should have been helping out.
zoegirl:	did u tell angela about "my girl"?
mad maddie:	**why? it would just make her feel bad.**
zoegirl:	it breaks my heart to think of u sitting there, wiping away angela's vomit, when the song came on. and ian looking everywhere but not finding u!
mad maddie:	**and—don't forget—he'd found out only 2 hours earlier that i for sure wouldn't be going to UGA with him.**
zoegirl:	that is *so* sad
mad maddie:	**do u know why he requested that song? he told me l8r that it was to say, "it's gonna be ok, let's just enjoy this nite, u'll always be mine regardless of where we end up."**
zoegirl:	oh, mads!
mad maddie:	**yeah, well**

mad maddie: i don't wanna keep him waiting, so i'm gonna go!

Monday, April 10, 10:12 AM E.S.T.

SnowAngel: there's a new sherrif in town, and her name is zoe barrett. 🤠

mad maddie: she's like on a bandwagon, man. i tried to talk her out of it, but no go.

SnowAngel: what?!

SnowAngel: i'm loving the fact that she's finally grown a spine. LOVING it. don't u dare talk her out of it!

mad maddie: she was not to be dissuaded, so chill.

SnowAngel: i feel bad about doug, tho

SnowAngel: a while ago she told me that she really really really needs praise, and i think the opposite is true, 2. if someone tells her she's "bad" in some way—like doug suggesting that she depends on him 2 much—she takes it waaaaay hard.

mad maddie: i know. she obsesses over it.

mad maddie: hold on—ms. hathoway's coming over

SnowAngel: do u have to get off?

mad maddie: yeah, i've gotta enter some quiz grades for her. sayonaras!

Tuesday, April 11, 5:15 PM E.S.T.

mad maddie: hiya, zo. get your history assignment done?

Send   Cancel

zoegirl:	*just* finished. there, i'm typing the very last . . . done.
zoegirl:	wassup?
mad maddie:	**saw u talking to doug today. u guys all mended?**
zoegirl:	i dunno. he knows he hurt my feelings, and he's being very sweet to try and make up for it. like leaving notes in my locker and meeting me after class.
zoegirl:	but even tho he's being so nice, i feel like i have to keep a wall up b/w us . . . otherwise he's gonna think i'm 2 "dependent" on him again.
mad maddie:	**a LITTLE dependent's ok. just not whole hog.**
zoegirl:	his side of things is that it was prom, it was a party, he wanted to hang with his friends *and* be with me. i'm like, yeah, i get that. but at the same time i'm thinking, "we made love for the 1st time 24 hours earlier. LESS than 24 hrs! shouldn't that count for something?"
zoegirl:	but i can't SAY that, cuz . . . u know.
mad maddie:	**2 dependent**
zoegirl:	yeah
mad maddie:	**have u made any progress with your jana plan?**
zoegirl:	yes, actually, cuz when i work on that i *don't* feel loser-ish. in my head i'm like, "c? i can be brave. i can take action."
mad maddie:	**and what form has that action taken?**
zoegirl:	to be honest, no actual action yet. but here is my brilliant idea: steal jana's car!
mad maddie:	**pardonay moi?**
zoegirl:	not STEAL it steal it. just borrow it . . . and then leave it at a sex addicts anonymous meeting!

mad maddie: oh, zoe, ur priceless

zoegirl: i know! it's perfect! sex addicts anonymous, that's *so* jana. she'll be humiliated just like angela!

mad maddie: sigh. must i always be the lone sage in the wilderness?

zoegirl: huh?

mad maddie: how r u gonna "borrow" her car, zo? and say u DO manage to get your paws on the heapmobile. do u actually have a sex addicts meeting in mind to drop it off at?

zoegirl: well . . .

mad maddie: and how is jana gonna know that's where it is, so that she can go retrieve it and be humiliated?

zoegirl: i guess i would

zoegirl: somebody could just

mad maddie: mmm-hmm

zoegirl: don't say that! it's a great plan!

mad maddie: your instincts r great, your plan is horrible

mad maddie: back to the drawing board, dude!

Wednesday, April 12, 8:12 PM E.S.T.

mad maddie: so check this out: vincent told me that things r NOT going well with jana and logan. good news, eh?

SnowAngel: grrr, i suppose

SnowAngel: but don't give me any details. i don't wanna hear about it.

mad maddie: pourquoi?

SnowAngel:	cuz i don't care. or rather, i DO care, but i don't wanna. i've gotta start somewhere.
mad maddie:	**uh . . . ok**
SnowAngel:	seriously, if zoe can learn to stand on her two feet, then surely i can 2.
SnowAngel:	when i think about logan and how much mental energy i've wasted on him . . . it's ridiculous!
mad maddie:	**well, yes. yes, it really is.**
SnowAngel:	but the reason it hurts so much is that now my friend is gone, u know? cuz logan WAS a good friend. just not a kissing friend, and i should have made that clear from the get-go. i realize that. but it's 2 late now, and that makes me unbelievably sad.
mad maddie:	**if it makes u feel any better, logan wants to get back together with u. that's what vincent heard from jana.**
SnowAngel:	i told u i didn't want details!
SnowAngel:	anyway, we're NOT getting back together. i mean, god, that would be a mistake on so many levels.
mad maddie:	**that's what i told vincent**
SnowAngel:	did logan tell jana that to her face, that i'm the one he really wants?
mad maddie:	**i thought u said . . .**
SnowAngel:	fine! fine. *strolls nonchalantly down promenade, whistling merry tune*
mad maddie:	**vincent also said that jana found out who her stepmonster's doing the nasty with. it's some guy who works at a liquor store.**
SnowAngel:	and i care becuz . . . ?

mad maddie: she found the guy's work shirt in her stepmonster's car. it smelled like her stepmonster's perfume.

SnowAngel: speaking of perfume, did u get glendy's latest spam offering? about the bad guys who go around with fake perfume samples, only really it's ether?

mad maddie: u read it? i thought u automatically deleted her emails.

SnowAngel: well, i've been showing a little more caution recently, after she called me all giddy to tell me her spiffy new trick. get this: she's learned how to dump some bug on ppl's computers which makes them shut down and reboot automatically. and when they reboot, they relay the owners' log-on names and passwords straight to glendy.

mad maddie: dude, that's some serious hacking. why???

SnowAngel: cuz apparently some ppl have had the audacity to block her (incroyable!), and this way she can go to MySpace or live journal or whatever and UNblock herself. can u imagine? *pretending to be glendy: hi!!!! i'm baaaack!*

mad maddie: jesus

mad maddie: doesn't the fact that she's been blocked in the 1st place tell her anything?

SnowAngel: so u better stay on her good side . . . or else!!!

Thursday, April 13, 8:13 PM E.S.T.

mad maddie: hey, babe. wanna hear about my healthy dinner? a reese's big cup and a glass of nestle quik.

Send   Cancel

229

zoegirl:	mmmm . . . nutritious *and* delicious
mad maddie:	**the rents r playing bridge with their buddies, so i'm on my own. u should come over!**
zoegirl:	sorry, charlie. gotta finish my physics so i can keep my "A." i do NOT wanna take the final exam!
mad maddie:	**r u gonna have to take any finals at all?**
zoegirl:	i don't think so. straight "A"s all the way . . . yeah!
zoegirl:	i did, however, take a study break to watch big bunny episodes 5 & 6. big bunny finally ate the kitty!
mad maddie:	**au contraire—the kitty went away on a business trip! the kitty has a very good head for figures, remember?**
zoegirl:	do u have every episode memorized? ur freaking me out.
mad maddie:	**heh heh heh**
zoegirl:	what freaked me out even more were those psychotic squirrels who hacked up the other forest creatures and turned them into pie . . .
mad maddie:	**"chop chop chop went the squirrel. slice slice slice went his associates."**
zoegirl:	so guess what? i heard back from UGA, about my late application.
mad maddie:	**WHAT?**
mad maddie:	**wait a sec—u actually did that? used angela's idea about writing the prez of the university?**
zoegirl:	uh huh. i used my mom's letterhead.
mad maddie:	**holy frickin shit, zo. u R taking a stand!**
mad maddie:	**what did they say?**
zoegirl:	that i've got a spot if i want it. whaddaya think of that?
mad maddie:	**what about the Hope Scholarship?**

Send   Cancel

zoegirl:	yep. they said my transcript demonstrates "the academic excellence the Hope Scholarship is in place to support." so i could do it, if i want. i could honestly and truly go to georgia.
mad maddie:	**free ride, baby! tell your mom to put THAT in her pipe and smoke it!**
zoegirl:	i know. it's incredible. i can't wait to c her face when i tell her.
zoegirl:	well, no, that's not true. i'm totally nervous about telling her, cuz it'll be me fighting back in a real way. me saying, "r u *sure* ur not willing to pay for kenyon?"
mad maddie:	**ahhhh, a power-play**
mad maddie:	**smart smart smart, little zoe**
zoegirl:	we'll c. i've gotta play it just right if it's gonna work.
mad maddie:	**SHOW NO FEAR**
zoegirl:	but i'm not gonna tell angela till it's done, cuz she'd just latch onto the UGA part and refuse to let go. u know.
mad maddie:	**uh, yeah. been there, done that.**
mad maddie:	**what about your jana revenge plot? making any progress?**
zoegirl:	i'm tossing some ideas around, but i'm not telling what they r cuz u'd just tell me they wouldn't work. for now i'm just . . . letting her get her confidence up.
mad maddie:	**uh, i think her confidence IS up**
zoegirl:	i'm just waiting for the right opportunity. and for a chance to talk privately with vincent.
mad maddie:	**vincent?!**
zoegirl:	nite!

Send   Cancel

Friday, April 14, 4:02 PM E.S.T.

SnowAngel: my graduation announcements came today! they're so beautiful!

zoegirl: cool!

SnowAngel: now i just have to address them and stamp them and trudge off with them to the post office. *slumps shoulders*

SnowAngel: but they're so beautiful! *perks back up*

zoegirl: mine aren't here yet, cuz my mom made a last-minute decision that they should be ivory instead of cream. did i have any say in this? no. so now they're like on a rush job.

SnowAngel: zoe! u have gotta learn to stand up to that woman!

zoegirl: i know, i know. and actually, she and i are supposed to have "a chat" this evening. i have something i wanna tell her. about college.

SnowAngel: that ur gonna blow off princeton altogether and come live with me in athens? *smiles charmingly* that ur gonna get a job as a waitress and learn how the other half lives?

zoegirl: er . . . not exactly. i'll tell u after we talk, ok?

SnowAngel: okey-dokey, smokie

SnowAngel: off to address envelopes. tootles!

Friday, April 14, 9:00 PM E.S.T.

SnowAngel: waaaah! waaaah! why does everybody have to be so frickin *independent* all the time?!!

Send   Cancel

mad maddie: **independent? the horror!**

SnowAngel: zoe just called and told me about georgia, which i know u already know, so don't rub it in. i can't believe she got accepted and yet she's not going to go!!!

mad maddie: **hold on, i don't know this part. did she talk to her mom???**

SnowAngel: yes *sniffs*

mad maddie: **and her mom caved? omfg!**

SnowAngel: apparently there were tears and yelling and a big fat scene, which as we know is not zoe's strong point.

SnowAngel: but zoe stayed strong, and her stupid mom finally gave in. she decided she'd rather c zoe go to kenyon than UGA—how snobby and hypocritical is that? she won't pay for kenyon, and now all of a sudden she will, just so her daughter doesn't have to go to a state university?

mad maddie: **angela . . . zoe was never going to go to georgia.**

SnowAngel: i think mrs. barrett should have held her ground and refused to pony up. then zoe would have HAD to go to georgia!!!!

mad maddie: **i hope u didn't act like this when she told u. i hope u were supportive, even if u had to fake it.**

SnowAngel: *turns up nose* hmmph

mad maddie: **dude, i'm gonna call and congratulate her.**

SnowAngel: yeah, u do that. and don't worry about me! just leave me in the dust!

SnowAngel: maddie?

SnowAngel: don't i need support? i'm the 1 who's gonna be all alone in athens! alone and lonely! all by myself!

Send   Cancel

SnowAngel: waaaaaah!!!!!

Saturday, April 15, 6:13 PM E.S.T.

zoegirl: hey, mads. u think angela's gonna be ok?

mad maddie: about what?

zoegirl: u know, about my going to kenyon.

mad maddie: she HAS to be. she has no choice.

zoegirl: i kinda felt like i was kicking her when she was down, when i told her last nite.

mad maddie: listen. u can't base your life around angela, any more than u can around doug.

zoegirl: i know, i know

mad maddie: it's AWESOME that u get to go to kenyon. U made it happen, u know? i'm so incredibly proud of u.

zoegirl: thanks, mads. i'm proud of me 2.

zoegirl: and to my mom's credit, she's being cooler about it than she could have been.

mad maddie: oh yeah?

zoegirl: this morning, when we were both feeling a little calmer, she told me that even tho kenyon's not the school she would have chosen for me, she admired my spirit. like, it surprised her what i'd done.

mad maddie: i bet it did!

zoegirl: she admitted that *maybe* she'd been too controlling about it all, and that *maybe* my own desires should factor into the equation. novel concept, huh?

234

mad maddie: well, blow me down. maybe she's growing up as well.

zoegirl: doug's excited for me, too. angela was all, "ur picking him over me," and i had to remind her that no, actually, he's still gonna be 2 hours away. we'll be apart no matter what. but we'll just take it as it comes, u know?

mad maddie: tell me about it. it's so hard, with ian, knowing that the time is ticking down. tick tick tick.

zoegirl: doug and i have a "hot date" tonite. i'm assuming he wants to have sex.

mad maddie: does this mean things r back to normal?

zoegirl: i suppose. i just have to be careful what i say and how i act, that's all.

mad maddie: oh, well in that case, no prob . . . i just have to totally change my personality.

zoegirl: it's sad, cuz i feel like i can no longer open my soul and let my true feelings out. but 2 bad—he's the 1 who made it happen.

mad maddie: and yet ur still gonna have sex with him

zoegirl: yeah. maybe it'll bring us closer.

mad maddie: i just hope u have the Big O this time. i'm rooting for ya, girl!

Saturday, April 15, 11:23 PM E.S.T.

mad maddie: Big O? ian & i wanna know!!!

Send   Cancel

235

Sunday, April 16, 12:02 AM E.S.T.

zoegirl:	*just* got in. my mom was sitting at the door with a clock.
mad maddie:	**honest?**
zoegirl:	no, but i had to go check in with her and let her know i'd arrived home safely, groan groan groan. u'd think things would be different now that she knows i'm an actual mature individual, but no.
zoegirl:	doesn't it seem silly to have a curfew when we're about to graduate and be on our own?
mad maddie:	**yes**
zoegirl:	u didn't really tell ian about me and doug, did u?
mad maddie:	**no, u goof**
mad maddie:	**but did u? have an orgasm?**
zoegirl:	well . . . no
mad maddie:	**damn!**
zoegirl:	but i'm fine with it, i really am. it's about more than just physical pleasure.
zoegirl:	anyway, u talking about it kinda makes me feel loser-ish.
mad maddie:	**oh, zoe! that's not what i meant.**
mad maddie:	**listen. ur having sex—making love—with someone u truly care about. ur not having 1-nite stands or being a slut machine, like some ppl we know. of course it's about more than whether u got off or not!**
zoegirl:	could u plz not be so graphic?
mad maddie:	**oopsy-daisy**

Send   Cancel

zoegirl:	i *wish* i was someone sex came easily to . . . but i'm just not.
mad maddie:	**that doesn't mean u never WILL be. u just gotta keep practicing.**
zoegirl:	it's still fun, don't get me wrong. and doug's skin is so incredibly smooth . . . and warm . . . and there's this one spot, right below his hip bone . . . it's like, wow. just to be so close to another human being—that's worth it, right?
mad maddie:	**u bet**
mad maddie:	**i truly didn't mean to make u feel bad, zo. i was just being my normal obnoxious self.**
zoegirl:	i love your normal obnoxious self. nitey-nite!

Monday, April 17, 11:43 AM E.S.T.

SnowAngel:	it's happening, our 2nd to last week of school! aaaaahhhhh!
SnowAngel:	i STILL don't have my senior quote. do u?
mad maddie:	**i've been using class time to think about it, since it's not as if anybody's doing any actual work. but everything i come up with sounds 2 corny or 2 cliche.**
SnowAngel:	i'm in the same exact boat. grrrr . . .
SnowAngel:	did u hear what jana did today? she swiped megan's hw during mr. bradley's class, right off her desk, and threw it out the window!
mad maddie:	**what?!**

237

SnowAngel:	for no reason at all! cuz megan made 1 small comment about jana's handwriting or something.
SnowAngel:	so megan yelled at her, and then MEGAN got yelled at by mr. bradley.
mad maddie:	**dude, that is just ridiculous**
SnowAngel:	i don't understand how jana can be such a bitch and get away with it. i truly don't.
mad maddie:	**well, yeah. i guess no one wants to take her on cuz they've seen how futile it is.**
SnowAngel:	i s'pose
SnowAngel:	zoe's not gonna beat her up for me after all, is she?
mad maddie:	**she WANTS to, but she hasn't worked out the details. i keep telling her to forget the details and just go for it, but u know zoe.**
SnowAngel:	🙁
mad maddie:	**but don't give up on her completely. sometimes ol' zo can pull 1 out of her butt at the last minute!**

Tuesday, April 18, 9:19 AM E.S.T.

zoegirl:	our graduation gowns r in! come to main office if u wanna c!
SnowAngel:	omg. and square hats? w/ tassles?
zoegirl:	mortar boards, that's what they're called.
SnowAngel:	can we try them on?
zoegirl:	that's what everybody's doing. get over here!!!

Send   Cancel

Wednesday, April 19, 10:45 PM E.S.T.

mad maddie: ur not gonna believe this.

SnowAngel: what?

mad maddie: my laptop got stolen! ian and i were at starbucks, and when ian got up to get some sugar, this guy came over and grabbed my laptop right off the table. and then he ran out the door!

SnowAngel: noooooo!

mad maddie: yesssss!

SnowAngel: that's awful! what did u do?

mad maddie: i just sat there, flabbergasted. ian, on the other hand, went all noble and tried to rescue it. it totally cracked me up.

SnowAngel: did he get it back?

mad maddie: he chased the guy into the parking lot, but the guy made it to his car and started the engine. so ian flung himself onto the guy's hood!!! the guy starts swerving, and ian's spread-eagled on the hood, and i'm like, "omfg!!!"

SnowAngel: jesus, maddie!

mad maddie: finally the guy turned on his windshield wipers, and ian bounced onto the pavement. all that for my crappy laptop which doesn't even turn on half the time!

SnowAngel: i can't BELIEVE ian jumped onto the car. i'm so glad he's ok!

mad maddie: he's more than ok. he's wonderful. after we stopped laffing, he took my hands and looked at me with his sweet brown eyes. and u know what he said? he said, "ur the 1, maddie."

SnowAngel: ohhhhh! *melts into warm gooey puddle*
mad maddie: i knew u'd get mushy
mad maddie: it made me pretty mushy, 2
SnowAngel: ian is wonderful, maddie. yaaaaaay! 😊

Thursday, April 20, 7:12 PM E.S.T.

zoegirl: hey, angela. i just wanted u know that i haven't forgotten about u.
SnowAngel: as if! how could u ever possibly forget about ME?
zoegirl: the jana thing, i mean. i saw how she was throwing her arm over logan's shoulder on the senior patio. she was totally doing it to taunt u.
SnowAngel: logan texted me in 6th period to tell me they're no longer going out, on the off chance that i cared. but megan heard from carrie that they still hook up, so whatever.
zoegirl: i *do* feel bad for logan. i can't help it.
zoegirl: do u c yourself ever being buds w/ him again?
SnowAngel: no, i really don't
zoegirl: so sad. but i understand.
SnowAngel: maybe i'll feel differently, 1 day in the very distant future.
SnowAngel: but i'm not there yet. not even close.
zoegirl: well if it helps, i'm almost there in terms of my plot against jana. i met with vincent about it this afternoon, believe it or not. altho it didn't exactly go as planned.

Send   Cancel

lauren myracle

SnowAngel:	i'm so intrigued! explain!
zoegirl:	i wanted him to hotwire jana's car for me, so that i could drive it onto the school's front lawn. i had this great idea of strewing it with beer cans and condoms—wouldn't that have been awesome?
zoegirl:	but vincent wouldn't do it
SnowAngel:	aw, man! why not?
zoegirl:	1st he acted indignant that i assumed he knew how to hotwire a car. except he admitted he *does* know how . . . so it's not like he had a leg to stand on.
SnowAngel:	busted!
zoegirl:	huh? who's busted?
SnowAngel:	both of u! u for assuming that cuz he's puerto rican he'd be a car thief, and him for being able to steal a car if he had 2.
zoegirl:	i never called him a car thief!
SnowAngel:	*adopts sing-song tone* racist! racist! zoe's a closet racist!
zoegirl:	oh god, now i feel terrible. i didn't mean it like that, i swear! u know i'm not racist!
SnowAngel:	so why wouldn't he do it? is it cuz he's friends with jana?
zoegirl:	i didn't c him as the type to get hung up on morals, since all along he's been amused by the jana war. and he's never taken sides 1 way or another. but when i brought that up, he gave me this pointed stare and was like, "yeah, that's right. i never took sides."
zoegirl:	then he put his hand on my knee (he really is quite hot)

Send   Cancel

241

	and said, "u guys r funny and all that . . . but, amiga, eventually u gotta let it go."
SnowAngel:	oh god help me. maturity lessons? from vincent???
zoegirl:	he was like, "u wanna know what the best revenge is? happiness. *that's* the best revenge."
SnowAngel:	easy for HIM to say
zoegirl:	i know, i know. i mean, he's got a point . . . but ur *not* happy. and how can i be happy if my angela's not happy?
SnowAngel:	yeah!
zoegirl:	he invited us to come over saturday, btw. he's having a party.
SnowAngel:	r jana and her minions gonna be there?
zoegirl:	terri and margaret: yes. jana: no. apparently terri and jana r in a snit again, and jana refuses to be in the same room as her until terri grovels at her feet.
SnowAngel:	that is so pathetic
zoegirl:	truly
zoegirl:	so, wanna go? could be fun.
SnowAngel:	not with terri and margaret there, it wouldn't. not for me.
zoegirl:	oh
zoegirl:	i was hoping u'd, u know, not let that get in the way of your good time.
SnowAngel:	wouldn't that be nice *tilts head and considers alternate-reality version of enlightened and transcendent self*
SnowAngel:	but, nope
zoegirl:	well, then i won't go either. u and maddie and i can rent a movie instead, whatever u want.

SnowAngel:	no, no, u go on. just cuz i'm a big huge loser doesn't mean y'all have to be, 2.
zoegirl:	like we'd really wanna go to a party without u. give me a break.
SnowAngel:	god, i'm pathetic
zoegirl:	oh, angela
zoegirl:	just . . . hold on, k? i'm *this* close to the absolute perfect plan, better than all the others combined. cuz finally i thought to myself, "what does jana care about? what would hurt her the most?"
SnowAngel:	and . . . ?
zoegirl:	i just have to work out 1 last kink. i can't do it in the school parking lot, cuz the only time she parks there is in broad daylight. and i can't do it at her house, cuz if her car's there, then obviously she'd be there 2.
SnowAngel:	can't do WHAT?
SnowAngel:	no, nvm. i believe u when u say ur trying, but i'll believe it MORE when i actually c results!

Friday, April 21, 6:30 PM E.S.T.

mad maddie:	**why did my coffee drink fizz all over when i opened it? WHY?**
SnowAngel:	???
mad maddie:	**it's a starbucks double shot in a can. but espresso really shouldn't fizz.**
SnowAngel:	*le shrug*
mad maddie:	**it's scary how much $ i spend at starbucks.**

Send   Cancel

mad maddie: omg, they should buy me a new computer! with all the money i've given them, they totally should!

SnowAngel: yeah, good luck with that

mad maddie: so wanna come hang with ian and me tonite?

SnowAngel: what r u doing?

mad maddie: er ...

SnowAngel: lemme guess. *starts cracking up* going to starbucks!

mad maddie: fine, make fun. do u wanna come or not?

SnowAngel: nah, i'd just be the sad pathetic tag-along. i'm already making y'all miss vincent's party to babysit me tomorrow nite—i refuse to burden u twice in a row.

mad maddie: oh, plz

SnowAngel: 1 day i need to get up off my butt and take MYSELF out. no one but me. only it always seems easier to just stay put.

mad maddie: if u change your mind, u know where to find us!

Saturday, April 22, 6:30 PM E.S.T.

SnowAngel: i just played a trick on aunt sadie, tee hee. remember that sex toy party her friend wanted to have?

zoegirl: vaguely. i remember the pole-dancing party.

SnowAngel: uh huh, the sex toy party is part of that whole lineup. aunt sadie finally agreed to host it, and it's set for next thursday!

SnowAngel: anyway, emma, she's the sex toy woman, has been calling endlessly to pester aunt sadie about details.

Send   Cancel

244

would aunt sadie be willing to pose in lingerie? how many pairs of handcuffs should she bring? what about s&m, is that going 2 far?

zoegirl: good god. r they actually gonna try the stuff out at the party?

SnowAngel: i think the idea is to "normalize" the sex toys so that the women wanna take them home to spice up their sex lives. but aunt sadie's insisting that emma only bring the catalogue. she can do a pole dance for her innocent niece, but she's too embarrassed to pass around a vibrator!

zoegirl: oh, wow. this is *so* not my mother's pampered chef party!

SnowAngel: so a few minutes ago aunt sadie was in the shower, and her celly beeped. i picked it up and it was a text message from dilemma33. dilEMMA, get it? and the msg was "sadie, 5pm good?"

SnowAngel: so i typed back, "5pm great, but changed mind about dildos. bring lots—all sizes!" ☺

zoegirl: angela!

SnowAngel: so now emma's gonna show up next thursday with a humongous box of dildos! i love it!

zoegirl: i don't understand the point of a dildo. doesn't it just sound gross, a fake penis that flops around in your hand?

SnowAngel: i don't get it either. altho i don't think it "flops."

SnowAngel: do u think they make fake vaginas for men to use?

zoegirl: ewwwww!

zoegirl: i don't like the thought of any of that stuff. can u imagine

245

what doug would say if i whipped out a pair of handcuffs the next time we were fooling around?

SnowAngel: THAT would prove ur not submissive! zoe the dominatrix, yeah!

SnowAngel: *cracks whip* sshwing!

zoegirl: nice whip noise

SnowAngel: thanks! ☺

SnowAngel: u guys still coming over to watch "pride & prejudice"?

zoegirl: u betcha

SnowAngel: i DO appreciate it, even if i don't always show it.

zoegirl: angela, it's our pleasure. i'll be over in about an hour!

Saturday, April 22, 6:58 PM E.S.T.

SnowAngel: uh oh *giggles uncontrollably*

zoegirl: what?

SnowAngel: that woman who called? turns out it wasn't emma-the-sex-toy-guru. it was emma, aunt sadie's personal banker!

zoegirl: oh no!

SnowAngel: they've got a late meeting tomorrow. THAT'S what she was referring to!

zoegirl: and u told her to bring dildos! lots—all sizes!

SnowAngel: why would a personal banker have the screen name "dilemma"?! would u trust a banker who called herself "dilemma"?

zoegirl: maybe the point is that she *solves* dilemmas

Send   Cancel

SnowAngel:	or maybe she's just stupid!
SnowAngel:	she gave aunt sadie this huge lecture on identity theft after aunt sadie explained the dildo comment. *rolls eyes* like i'm gonna use aunt sadie's celly to do something evil—yeah right!
zoegirl:	except u did. u used her celly to
zoegirl:	omg . . . that's it!
SnowAngel:	i could maybe pretend to be her and order a pizza, but i'd still have to come up with the cash to pay for it, u know? i'm thinking emma-dilemma needs to take a chill pill.
zoegirl:	no, i mean about jana! that's totally how to make it work!
SnowAngel:	by ordering a pizza on aunt sadie's celly?
zoegirl:	g2g. i have to catch maddie and tell her the movie's off—she needs to go to vincent's party instead.
SnowAngel:	the movie's off? why????
zoegirl:	um, cuz i'm seizing the moment, and it's all due to brilliant u!
zoegirl:	i'll call u after i kidnap Boo Boo Bear!!!

Saturday, April 22, 10:33 PM E.S.T.

zoegirl:	r u at vincent's? r u, r u, r u?
mad maddie:	**zo! be a little more obvious, will ya?**
zoegirl:	well that's why i'm texting! duh!
zoegirl:	do u have terri's cell???

Send   Cancel

247

mad maddie: no, but just saw her put it down on pool table. about to make my move.

zoegirl: remember, keep the message u send short and sweet. something like, "jana, this is your biyatch here. i'm prepared to grovel."

mad maddie: ok, uh, zo? on scale of 1 to not-cool, that is SO not cool. "this is yr biyatch here???"

zoegirl: fine, just make it sound like terri

mad maddie: i will

zoegirl: tell her to go to the buckhead barnes and noble and say that u'll be INSIDE. inside, got it? so that jana has to physically get out of her car.

mad maddie: i WILL

zoegirl: and afterward, be sure to delete jana's number from terri's call list. and put her phone back right where u found it!

mad maddie: i can't till u quit yer yammering!

zoegirl: right. very good.

zoegirl: call me when u have news!!!

Saturday, April 22, 10:46 PM E.S.T.

zoegirl: just talked to maddie—she's at vincent's right this very second! she's setting up the sting!

SnowAngel: eeek!

zoegirl: i'm so nervous . . . and nothing's even *happened* yet!

SnowAngel: except for the fact that u used the word "sting." u've been watching 2 many episodes of the sopranos!

zoegirl:	this is not the time to make fun of me. i'm about to steal her most cherished possession, don't u get it?
SnowAngel:	isn't it kinda mean to trick her into thinking terri wants to make up, tho?
zoegirl:	um . . . well . . .
SnowAngel:	oh, what am i saying??? *throws conscience to the wind* trick away, u tricky girl!
zoegirl:	omg, maddie's calling my cell! brb!
SnowAngel:	zoe!
SnowAngel:	can't u type AND talk?
SnowAngel:	u can't leave me hanging like this!!!!
zoegirl:	maddie texted jana from terri's phone, and jana went for it! only jana nixed barnes & noble and said to meet at a coffee house in little five points called aurora. as in *now*!!!
SnowAngel:	then go! go go go go go go!

Saturday, April 22, 11:15 PM E.S.T.

SnowAngel:	zo, where r u? why aren't u answering your phone???

Saturday, April 22, 11:17 PM E.S.T.

mad maddie:	hey, a, got your message. what's going on?
SnowAngel:	it's been half an hour and zoe hasn't checked in. all she was gonna do was get to the coffee place, get the bear, and get out. where IS she?

Send   Cancel

mad maddie: have u called her?

SnowAngel: 200 times, plus i sent a text. no reply.

mad maddie: maybe she's somewhere where she can't talk

SnowAngel: but where? and why couldn't she at least respond to my text???

mad maddie: hmmm, good question

SnowAngel: listen, your job at vincent's is done, so i think u should say g-bye and come be with me. i can't handle being on my own and not knowing what's going on!

mad maddie: u got it. see ya in 5!

Saturday, April 22, 11:20 PM E.S.T.

SnowAngel: zoe, plz answer! ur scaring me!!!

zoegirl: i'm ok. don't worry.

SnowAngel: oh thank GOD. i've been imagining all these awful scenarios, like that jana caught u and stabbed u to death with her eyeliner.

SnowAngel: did u get the bear? did she c u?

SnowAngel: zoe, ur not answering again!

SnowAngel: zoeeeeee!

Saturday, April 22, 11:31 PM E.S.T.

zoegirl: mads, i need u to come get me. call me!

Saturday, April 22, 11:35 PM E.S.T.

SnowAngel: oh great, maddie. now UR not answering. it's been way longer than 5 minutes since u left vincent's . . . WHERE R U????

Saturday, April 22, 11:50 PM E.S.T.

zoegirl: angela—we're here. we're safe. *please* don't be mad!

SnowAngel: don't tell me not to be mad! i AM mad!

SnowAngel: and who's the "we"? u and Boo Boo Bear?!

zoegirl: no, not Boo Boo Bear. maddie. she had to drive me home so i'd make curfew.

SnowAngel: drive u home from where? why didn't u drive yourself home?

zoegirl: hold on, maddie's talking to me . . .

zoegirl: she's gonna head out, she says she'll call u tomorrow. and if u calm down, i'll tell u everything.

SnowAngel: *taps foot verrrrrrry impatiently*

zoegirl: ok, let's c. the last time we talked was when i was leaving for the coffee house, right?

SnowAngel: yes, and what i wanna know is how u got from there to going incommunicado. why didn't u call or text or something?!!

zoegirl: well . . . cuz i was trapped in the back of jana's station wagon.

SnowAngel: WHAT?!!

zoegirl:	i sent u that 1 message cuz i didn't want u flipping out, but even with my key pad noise turned off, i didn't wanna risk any more.
SnowAngel:	fyi, the not-flipping out thing? totally ineffective! i was flipping out then, and i'm doubly flipping out now!
zoegirl:	u can stop. like i said, i'm fine!
SnowAngel:	how in the world did u end up in the back of jana's station wagon???
zoegirl:	i drove to that coffee house called aurora, and there was jana, just that second heading inside. i was like, "all right, zoe. GO."
SnowAngel:	*bites nails nervously* aye-yai-yai!
zoegirl:	she luckily had NOT locked her car, just as we expected. cuz who'd wanna steal anything out of that heap?
zoegirl:	well . . . other than me
zoegirl:	but, whatever. i crawled into the backseat to look for Boo Boo Bear, and i pulled the door shut behind me so that anyone in the parking lot wouldn't wonder what was going on.
SnowAngel:	oh no. oh no!
zoegirl:	uh huh—jana came back a lot sooner than i thought. i didn't even hear her until she was opening the front door.
SnowAngel:	holy shit!
SnowAngel:	i'm like totally having an insane nervous-laughter attack as i'm reading this, i want u to know. aunt sadie prolly thinks i'm possessed!
zoegirl:	so i dove under that ratty army blanket she has and

Send Cancel

	covered myself up as best i could . . . and btw i *did* find Boo Boo Bear. he smelled like spit, just like terri said.
SnowAngel:	ok, zo? soooo not interested in Boo Boo Bear. far more interested in what the hell happened next!!!
zoegirl:	well, jana cursed and slammed the car into reverse. it was obvious she was in a huge hurry, which i understood later, but right then all i could think was, "oh CRAP."
SnowAngel:	keep telling! keep telling!
zoegirl:	she drove down peachtree and turned left on some side street, and the whole time she was muttering "that bitch" over and over. i thought she was talking about maddie. i was like, "yikes, she found out maddie set her up, and now she's going to hunt her down."
zoegirl:	but it *wasn't* maddie she was talking about. it was her stepmom.
SnowAngel:	???
zoegirl:	have u ever seen the liquor store that's a couple stores down from aurora?
SnowAngel:	no
zoegirl:	turns out that's where that guy works, the guy jana's stepmom is having an affair with. and what i've pieced together, now that it's all over, is that jana must have spotted him from inside the coffee house. maybe he was getting off work, maybe that's why she picked aurora in the 1st place. maybe she's been trying to catch him with her stepmom for a while.
SnowAngel:	and did she?
zoegirl:	uh huh. jana's stepmom was waiting in his car—that's why jana tailed them.

SnowAngel:	u saw them with your own 2 eyes? jana's stepmom with the liquor store guy?
zoegirl:	she followed them to an apartment parking lot, then killed her engine. all this time i was absolutely frozen, trying not to breathe and watching as more and more frantic messages popped up from u.
zoegirl:	finally jana said "f***" under her breath and got out of the car. i waited a few seconds, then peered over the seat and saw her striding to the guy's truck.
SnowAngel:	omg
zoegirl:	she yanked open the passenger side door, and her stepmom and the liquor store guy jerked up like deer in headlights. and . . . well . . . there was pretty much no question what they'd been doing.
SnowAngel:	oh my GOD
zoegirl:	and then it was awful, cuz jana was yelling and her stepmom was yelling and the liquor store guy was holding his hands out and going, "whoa, whoa, whoa!"
SnowAngel:	geez louise, this is like a jerry springer episode
SnowAngel:	can u imagine something like this happening to 1 of us? i mean, seriously. can u imagine 1 of our moms having an affair with some random liquor store guy?
zoegirl:	i can't. it made me feel very . . . lucky.
zoegirl:	it also made me feel like i better get the hell out of there. i tried, i almost made it, but then liquor store guy's truck roared off and jana screamed "f*** u" at the taillights. then she stormed back and kicked her tire. she was literally shaking, angela.
SnowAngel:	oh man. and then . . . ?

Send   Cancel

zoegirl:	and then she saw me. i was crouched by the car and wearing the world's most shell-shocked expression, i'm sure.
zoegirl:	it was 1 of those out-of-body experiences where we were both like, "oh shit," and at the same time, "is this real? is this really and truly happening?"
SnowAngel:	of all the ppl in the world to be stuck with in that situation . . .
zoegirl:	i know! and with Boo Boo Bear watching it all!
zoegirl:	it was a crazy stretched-out moment, and neither of us knew what to do. then time snapped back to normal and jana lunged for me and i tripped on a beer bottle and fell on my butt. i was like, "wait! i can explain!"
SnowAngel:	yeah sure. "i can explain why i was hiding in your car when u caught your stepmonster doing it with the liquor store guy."
SnowAngel:	that's gonna go over real well!
zoegirl:	i was so far gone, i didn't care. i mean, i *cared*, i didn't wanna be the horrible and-then-she-killed-her-fellow-student ending of the jerry springer show. but i also knew i was screwed no matter how i played it.
SnowAngel:	so what did u say???
zoegirl:	i told her the truth—that i was trying to get her back for everything she did to us. she was like, "the shit u were." so i explained about the kidnapping plot, which didn't come out making the slightest bit of sense, and in fact the whole convo seemed out-of-place and wrong.
SnowAngel:	if she hadn't slept with logan and done all that other stuff, u wouldn't have been there. it's her own fault.

Send Cancel

255

zoegirl:	i brought that up, actually. and angela, ur not gonna like this next part.
SnowAngel:	what?
zoegirl:	i came to the part about the dead bird, and she was like, "what dead bird?"
zoegirl:	"the dead bird u put in angela's jeep," i said. "if u hadn't done that, the whole revenge thing would have been over. we would have let it go. but u did, which is why angela mailed u the baby chicks. which led to that comment u made about angela not putting out, which led to the fake health service letter, which led to u proving ur a slut by sleeping with angela's boyfriend."
SnowAngel:	damn. u go, girl!
SnowAngel:	what did jana say to that?
zoegirl:	she said, "ur f***ing pathetic, all 3 of u. i never put a dead bird in angela's jeep."
SnowAngel:	what?! she's such a liar!
zoegirl:	she didn't deny any of the rest of it, just that.
SnowAngel:	but . . .
SnowAngel:	if she didn't put the dead bird in there, then . . .
SnowAngel:	ohhhh *turns very tiny*
zoegirl:	maddie was in hysterics when i told her this part, btw
SnowAngel:	oh yeah, i bet she was. *crawls into hole*
zoegirl:	u left the window down. the bird flew in and rammed into the dashboard. then it died.
SnowAngel:	jana had nothing to do with it?
zoegirl:	jana had nothing to do with it.
SnowAngel:	*slinks away . . . then turns around and comes back*

lauren myracle

SnowAngel:	she's still evil
zoegirl:	yep, she is
SnowAngel:	she still slept with logan!
zoegirl:	she did, it's true.
SnowAngel:	r u sorry u went after her?
zoegirl:	it didn't end the way i thought it would, that's for sure. but it *did* end, i think.
zoegirl:	i saw her stepmother cheating on her dad. it made kidnapping Boo Boo Bear seem pretty meaningless.
SnowAngel:	so what was the final scene b/w u? what happened after the dead bird remark?
zoegirl:	jana looked at me like i was dirt, and then she got in her car and left. and then i called maddie . . . and u know the rest.
SnowAngel:	ur not dirt, zoe
zoegirl:	i know, neither r u. but i *am* completely worn out. i'm like a typing zombie.
zoegirl:	we'll talk more in the morning, k?
SnowAngel:	u better believe it. we'll be rehashing this for days and months and years!
SnowAngel:	i love u, zo! UR MY HERO!!!

Sunday, April 23, 10:02 AM E.S.T.

mad maddie:	**hey, a. found any dead birds recently?**
SnowAngel:	ha ha
mad maddie:	**just messing with ya. so can u graduate in peace, now that zoe finally went to bat for u?**

Send   Cancel

257

SnowAngel: why yes, i can. *smiles radiantly*

SnowAngel: i woke up this morning thinking, "something good happened—what was it?" and then i was like, "right! zoe caught jana's stepmom macking with the liquor store guy!"

mad maddie: **kind of a terrible thing to be glad about, but what is it they say? 1 person's pain is another's pleasure?**

mad maddie: **what do u think jana's stepmonster is gonna do, now that jana knows?**

SnowAngel: make jana's life a living hell?

mad maddie: **i wonder if jana's gonna tell her dad. what do u think he'll do?**

SnowAngel: ya got me

mad maddie: **talk about an awkward conversation. can u imagine having to tell your dad that his wife's been whacking the liquor store guy's salami?**

SnowAngel: *narrows eyes* STOP! it's possible i feel a tiny bit sorry for jana's dad, but not for jana and certainly not for her stepmom.

mad maddie: **hmm, u make a good point**

SnowAngel: if i feel sorry for anyone, it's zoe. she's the 1 who went thru it all.

mad maddie: **when i showed up at the parking lot, her face totally collapsed in relief. and then she burst into tears. like she'd been holding it together and holding it together, and could finally let go.**

SnowAngel: i'm so glad u were there for her. if i still had the jeep . . .

SnowAngel: grrrr!

Send   Cancel

mad maddie: she said something cool in the car. she was like, "being there in such an awful situation DID make me realize something, tho. that no matter what i'm feeling, i get to choose how to act."

SnowAngel: meaning what?

mad maddie: she said her heart was pounding so hard she thought she might die, but she thought, "what would maddie do? what would angela do?"

SnowAngel: hey now—why do U get to be 1st? does she think ur braver than i am?!

mad maddie: yes, cuz i am

mad maddie: and it was like a revelation to her that SHE'S the one who gets to define what kind of person she is, despite being scared or anxious or whatever.

SnowAngel: ohhhh! like last year when i decided i'd had enuff of california, so i just took off. it was so liberating to realize that i could make such a bold move and not be struck down by lightning.

mad maddie: it sounds dumb when i write it down in words, cuz of course we're the ones who get to decide how to live our lives.

mad maddie: but still. it seems important.

SnowAngel: it IS important. it's not dumb at all.

SnowAngel: so should we call zo and tell her how great she is? i tried her once, but she wasn't awake.

mad maddie: ah, let her rest. she deserves it. but tonite let's take her to din-din.

SnowAngel: thumbs up, big buddy!

Send   Cancel

259

Monday, April 24, 8:45 AM E.S.T.

SnowAngel: OMG, it's officially our last wk of skool! 4evah!!!!

zoegirl: and mad's sleeping in. go fig.

SnowAngel: lame x 100. cya at grad rehearsal!

Monday, April 24, 9:01 AM E.S.T.

SnowAngel: wake up, u lazy bum!!! i'm calling yr land line over & over till u do!!!

Monday, April 24, 3:55 PM E.S.T.

zoegirl: did u c jana at graduation practice?

mad maddie: yeah. so?

zoegirl: she was smirking at me. snidely. she was snidely smirking at me.

mad maddie: and again i say . . . so?

mad maddie: u didn't expect things to change b/w u, did u?

zoegirl: well . . .

mad maddie: she snidely smirked at me and angela 2. AND she whispered something to terri about my tevas, which i ignored.

zoegirl: i think it was something about how u weren't as dressed up as everyone else. i couldn't quite hear, but i *think* that's what it was.

Send   Cancel

mad maddie:	**whatevs, i'm just glad my fashion statement could bring jana and terri back together again. nothing like a catty remark to mend a friendship, that's what i say.**
zoegirl:	i told jana it wasn't really terri who called, btw. that night in the parking lot.
mad maddie:	**well aren't u sweet**
zoegirl:	i didn't want her thinking terri had stood her up, that's all.
mad maddie:	**listen, jana and terri will do their dysfunctional dance till the end of time. and if 1 day they realize they've wasted their lives being nasty? tuff tootle birds for them.**
zoegirl:	"tuff tootle birds"?
zoegirl:	maddie, i'm gonna miss u soooo much.
mad maddie:	**oh god, here we go. 1st angela with her waterworks . . . now UR getting mushy?**
zoegirl:	it was the graduation music that got me. otherwise i would have been fine!
mad maddie:	**curse marching in 2 by 2! curse "pomp and circumstance"!**
zoegirl:	u got teary too, don't try to deny it. and i *am* gonna miss u. and angela, of course. and mary kate and kristin and DOUG . . . i'm gonna miss everybody so much!
mad maddie:	**ian and i had another talk about next fall, btw.**
zoegirl:	and?
mad maddie:	**he said we'll make it work no matter what. that we just have to be honest with each other and tell each other what we're feeling.**
zoegirl:	awww
zoegirl:	i hope u guys *do* make it. and doug and me, 2. do u think we will?

mad maddie:	i don't know. but at the same time, i don't c why not.
zoegirl:	yeah. i like that way of thinking about it.
mad maddie:	what did doug say about your jana adventure?
zoegirl:	he was shocked. and he told me how stupid it was, which was oddly gratifying. he was being mr. protective.
mad maddie:	a little 2 late for that, bucko
zoegirl:	it changed the way he looked at me, i think. in a good way.
mad maddie:	that's awesome
mad maddie:	and now, over and out. byeas!

Tuesday, April 25, 5:45 PM E.S.T.

SnowAngel:	heya, zo. i'm IMing on this beautiful day to tell u that even if u super-duper want to, u can't ask me out for dinner tonite.
zoegirl:	uh . . . ok. only i never was planning on asking u to dinner. was i?
SnowAngel:	i'm just saying that if u got a wild hair and suddenly needed to go out for burritos, u'd have to call mads. not me. k?
zoegirl:	right. well. that was out of nowhere, but sure.
zoegirl:	anything else going on? did mrs. evangelista decide whether your exam's gonna be take-home?
SnowAngel:	*huffs in indignation* i can't believe ur talking about exams instead of asking me to dinner. do u not WANT to ask me to dinner?

Send Cancel

zoegirl:	u just told me NOT to!
SnowAngel:	so?
SnowAngel:	i make this big deal out of telling u and maddie that i'm not available for dinner, and do either of u even fight it? nooooooo, ur both just like, "sure, whatevs, is your exam gonna be a take-home?"
zoegirl:	sweetie. r we having an angela moment?
SnowAngel:	it's like ur not even aware that we only have 3 more days of school. THREE MORE DAYS to enjoy just being us, and then come exams, followed by graduation, followed by 5 billion zillion graduation parties. and the parties will be fun, but they won't exactly be winsome-threesome intimate. i'm just SAYING.
zoegirl:	oh good heavens
zoegirl:	angela . . . would u like to go to dinner tonite?
SnowAngel:	oh, thank u so much for asking! that is so thoughtful! *hugs zoe and smothers her with smooches*
SnowAngel:	but no, i can't. sorry.
zoegirl:	!!!!!!!!!!!!!!!!!!!!
SnowAngel:	i'm taking *myself* out, that's why. this is STAND TALL FOR ANGELA DAY, and in my brain i will be saying "hahahaha" to logan and every other boy on the planet, cuz i do not need a boy to be complete.
SnowAngel:	i'm going to have a lovely time if it kills me, and that's why i can't drag u or maddie along. make sense?
zoegirl:	yes, altho u could have just said that.
SnowAngel:	g2g. gotta go primp for my hot date—with myself!!!

Wednesday, April 26, 4:45 PM E.S.T.

zoegirl: hola, madikins. big bunny is gone 4ever, squeezed out by the Crusty Pines Executive Housing Complex, Phase III.

mad maddie: ah, the end of an era. and with big bunny gone, susie, lulu, and round-headed boy r safe and sound.

zoegirl: they wouldn't be if it wasn't for susie

mad maddie: so true. we can learn a lot from susie, can't we?

zoegirl: like what?

mad maddie: like ... hmm

mad maddie: that the forest is out there whether we like it or not, and we can't just stay in our pretty houses and lock the doors. we have to make the bold move. but what we CAN do, when we venture bravely forth, is be aware of giant pink bunnies. that's the lesson we all should heed!

zoegirl: ohhhhh. i thought it was that only a few ppl like bunnies and trees, but everybody likes executive housing complexes.

mad maddie: look at u, quoting the bunny! nice!

zoegirl: tina and arlene came by today. the jehovah's witnesses. i think we've reached the end of an ear there, 2.

zoegirl: oops—end of an ERA.

mad maddie: if it was the end of an ear, they'd be like vincent van gogh, who cut off his own ear. did u know that?

zoegirl: as a matter of fact i did

mad maddie: can u imagine cutting off your own ear? and then afterwards holding it in your hand and being like, "huh. not so sure why i did that ... "

Send   Cancel

zoegirl:	not something i c myself doing, actually
mad maddie:	**no, i suppose not**
mad maddie:	**so why was it the end of an era with tina and arlene?**
zoegirl:	i think they've had enuff of me and my heathen ways, that's all. even tho in reality i'm so *not* a heathen.
mad maddie:	**let's consider. u lied to your parents about your princeton application. u had (and r continuing to have) pre-marital sex. u hitched an illegal ride in the back of jana's car . . .**
mad maddie:	**ur sure ur not a heathen?**
zoegirl:	God is bigger than all that—what's important is that we try to be good ppl. that's what i told tina and arlene.
mad maddie:	**did u tell them about the pre-marital sex part?**
zoegirl:	yes. bet u thought i didn't, huh? but i'm not ashamed of it.
mad maddie:	**what did they say?**
zoegirl:	arlene looked extremely disapproving, and tina—she's the young 1—looked shocked. arlene said something like, "well, everything happens for a reason," implying that i could learn from my mistakes. but i was like, "i don't believe that."
mad maddie:	**u don't believe we can learn from our mistakes?**
zoegirl:	no, i don't believe everything happens for a reason. ppl who say that r imagining God up in the sky, making things happen. but in reality, WE'RE the ones who make things happen. and when crappy things happen anyway, WE choose how to respond. that's what i meant.
mad maddie:	**tell that to glendy, will ya? she's definitely a "hand in the sky" kind of gal, altho for her it's more superstition than God.**

Send   Cancel

zoegirl:	she sent u another chain letter?
mad maddie:	**yeah, but this one's FOR REAL!!! (note ironic use of all caps)**
mad maddie:	**i'm supposed to tell everyone i love how much they mean to me, and if i don't, i'll have bad luck for the rest of my lifelong days. oh, and i was supposed to do it within the hour. woops.**
zoegirl:	i can't believe u didn't. don't u love me???
mad maddie:	**of course i do, i just don't need any stupid email telling me to proclaim it.**
zoegirl:	awwww
zoegirl:	u honestly can block her name from your account, u know.
mad maddie:	**she'd just hack her way back in.**
mad maddie:	**anywayz, it'd be a shame to let such drivel go to waste. 1 of these days i'm gonna come up with a genius use for glendy's crapmails, just wait and c! 1 of these days i'm gonna**
zoegirl:	ur gonna what?
mad maddie:	**ooo, baby, yeah! gots to go—i's been inspired!**

Thursday, April 27, 6:08 PM E.S.T.

SnowAngel:	tomorrow's senior mudslide! yeahhhhhhh! *takes flying jump onto oozing hill of mud*
mad maddie:	**what a great way to go—last day of classes and an oozing hill of mud.**
mad maddie:	**u gonna try to pull anybody in?**

lauren myracle

SnowAngel:	heck yeah! mrs. evangelista, if she's foolish enuff to come near me. that'll be her payment for sticking us with our sucky take-home exam!
mad maddie:	**i'm so jealous of zo. after tomorrow, she's DONE. as in, kaput, finito, no more classes and not a single exam. so unfair!**
SnowAngel:	quit complaining. at this point, final exams r just a formality. it's all about closure, baby. 😁
mad maddie:	**so. dude. u said something in the parking lot about an idea u had—then zoe came up and the convo somehow veered off. what's the scoop?**
SnowAngel:	right, i'm so glad u remembered!
SnowAngel:	friggers, i just spilled my coffee all over my frickin keyboard. 1 sec.
SnowAngel:	k sorry, i'm back
mad maddie:	**i once spilled an entire dr pepper into my keyboard. totally ruined it.**
SnowAngel:	ooo, sux for u
mad maddie:	**so, yer idea?**
SnowAngel:	well . . . i think we should all wear our hair in pigtails tomorrow! for National Pigtails Day!
mad maddie:	**i'm drawing a blank. nat'l pigtails day?**
SnowAngel:	from zoe's princeton essay! when we say "screw it" to being a grown-up and wear our hair in pigtails and slide down the mud hill and just have fun!!!
mad maddie:	**ohhh**
SnowAngel:	plus we would look so cute. plus it would be a way of saying "yay for us," cuz sure, we're graduating from

Send   Cancel

267

high school, but that doesn't mean we're letting go of our carefree youth.

SnowAngel: u in?

mad maddie: YEAH!

mad maddie: should i be pumping my hand wildly in the air? somehow that seems appropriate.

SnowAngel: pump away, babycakes. and then call zo and tell her our plan, now that we've both agreed. i can't, cuz i've gotta help aunt sadie get ready for her SEX TOY PARTY which is tonite. ahhhhhh!

mad maddie: buy me some fudge-flavored body icing? plz plz plz?

SnowAngel: to use with ian? ooh-la-la!

SnowAngel: OH, and don't forget to turn in your senior quote! tomorrow's the last day to get it in if u want it included in the graduation program!!!

Friday, April 28, 4:55 PM E.S.T.

SnowAngel: u outta the shower?

mad maddie: yeb'm, altho that mud took some serious scrubbing.

mad maddie: shall i come get u for our supa-dupa celebration?

SnowAngel: 1st let's enjoy the moment . . . altho we can't w/o zoe, now can we? hold on . . .

You have just entered the room "Angela's Boudoir."
mad maddie has entered the room.
zoegirl has entered the room.

Send Cancel

zoegirl:	hello, my friends!!! i was hoping u guys would be on-line!
mad maddie:	**heya, zo. were u able to salvage your sneaks?**
zoegirl:	no, they're goners. oh well.
SnowAngel:	u should have gone barefoot *wags finger in zoe's face*
SnowAngel:	u looked adorable in your pigtails, tho
mad maddie:	**ahem. and me?**
SnowAngel:	yes, maddie, u looked adorable 2. we ALL did. *preens happily*
zoegirl:	u guys, i can't tell u how much i loved it that we did that. i'll print up my phone pics tomorrow and make copies.
mad maddie:	**i got a good shot of when doug pulled u in from the side, heh heh heh**
SnowAngel:	omg, that was so funny!
zoegirl:	to u, maybe! u weren't the 1 tumbling headfirst into the slime!
SnowAngel:	u know u loved it ☺
SnowAngel:	seems like things r better than ever with u guys, yeah?
zoegirl:	huh, i guess so
zoegirl:	i still get worried about next year—sometimes to the point of hyperventilating—but then i just slow down and *breathe*. it is what it is, u know?
SnowAngel:	and what it IS is fabulous, schweetheart.
SnowAngel:	think about it: for all intents and purposes we r DONE WITH HIGH SCHOOL 4-EVAH!!!
mad maddie:	**and tonite we're celebrating with just us 3, right?**

269

SnowAngel:	correctamundo
mad maddie:	**no ian**
zoegirl:	no doug
SnowAngel:	and NO JANA. i have washed my hair of that girl once and for all!
zoegirl:	altho i DO have something to say about her, real quick
SnowAngel:	nooooo *covers ears*
zoegirl:	no, this is good
zoegirl:	i couldn't help but notice her today, since she was totally showing off and playing to the crowd, and u know what i realized?
mad maddie:	**that her thong was tracking mud into her woo-woo?**
SnowAngel:	ewww!
zoegirl:	no, what i realized was that jana never won, even when we thought she did.
mad maddie:	**how do u figure?**
zoegirl:	think about it. maddie's back with ian, and they're like the couple of the century. i've gotten over (or at least am getting over) my codependency issues. and yes, jana slept with logan, but angela, u took yourself out for a solo date to houston's, cuz that's how strong u r!
SnowAngel:	hate to point it out, but i didn't take myself to houston's until AFTER u and jana had your show-down.
zoegirl:	the key elements were already there. u DID break up with logan before the show-down, after all. which was also before u knew he and jana had slept together.
mad maddie:	**it's true, babe. jana was beaten before she even began. and speaking of . . .**

Send   Cancel

SnowAngel:	yesssss?
mad maddie:	**well, even tho zoe is absolutely right, i decided jana needed a touch more winsome-threesome love to take with her after graduation. so i put in a little email to our friend the glendinizer.**
SnowAngel:	no!
mad maddie:	**i told her hi, and that i sure have appreciated her chain letters over the months. i mentioned that as matter of fact, i knew a girl who could really benefit from said chain letters. i told her all about jana's tortured past, and suggested that deep down what jana needs is to be showered with love.**
SnowAngel:	maddie!!!! *shrieks and has a coronary*
mad maddie:	**i passed on all of jana's deets, and here's the real stroke of genius. i told glendy not to ever EVER give up, and that if anyone knows how to connect with others, it's her. think that pushed the right buttons?**
SnowAngel:	jana's gonna have glendy latched on for life! 😊
zoegirl:	ur awesome!
mad maddie:	**aren't i?**
SnowAngel:	*flings self to ground and hugs maddie's knees* i love u so much!
SnowAngel:	*hugs zoe's knees 2* and u, of course! i have the 2 bestest friends in the universe, and we will ALWAYS be there for each other . . . even if u guys r stupid idiots who feel compelled to go far far away to college, u naughty children!
mad maddie:	**ur not gonna start guilt-tripping us again, r u? cuz angela, ur gonna have to get over it 1 day. u know that, don't u?**

Send   Cancel

271

SnowAngel:	actually . . . i do
zoegirl:	u do?
SnowAngel:	just lemme explain something, something i've been thinking a lot about. when i lived in el cerrito last year—i have never been that lonely in my life. i missed u guys sooooo much.
mad maddie:	**we missed u 2**
SnowAngel:	yeah, but u guys had each other. i was all alone. and it made me feel . . . un-whole. and i'm so afraid that's gonna happen again this fall.
zoegirl:	oh, angela!!!
SnowAngel:	but like i said, i've been thinking a lot about it, and—*gulp*—i'm gonna try really hard to stop being such a baby about it.
mad maddie:	**u haven't been a baby about it, u've just . . .**
SnowAngel:	been a baby about it. yeah.
SnowAngel:	but just cuz we're splitting up doesn't mean we're "splitting up". i mean, we can visit each other, right?
zoegirl:	of course
SnowAngel:	and we have to IM each other every single day!!!
mad maddie:	**DUH!**
SnowAngel:	well ok then *straightens spine in a queenly fashion* maddie, u may go to santa cruz. and u, zoe, may go to kenyon. i give u my permission.
zoegirl:	thanks, angela. your support means the world to me.
mad maddie:	**ah, dudes. life is good. in fact i had a zen moment about this very thong, when i was driving home from school all muddy and disgusting.**

Send   Cancel

lauren myracle

SnowAngel:	this very "thong"?
mad maddie:	***THING*, u freak**
mad maddie:	**the window was down and my music was blasting and i was like, i am the sun on my skin. i am the clouds in the sky. i'm everything i've ever seen or done or felt or heard, and one day i will be gone.**
SnowAngel:	now THAT'S cheerful
mad maddie:	**no, just . . . we're our own destiny, that's all. and 1 day we WILL be gone, so we better appreciate life while we can.**
SnowAngel:	i get it. it's like my senior quote, from that beetles song: "blackbird singing in the dead of night, take these broken wings and learn to fly. all your life, u were only waiting for this moment to arise."
zoegirl:	i love it! that's a *great* quote, angela!
mad maddie:	**but it's BEATLES, u doof. not scurrying little insects.**
zoegirl:	mads, what'd u put for your quote?
mad maddie:	**after much deliberation, i went with a classic that perfectly captures my life philosophy.**
zoegirl:	which is?
mad maddie:	***"there's something strange about that giant pink rabbit . . ."***
zoegirl:	HA!
SnowAngel:	huh?
zoegirl:	i can't believe u . . . but then again, i totally can.
SnowAngel:	i don't get it. will someone plz explain?
mad maddie:	**they're words of wisdom from my role model, the great and wonderful susie.**
zoegirl:	who dared to enter the forest, and who triumphed despite all odds.

Send   Cancel

273

SnowAngel:	what forest? what odds?
mad maddie:	**go to big-bunny.com and all will be revealed.**
mad maddie:	**what's yours, zo?**
zoegirl:	originally i was gonna use that quote from shakespeare. *"this above all, to thine own self be true."*
SnowAngel:	aw, that's nice
mad maddie:	**gross, barf, vomit. and the character who said it, that polonius dude? total windbag! u can't use something from him!**
zoegirl:	well, i didn't. i ended up going with something from dr. seuss: *"don't cry because it's over. smile because it happened."*
SnowAngel:	oh, zoe!!! *blinks back tears unsuccessfully*
mad maddie:	it's absolutely perfect . . . even tho thanks a lot, now u've got ME all weepy!
zoegirl:	me 3. i can't help it!
mad maddie:	**NO! STOP! the point is to REJOICE, not fall to pieces.**
SnowAngel:	omg, ur so right *lifts chin and sniffs in snot bubble*
zoegirl:	i'll try if y'all will
mad maddie:	**damn straight we will**
mad maddie:	**so what r we waiting for? it's time to party!!!!!**
SnowAngel:	*flings mortar board jubilantly into sky*
SnowAngel:	come pick me up, ya big softie!
zoegirl:	and then me! i'll be waiting at the door!
mad maddie:	**u sure as heck better be**
mad maddie:	**l8r, g8rs!!!**

Send   Cancel

About the Author

Of writing *l8r, g8r*, Lauren says, "Oh, my little muffins, what a ride it's been. I'm not ready to say good-bye to my girls—just as I *know* they're not ready to say good-bye to each other! But my editor, who is beyond wonderful, called up Winnie-the-Pooh to help me through this time of sorrow. *sniff, sniff* 'Wherever they go,' she said, quoting A. A. Milne, 'and whatever happens to them on the way, in that enchanted place on the top of the Forest, a little boy and his Bear will always be playing.' And that is what I leave with you guys, you who have your own times of sorrow to get through. (And times of joy and laughter and craziness, of course. We can't forget that!) Wherever they go, and whatever happens to them along the way, in that magical land of the Internet, three girls will always be playing."

Lauren can be reached through her Web site at www.laurenmyracle.com. She is quite needy and would appreciate your virtual hugs.

The text in this book is set in 10-point Georgia, TheSans 9-Black, and ComicSans. The cell phone icons and many of the smiley faces were created by Celina Carvalho.